Other works

Daughters of the Crescent Moon Series

Destiny's Past

Destiny's Present

Destiny's Future

Sadie Hawkins Series

First Gear

Phoenix Literary Publishing
phoenixlitpub@gmail.com

This book is a work of fiction. Any references to historical or current events, real people or real places and events are products of the author's imagination, and any resemblance to actual events or places or persons, living or dead, is entirely coincidental.

Cover picture: Texas Big Bend National Park over the desert – Creative Commons Public Domain

ISBN: 9781777156350 print

Praise for First Gear

"A brisk, enjoyable tale of a resourceful amateur investigator." *Kirkus Reviews*

"Rollicking, gritty and just plain wonderful! I LOVE THIS NOVEL!! Sadie Hawkins is the perfect character for a series. She has enough baggage to be endearing and enough grit to make me wonder what she'll do next." *S. Harrison, New York Times bestselling author*

"As unlikely a heroine as you're going to encounter! Lee has started what promises to be a great series, with some humour, lots of twists, and enough excitement to keep me turning pages. I can highly recommend First Gear, and am looking forward to the next in the series!" *R. Tarantini*

Praise for the Daughters of the Crescent Moon Series

"5 stars***** Patricia C. Lee has created an enthralling story with all the characters of Destiny's Present. I was riveted to the pages from the first to the last ...I want to know more. I enjoyed this book a great deal. I would highly recommend it." *Kathryn Bennett for Reader's Favorite*

Read2Review on Destiny's Past: "The flow of the story was very well planned; I didn't want to stop reading! I loved the characters; each one had heart and their own voice. However, what really stuck out for me was that while I was reading I could actually picture the places the story was set in and I could clearly picture the characters. Patricia's use of description, for me, helped bring this brilliant story to life."

From the Paranormal Romance Guild: **Reviewer's Choice 2016 2nd place winner** "This is an amazing series and I can't recommend it enough...it has everything you could want if you love paranormal and fantasy." *Linda Tonis*

"Patricia C. Lee has a gift for plot and character, and readers won't need to read much into the work to realize this as they are immediately swept away by the engaging descriptions, the poetic allure of her language, and the powerful narrative voice right from the opening lines of this beautiful story. The story also touches on a good number of very interesting themes and they will speak to many readers because they are very close to their own experiences. Love, sacrifice, betrayal, and a sense of duty are among the most recurrent ones. I loved the way the characters evolved throughout the story. They are engaging and fully-fledged. Destiny's Future is one of the very few novels I have read that deals with time travel, and I found it greatly satisfying." *Christian Sia for Reader's Favorite*

IDLE

A Sadie Hawkins Mystery

by

Patricia C. Lee

ACKNOWLEDGMENTS

My thanks go to the people who assisted me in forming this book: my editor, for the suggestions and guidance. Ashley Boler - Creative Director, sista, and one of my beta readers and Meghan Sloane – another sista, converted romance reader and good friend – thank you for the help. Fearless leader, Narelle and the crew from GMBOT, and also to Susan Smith for your support, guidance and paying it forward – many thanks.

DEDICATION

For Dianne Burns, author, wine buddy, my go-to shot-in-the-arm-person and good friend. I promise to 'just keep swimming' for the both of us. I miss you.

To my readers...thank you for waiting. It's been a challenging four years.

And for *K* – always and forever my love.

CHAPTER ONE

Stepping out of the cool interior of the van, the Texas heat welcomed me as I made my way to the front door of my company. Hawkins Freight was in the semi-industrial outskirts of Houston with other offices and tech companies housed in nondescript cookie-cutter strip malls. It had come into my possession via a circuitous, troubling route and consisted of an office, a bathroom and a holding bay/garage where we kept the cube van. I dreamed of an expansion in the future, some more vans, perhaps even a big rig with a couple of containers to travel long haul. For now, one van sufficed.

It had been a long day, driving a client and her six poodles from Amarillo to Houston and I was hot, sweaty, tired and grumpy. That was probably why it took me a minute to register that the front door to the office was not latched properly. I was pretty sure I had locked the door before I left, but it occurred to me that Blaine, my brother and mechanic, might have stopped by before he left with his very pregnant wife and two-year-old daughter to visit the in-laws. Maybe in his haste he hadn't made sure the door was closed.

However, once I drew near, the telltale scratch marks of forced entry said otherwise.

Well, hell.

I could call the police, but if they arrived and found no issue, I'd feel like an idiot. And they had much more serious crimes to investigate. I'd have a faster response time with the volunteer fire department from my hometown in Alabama.

Using the end of a key, I gently pushed on the portal, which opened with a slight creak. My eyes scanned the broom-closet size of an office; desk, two beat-up vinyl chairs in olive green, and a four-drawer filing cabinet with a framed picture of my father and his brother, Stan. Nothing seemed out of order, no broken glass, no strewn files. It was as I had left it the other day, right down to the stack of ever present bills in the plastic inbox.

So far, so good.

Eyes peeled and ears perked, I crept to the connecting door that led into the bay area. The insane part of my brain wondered why I was tiptoeing in my Dan Post turquoise triad water snake cowboy boots instead of barging through the door with a baseball bat, hell bent on catching the culprits red-handed. Surely if anyone was still here, they would have heard the vehicle pull up outside and be long gone through the bathroom window. Mind you, this was how they did it in the movies.

The sane part of my brain tapped me on the shoulder and suggested it would be a smart to fetch Louis, my Louisville slugger from the van. The bat came with me wherever I went because, as an independent woman under five and a half feet, I took steps to protect myself. I had considered self-defense classes but hadn't gotten around to investigating it further. Most people would suggest a gun, but given my recent experience of being a reluctant witness to the up close and personal effect of a bullet plowing into a person's heart, firearms were a no-go. Memories of seeing the victim's wide-eyed shock, having their warm blood hit my face made a shudder of revulsion slither up my throat. The vision receded to the edge of my brain while I backtracked to the van, quietly opened the door and retrieved Louis from under the seat.

My passion was baseball, which I played for most of my life and reached the Single A fastball league in Texas. I was also the best female batter in the state and second best overall in the league before I got married. The thirty inches of solid ash was like an extension of my arm, and I held it like a weapon. At the connecting door to the garage/bay, I inched it open, knelt down, and peered through the slit.

Nobody. Not even a shoe scuffle of noise.

I took a deep breath and carefully pushed the door open until it met the wall. An empty garage greeted my view. Empty, as in no people, but Blaine's large black tool chest stood at the end of a bench along the far wall. The moving van hadn't moved. I squatted down and peered across the floor to see if someone hid on the other side.

All clear except for a darkish spot under the front part of the engine.

Even though it appeared no one else was here, I held my bat raised and ready and closed in on the cube van. Someone could be crouched behind the tires, masking their presence, so I sidled up to the side facing me, doing the same, and waited. One minute stretched to two, then longer, but all was silent.

Until the cell phone in my pocket warbled, *Take Me Out to the Ballgame.*

With a shriek like a soprano from the Vienna Boys Choir, I dropped the bat and almost passed out from hyperventilation. Any semblance of surprise to someone still lurking about was gone, so I zipped around to the other side of the van but the garage was empty.

I yanked the phone up to my ear. "Hello?" Yup, still sounded like a singing soprano.

"Hello?" I swallowed, tamping down my rampaging heart.

No answer.

The caller's number had flashed off. Thumbing through the log, the last number dialed in was unknown. It didn't even show any digits.

How was that possible?

I did a fast spin, eyes darting around the garage. Did someone dial the wrong number and just hang up, or were they watching me? Goose bumps two-stepped along my skin and it was probably a good idea to lock up, get out fast and call the police, but what was there to say? It is *possible* someone broke in but it looks like nothing was disturbed?

I marched over to Blaine's toolbox and started yanking open drawers. The full extent of his inventory was unknown to me but it seemed everything was still there. No big empty spaces where tools may have rested. Most of the drawers were full but in order.

The bathroom door hung wide open and because it was so small, there was no place for anyone to hide and the window was shut, still locked in place.

If anyone was here, the last place left to hide was the back of the cube van, which could only be accessed by the back doors. Not taking any chances, I grabbed a screwdriver and slid it through the hole where the lever handle rested against the bumper, using the tool as a lock so the lever couldn't release from the inside.

Back in my office, a quick search of my filing cabinet showed everything was pristine, nothing missing or out of order.

Was I being paranoid? I returned to the bay and did a very slow turn, inspecting every corner of the room. Nothing was out of place. My gaze passed over the floor under the front of the van. Although not perfect, we tried to keep the floor as clean as possible in case we have to stow items that needed hauling. I grabbed a flashlight, knelt down, and peered under the engine section. A fair-sized glob of pink shone dully in the beam's reflection. I dipped my finger in the slimy substance and brought it to my nose. Engine coolant. Blaine would need to know about this to circumvent major problems later. Besides helping me with the moves, my brother was an excellent mechanic. He understood the importance of keeping this business afloat and was adamant about maintaining our vehicles in top running condition. At lease he was only gone for a few days before his wife, Karen's due date.

After replacing the flashlight and cleaning my fingers of the coolant, I questioned the break-in even more. Had the scratches at the office entrance always been there since I took over the business and I'd just forgotten because at the time there were irrelevant? And as for the door being left open, it was plausible Blaine had visited the shop before he and his family left earlier that day and hadn't locked the door. I hated to bother my brother but knew if I didn't call him it would bother me until he came back.

He picked up on the third ring. "Hey."

"Hi yourself. You there yet?"

"Yes, arrived about an hour ago. What's up? How was the doggy delivery?"

The grimace was still on my face from the four-legged howling little heathens. "Fine. Listen, did you go into the shop today before you left?"

"Yeah, to redirect the calls to your cell."

Good, he'd been in here.

His voice held a hint of concern. "Why? Anything wrong?"

I paused. If I told him about the door and a possible break in he'd immediately want to return. He'd always been the big brother every sister wanted but ever since the attempt to frame me for murder he'd been protective. Make that almost over protective and the last thing he needed was to come charging back here.

"No. Just making sure you did because no calls came to my cell." The lie didn't taste bitter on my tongue. The man needed a break and once his wife gave birth to their second child, he wouldn't get a chance for a while. "How are Karen and my favorite niece, Shanty?"

"She's your only niece and she's fine. They're both taking a nap."

Before he could get suspicious, I brought the call to a close. "Have a good time and don't worry about a thing."

"Okay, talk to you soon," he said.

"Take it easy, Blaine."

"And don't let Moose on the furniture," he added.

Moose was the Saint Bernard I rescued from its former owner the wicked-witch-wacko who tried to frame me for murder but because I lived in an apartment, the dog was better off at Blaine's house since he had a backyard. Doggie duty over the next week was payment for using Blaine's van, which was no big deal because Moosie was great and I loved him.

"What? I can't hear you, you're breaking up…"

"Sadie!"

The grin died on my face after hanging up as I stared at the vehicle. Maybe my brother hadn't made sure the door was locked when he left but should I take that for granted? Were culprits in the back of the cube van, waiting for me to leave and hoping someone would come back later to get them out?

Having had to take matters into my own hands in order to survive more than once in the past, I didn't want to tempt fate, so instead of phoning the police and looking like an idiot if the van was empty, I called Wayne.

Wayne Timmins was a cop and a friend. He came to my rescue after I had been thumped on the back of the head when thieves stole my load. Since then, I'd helped him move to Houston and we even went on a date. He was nice, in a boy-next-door kind of way and easy on the eyes. And he loved baseball, a big plus in the right column.

"Hey shortcake," he said.

I do not take kindly to people putting labels on me because of my size, but Wayne used the term as an endearment.

The warmth of his greeting brought a smile to my face. "Hi. How are you?"

"Good, you?"

"I'm fine."

"When are we going to go out for the double rain-check dinner?" he teased.

On moving day, we'd both wanted to spring for meals for the other, but ended up too tired after the day. We hadn't had time to collect on that yet.

My heart gave a light flutter. "How about tomorrow?"

"Sounds good," he said, an upbeat tic in his voice. "Is that why you called?"

"No, but that worked out well. I was wondering if you're busy."

"About to get off shift. What's up?"

"Well…" I hesitated, feeling sheepish making something out of nothing.

"Sadie?"

"Umm…when I got to the office, the door was open. Blaine was here this morning but he said he'd locked up."

Wayne's tone changed to a no-nonsense demeanor with a hint of curiosity. "Anything taken?"

"Not that I could see." Sheepishness tangled with foolishness. "Never mind. Forget I called."

"Are you alone?"

"Yes, the place checks out and everything is fine."

"You searched alone? Didn't you learn your lesson the last time?" he said, an edge to his voice. He was referring to how he'd first found me.

"I have Louis with me." I could end it at that, put on the brave no-nonsense front which was like a second skin. Yet perhaps the trauma of what had happened a few months ago affected me more than I cared to admit, manifesting phantoms that weren't there. A part of me demanded I confront my apprehension, fling open the doors of the van and face what might be inside. But if someone was waiting for me and things took a turn for the worse what would that prove?

I smothered a reluctant sigh. "The reason I'm hoping you'd come by is if anyone is still here the only place they could hide would be in the cube van. It's jimmied closed now but I would prefer not to open it by myself."

"Halleluiah for minor miracles. I'm done in about twenty minutes. Go outside and wait for me."

"They can't get out, Wayne." It was difficult calling for help; the damsel in distress was not part of my nature.

His voice hardened. "Wait outside."

I tamped down the urge to argue. What would it hurt whether I waited at my desk or in the van with the air conditioning running?

"Okay."

"I'll see you soon."

"Thanks, Wayne."

His tone softened. "You're welcome." He disconnected.

During my drive from Amarillo earlier with a client and her dogs, my phone had pinged multiple times with voicemails so I snatched a pen and some paper to make notes. In Blaine's van outside, I cranked over the motor, letting the blessed cool air drift past my face as I listened to the messages.

The first was from the previous night. I had been on the other line when my best friend, Tanya Woods, had called and then it got too late to phone her back.

"Sadie. It's Tanya." Her voice sounded odd, strained. My fingers tensed around the phone.

"I…I need…I need to see you. Call me tomorrow, please. You won't be able to reach me tonight." Another momentary pause. "It's important."

I'd heard that one last night already and moved to the next two, which were requests for moving quotes. I'd get back to them soon unless Wayne found someone in the van and there would be the inevitable delay of a police report.

After the two requests came three hang-ups. No big deal.

The next call had me sitting up straight in the seat.

"Sadie, it's Will. Call me. It's important." His tone was indicative that something was wrong.

Will Ellington was one of the rehabilitated convicts from StreetSmart that worked under my friend Tanya who was the organization's manager. He and another StreetSmart client were the main reason I was walking around as a free woman.

The last message began to play. "Sadie, it's Tanya again. Listen, I know things have been awkward lately, but would you contact me? Not on my cell. Will can give you the details." She halted, then went on with a soft hitch in her voice.

"Please Sadie. I'm scared. I'm in jail and the police believe I killed someone."

CHAPTER TWO

The words crashed through my brain, bringing flashes of memory from my ordeal, which still plagued me. Tanya? Charged with killing another person? No way. My hands shook so much it took two attempts to dial Will's number.

He picked up by the second ring. "I'm glad you called."

"Is it true?"

That was all I could get out. There had to be a mistake. Tanya was the most honest and unflappable person I knew. She followed all the rules to the letter, which was funny considering I didn't and yet we were best friends. Even to look at the pair of us, we seemed like total opposites; she, tall with a perfect figure, gorgeous brown skin, a face which could grace any fashion magazine and luxurious dark hair as compared to my short, very curvy stature, red hair and fair complexion. I loved her like the sister I never had and my heart seized at the thought that someone could charge her with anything, let alone murder.

"Yes," Will tersely replied. "I don't have a lot of details. She's still in custody."

My thoughts ricocheted around in my brain, refusing to assemble in some sort of pattern. "She left a brief message and told me she was accused of murder. She also called last night but it was so late. I..I didn't think to call her back."

Guilt's heavy burden rained down, like some of the torrential downpours from back home, fast and unrelenting. Despite the logic of not being able to help her, she must have felt lost when she reached out and I wasn't there. Some friend I was.

"There was nothing you could have done to help," he consoled, as if reading my thoughts.

"Have you spoken to her?"

"Early this morning," he replied.

Blood roared in my ears. This couldn't be happening. "I should go see her."

A pause and a soft exhale of breath came across the line before Will spoke again. "Before you do, can you meet me? I have some information but it shouldn't be discussed over the phone."

Of course he would say that. Will's apprehension regarding communications others could be privy to set him in the *Lone Gunmen* category. When he helped me with my case, we always met face-to-face when he had something important to share. As anxious as I was to see Tanya, to hold her and give support, I'd learned not to question Will's fixation for privacy.

"Sure. Where and when?"

"The usual place, say, in about half an hour?" he suggested.

That was Andros, an upscale restaurant and lounge on Capitol Street in downtown Houston where we had met numerous times to hash out plans on how we were going to prove my innocence. The staff knew him well there; he even had a regular table because of his father's prestige and influence. Will didn't follow in his father's social circles but received preferential treatment because of his association. And since it was late afternoon, a cocktail definitely was in order.

"Okay but it'll have to be in about an hour. I'm waiting on someone to help me with a…potential situation."

"What's going on, Sadie?"

"It's nothing," I scoffed out.

He suppressed a chuckle. "With you, it's never nothing."

His assessment made the corner of my mouth tilt upward. It seemed my life was one hurdle after another. "I've got it under control."

"Fair enough. See you then."

I hung up and stared out the windshield, letting my thoughts drift back to memories of Tanya and me sitting up late watching retro television shows, sipping Wild Turkey and smoking Davidoff Panetallas. The premium slim cigar was Tanya's vice, not mine and although my best friend had the odd glass of wine, she wanted nothing that could cloud her integrity regarding her involvement with the young adult offenders of StreetSmart. Other than her smoking habit, Tanya was such a straight arrow I had a hard time grasping this murder charge.

My mental musings ended when Wayne drove up in his black Dodge Ram super truck and parked beside me. I hopped out of the van and he came over and gave me a kiss on the forehead. Golden highlights layered his straight brown hair, which was cut short but not as severe as a military style. He had a broad forehead and dark eyebrows that rested over eyes a lighter shade than his hair. A straight nose sat above a mouth with a fuller lower lip than upper one and when he smiled a dimple popped out on the right side, which always made my heart skitter. The shadow of a beard sprinkled over his face and firm chin. He reminded me of the hottie co-star from the *Baywatch* movie.

Wayne had changed out of his uniform blues for a short-sleeved light grey polo shirt, which fit snug on his well-muscled shoulders but he didn't have the physique of a bodybuilder, more like someone who just liked to keep in shape. Blue jeans encased slim hips and traveled down to end just above clean black sneakers.

Our relationship was still in the beginning stages, sitting somewhere in the middle of friends and perhaps more, but neither of us had crossed the line into the romance category. I was still finding my feet after my amicable divorce and although Wayne never mentioned he had been married, and therefore gun shy, he didn't seem in any rush to take our friendship to the next level.

After a quick hug, all the while noticing how nice he looked and felt, I stepped back and gave him my most appreciative smile. "Thanks so much for coming. You didn't have to, you know."

He ruffled my hair, a favorite quirk of his, and grinned back. "For you, I prefer to err on the side of caution."

Gees, why did people always think I got into trouble?

The grin faded as he focused on the building. "So, what have we got?" A tense look tightened his features and his hands curled.

"The door wasn't latched all the way." I ventured toward it. "But I checked everything and like I said, nothing seems to be disturbed."

He moved to stand between me and the door. "Wait here."

I braced a hand on my hip and stared at him with disbelief. "Really? You're pulling the knight-in-shining-armor card? I have Louis with me." The bat I'd taken out of the truck when he arrived leaned against the door.

Wayne stared at me in mild frustration. "Just humor me, will you?"

I did my best eye roll and motioned for him to proceed. If this was some sort of crime scene, I shouldn't contaminate any evidence, although that was a moot point since I'd already checked for the culprits but one shouldn't step in the way of chivalry. Although it rankled, I waited outside, not wanting to start an argument.

He returned a few minutes later. "All clear."

"Did you check inside the moving van?"

"Yes. Nothing there. If anyone had been here, they're long gone and I didn't see any evidence of vandalism."

A flush of relief made my shoulders relax. "What now?"

He shrugged. "Not much to do. You said nothing was taken and since everything looks okay, there isn't anything here that would make up a crime other than breaking and entering. Have you checked your files, your computer?"

"Not to any extent. Let me see."

Back in the office I opened the filing cabinet and flipped through the contents more thoroughly. Everything looked exactly as it should be. I started up my computer and while it loaded checked the drawers of my desk. There was no cash on hand so if that had been the reason for the break in, whoever the unwelcomed guest had been was out of luck. When my computer finished powering up a quick scan through the drive and files showed all was fine but that made the whole situation stranger.

Wayne stood with his shoulder leaned against the door frame. "Anything?"

"No, nothing."

He straightened. "You ever think about installing an alarm system?"

I turned off my computer and snatched a couple of blank contracts. "No. Other than Blaine's tools there's nothing here of value. Perhaps I should reconsider, given the jimmied door. Maybe whoever got in was casing the joint for the next time."

He chuckled. "You've been watching too many old cop shows, Sadie. We don't say 'casing-the-joint' anymore."

He followed me outside and made sure the door was locked up tight. "If you don't have plans, did you want to catch a drink?"

"I'm sorry, I can't." I wanted to but had to see Will at Andros.

"Oh." Disappointment flashed briefly in his eyes and then was gone. "Okay. But we're still on for dinner tomorrow, right?"

"For sure." I reached up on tip-toe and gave him a peck on the cheek. "Thank you for coming right away, Wayne. I really appreciate it."

He brought me close for a quick hug. For a moment, while in his arms, I thought I heard him sigh but couldn't determine whether it was out of contentment or resignation. Before I could evaluate the cause, he released me and stepped back.

"Pick you up at seven?"

"Sounds good."

He opened the door to Blaine's van and handed me Louis. "Have a good night, Sadie."

I waved as he got into his truck and followed him out of the parking lot. He turned right and I ventured left toward the heart of the city.

The mass exodus from the downtown core was in full swing as I maneuvered my vehicle into a parking spot two blocks away from Andros. The steady hum of traffic muffled the echo of my boots hitting pavement. Before opening the heavy wooden paneled door at my destination, I glanced down at my clothes; customary short sleeved blouse, blue jeans, cowboy hat and frowned. Although what I had on was an improvement to the usual tee shirt and faded jeans worn while on a job, I still felt underdressed for this establishment. But since this meeting was for drinks and not dinner it would suffice.

My companion stood waiting for me inside the restaurant dressed in tan chinos and a soft yellow button down short sleeve shirt. He turned in my direction, and it startled me once more that this handsome young man, who seemed to have it all, had a record for tech crime. With his sandy blond hair, deep blue eyes that always held the hint of a mischievous twinkle and a face like Adonis, he could have a career in Hollywood. Instead, because of his past, his parole demanded he spend parts of his days doing community hours.

The host showed us to the same table from our previous visits, which was at the back of the lounge against a low standing wall that had a three-foot high screen made up of interconnecting squares to give the table some privacy. Wait staff were busy bringing drinks to the occupied tables from the long stand-up bar where two men and one woman constructed liquid concoctions from what seemed to be every kind of alcohol known to man. Light jazz music created a subtle undertone amid low laughter and murmured conversation.

"What will you have?" Will asked once we sat down. The ever present twinkle and usual smile didn't appear on his face. Not a positive sign.

"Depends on what the conversation will be. The last time called for dirty martinis." They had been part of the reason I went for a nose dive later into a dish of deep fried pickles in front of my ex-husband a few months back.

His lips pursed. "Consider something with a bit more teeth."

Which meant Wild Turkey. Definitely not a good sign. I ordered the drink. Will opted for a Glenmorangie and the waitress left with our order.

"You want to tell me what's going on with Tanya?"

"I will. Just need a shot of something first," he said, the corner of his mouth tilting upward. "How have you been?"

Liquid courage? Okay, the not-a-good-sign was now sliding into panic territory faster than a greased pig through a kid's hands at the fall fair.

My brow furrowed. He was stalling, which was odd. We never had this stilted awkwardness between us before and it made me uptight. I tamped down the urge to grit my teeth and bombard Will with questions but I knew from experience that he wouldn't divulge anything until he was ready. "Fine. How about you?"

He shrugged. "Okay, all things considered. I called you a short time ago. How's the business coming along?"

The call with no numbers on display. "Picking up."

What the hell? I was about to demand answers when our drinks came.

After Will took a long sip of his scotch, he rotated the glass in his hand, watching the amber liquid tilt from side to side as if searching for answers within the brew.

Wait time was over. "You're the one who wanted to meet so out with it."

He inhaled and met my eyes. "Tanya's been arrested and charged with the manslaughter of someone she knows. Her court-appointed lawyer is going to try to get bail but we'll have to wait and see what the judge says. On the plus side, Tanya's character will speak for itself; being manager of StreetSmart and not having a single brush with the law that I know of."

The bourbon's smooth heat slid down my throat, giving me the push to ask. "And the minus side?"

Will briefly shut his eyes briefly and when he open them, a deep pain filled them. "She was discovered over the body."

I gasped, unable to breathe for a moment. "Oh god. She…please tell me she didn't do it. Please."

Will shook his head. "When I spoke to her, she claims she's innocent. Unfortunately, the police learned she and the victim had a very heated argument earlier at Tanya's apartment the night of the incident. Raised voices brought the attention of the next-door neighbor who was on her way to see if everything was okay and the victim stomped passed in the hallway."

I shot back the rest of the booze. This just couldn't be happening.

He paused a moment, took another sip of his drink, pinned me with a narrowed gaze. "The victim was Tanya's lover, Crystal Sherridan."

Well, hell.

So Tanya's secret was out. I had known my best friend was gay for a long time but by Will's stare he did not.

"How long have you known?" he asked quietly.

"Since our mid teens." I waited and gauged his reaction before speaking. "Is that an issue?"

"Not for me. I don't care. It could, however, be a problem with the city, county or state."

"Because she's gay?" Come on, it was the twenty-first century.

"Because she's gay, she's Black and in charge of young adults, including women," he pointed out.

"Oh, for chrissake. Tanya and her lover are both adults and what they do on their own time is none of anyone's business." That was one thing I couldn't understand regarding the issue. What right did people have to judge what went on behind closed doors with consenting adults?

He drained his glass, signaled for another. "Agreed, but when has that ever made any difference?"

He had a point. Although same-sex sexual activity was legal in the state, no state law banned anti-LGBTQ discrimination. Some people had very strong opinions regarding the sensitive topic, which was why Tanya had always been very discreet.

My friend must be reeling. "I need to see her."

"I'll try to arrange it. She's asked the lawyer to funnel any information to me."

A jolt of disappointment speared through me that my best friend hadn't selected me as her contact. However, Will could give her information I wasn't privy to and she was so dedicated to her charges and the organization of StreetSmart, it was logical for her to turn to him for updates.

"Good. Right now, we need to help her in any way we can."

"Until we have a list of other suspects, no matter how remote, there isn't much I can do on my end," Will conceded. "What about you? Is there anything you know about Crystal that can help me or the authorities?"

"Not really. I met her once or twice, didn't know her all that well but she seemed nice. The relationship was fairly new and from appearances and the conversations I had with Tanya about them, they were getting along well."

He leaned back against his chair. "That's surprising. Don't girlfriends usually tell all?"

"Not always."

I knew everything about Tanya and although she never kept her lovers a secret, this one aspect of her life she was more reserved about. She wasn't embarrassed at being gay, far from it, but perhaps because she'd had to be so careful growing up in Alabama and then living here in Texas, keeping her love life shrouded in mystery had become a part of her makeup. I didn't have any such qualms about my personality and Tanya was privy to all of my deep, dark secrets.

Well, except one.

"Want another?" Will asked as I finished the last of my drink.

"No, thanks, it would put me over the limit."

"We can eat here if that's what you're worried about."

"I should get going because there is a stop I want to make before heading home. A lead, well more of a theory really, for Crystal's murder." I stifled a smile at the cop lingo. Ever since my brush with the law made me take an active part to prove my innocence, the *Miss Marple* side of my ego kept popping up.

He leaned forward, braced his arms on the table and lowered his voice. "What type of lead?"

"I have to see someone."

"Do you want me to come with you?"

My eyes widened. "Definitely not."

Will arched a brow. "Sadie, is this going to be dangerous?"

I scoffed and rose. "Nah."

He stood as well, mentioned to the bartender to put the drinks on his tab and followed me out. "I don't believe you."

Outside, we walked along the shadowed concrete and stopped at my vehicle. "I'll be fine, Will. Trust me."

He narrowed his gaze but said nothing.

I stuck my finger at him. "And no cyber-tracking either."

Will was a genius with computers, the internet and all things electronic. Unbeknownst to me, while helping clear my name, he had installed a tracker on my phone. At first, I was miffed because it felt like an invasion of privacy but since that program had saved me from almost getting caught breaking and entering, I couldn't blame the guy. Deep down, I appreciated having someone to watch over me, like an electronic guardian angel, but I couldn't confess that to him.

"Sorry, no promises." He continued over my attempt at protesting. "I won't follow you. Just…text me if you need any help."

"Fine."

We said goodbye and as he walked away, I considered my next stop. Dangerous? Maybe. On second thought, definitely but if it would help Tanya a little thing like danger wouldn't stop me.

CHAPTER THREE

I was ten minutes away from my destination when I got a text from Will.

Lawyer says you can visit Tanya. Arrangements made. Police station on Edloe.

God bless the man. I text back my thanks and for a moment, considering continuing on my task but decided seeing Tanya was more important.

At the rectangular two-story building, I walked through the doors, up a few stairs, through another door and strode toward the long counter that partitioned the rest of the room from access to the public. The gatekeeper, a tall slim Black man, watched me approach, his face an expressionless mask.

"I…" my voice caught in my throat and my hands shook slightly. This type of environment brought back too many memories, none of them pleasant. My throat constricted thinking about Tanya and why she was here.

"I..um…I'm here to see a prisoner." My breath hitched on the word. Prisoner. Geesus. "I believe arrangements were made with her lawyer. The person's name is Tanya Woods."

"One moment please," the officer instructed. He tapped a few keys on his computer, then nodded. "She'll be brought up from holding. You can see her in one of the interrogation rooms. This way, please."

My legs heavy, as if walking through a quagmire, I followed him to a room, which he opened. My heart was thundering against my ribs, banging to be released.

"Wait here. She'll be a few minutes," he said.

The small square room had a table and two chairs. Sitting lasted less than a minute because I was too keyed up for anything else but pacing and thinking of how things stood between Tanya and me. Our relationship was tenuous lately. I'd crossed a line by asking for help from two young adult offenders under Tanya's care in StreetSmart to help absolve me of murder charges—without her consent. Although she never found out, she had seen Will and me together several times and had come to the incorrect conclusion that we were seeing each other, despite the difference in our ages. I'd lied and said he had been helping me with some moving jobs because if Tanya ever found out that I'd asked Will to break his parole, which he did willingly, Tanya's and my friendship would be over. Period. My betrayal of her trust still bothered me, like a persistent pebble in a shoe, but I'd done what I had to for survival.

And now I hoped the eggshell feeling that cropped up over the past six months between her and me would be over so I could help her.

The door opened and I heard the metal clinking of handcuffs. I turned and took in my best friend, hands locked behind her back, her entire demeanor a mixture of confusion and sorrow. The guard unlocked the cuffs, brought Tanya's hands forward and cuffed her wrists again so that her hands were now in front.

"You have ten minutes," the female guard said and left the room.

Tanya stared at me, almost in incomprehension then her face crumbled and tears filled her eyes.

"Sadie," she cried.

I rushed forward and enveloped her in my arms, irritated at the barrier of her bound hands. "I'm here. I'm here."

She sobbed, her breath coming out in gasps, her shoulders shaking. Seeing her in such distress pulled me back to how we met as children in Oxford Alabama when she'd come careening around a corner on the run from a pack of girls bent on beating her up for whatever reason. Her wide eyes and tear-streaked face showed such fear that I shoved her into a nearby building and told the group of attackers she'd gone into the department store across the street. Once the coast was clear, the two of us escaped and I called my brother to come get us. We cleaned her scraped knees, took her home and from that day forward, Tanya and I had been best friends. Even after our family moved to Amarillo, we stayed in touch and eventually reconnected when Tanya's father got a transfer to Houston and I came down to attend the city's community college.

Tanya had needed me then and she needed me now. After a moment, I led her to the table, pulled out her chair and eased her down. I had a feeling the guard, who was watching, wouldn't like me bringing my chair right next to Tanya's so I went around the table and sat down opposite her.

"Are you okay?" An inane question but I couldn't think at the moment.

"I guess," she said in a defeated, thin voice.

I reached across the table. Screw the people who might think I was doing something I wasn't supposed to, and gripped her hands. "Tell me what happened."

Her forlorn gaze connected with mine. "I don't know where to start."

"The beginning."

She took a deep, shuddering breath. "Crystal and I had gone out for dinner before heading to the all night Indie movie event with the rest of the StreetSmart group."

"What time?"

"Nineish. The movies started at nine but we were late. The crew was already there and we sat in the row behind them."

"And then what?"

"We…we ended up leaving early," she said with hesitation.

Something in her tone made me ask. "Any reason? Were you tired, didn't like the movie?"

She paused. "No. We actually had an argument, well a continuation of the argument that started at dinner. I thought going to the movie fest would give us a break from it but Crystal had other ideas."

I pursed my lips. "Can you tell me what it was about?"

"Crystal wanted to take our relationship to the next level." Tanya scratched her nail on the smooth table. "I wasn't ready. That's why we were fighting."

"Take it to the next level, as in how? Move in together?"

She nodded. "Yes. She kept pushing me about why I didn't want us to live together, made insinuations I was seeing someone else but that's not true. "

I nodded. "Okay. What happened then?"

"We went back to my place. I was hoping a quieter setting would allow us to iron some things out but the argument escalated. Things got heated, words were said. Crystal left."

This coincided with what Will had said. "How was she when she left?"

She grimaced. "Angry. Furious."

"What time was this?"

Tanya pursed her lips. "A little after eleven. I remember because I clicked on the news and they were already into the headlines but the weather hadn't started."

I pictured the events in my head, like a movie. "Go on."

My friend sighed. "After watching the news, I took a bath, tried to relax after our fight. I didn't like how things ended between us, so I called her but she wouldn't pick up. Then I figured I'd try speaking to her face-to-face and called her again on the way over to her place but still no answer. I wanted to explain the reason for me not wanting to move forward had nothing to do with her. It was all me. I just wasn't ready."

"Do you remember what time that was?"

Tanya thought for a moment. "Maybe twelve-thirty or so."

I paused, thought. "Did anyone see you go into the building?"

"Some guy was leaving so I slipped in the main door."

Some guy. A neighbor? Visitor to another tenant? The murderer? "Did you give a description of him to the police?"

Tanya eyed me. "It was dark. I didn't get a good look at him and had other things on my mind."

"So you went up to Crystal's. She let you in?" I prompted.

My best friend bit her lip, eyes filling with tears. She shook her head quickly maybe in denial maybe as an answer to my question. "No. I…I have a key. Crystal gave it to…to me a few weeks back even though I didn't give her one of mine."

I waited, saying nothing.

"I…," she swallowed, started again. "I knocked first. No answer. Knocked again, louder, calling for her to let me in but she didn't come to the door. Because of the late hour, I didn't want to raise the neighbors so I unlocked the door and went inside."

She stopped taking deep breaths.

I lowered my voice. "What did you see?"

Tanya's hands shook, the clinking metal of the handcuffs as loud as rattling chains. "It was dark, well, not quite. A lamp was on."

"Where?"

She closed her eyes for a second. "In the corner, near the couch."

Muted lighting. Was the killer still in the apartment or had they left? "Did you hear anything, see anything odd?"

She shook her head.

"Okay. What did you do next?"

Tanya stared past my head, her gaze unfocused as if she were retracing the steps in her mind. "I walked in, called her name. Nothing. I thought she might be in her bedroom but as I walked by the living room, I saw a dark shape on the couch."

Her last words put a high, reedy edge to her voice. I squeezed Tanya's hand and she held mine in an iron grip.

"As I got closer to her, I noticed things strewn around."

My eyes sharpened on her. "What things?"

"A wine bottle on the glass coffee table and an empty bottle of something on the floor by the couch. Some books on the table and on the floor; her award for creative design."

"Were there glasses?"

Her gaze returned to me. "What?"

"Were there wine glasses or any other type of glass anywhere?" If more than one glass, perhaps someone had been there prior to Tanya arriving?

She frowned. "Umm. I don't remember."

"Okay. What did you do when you saw all this?"

She gave a short laugh of incredulity. "I picked everything up, put them on the coffee table because I didn't want her tripping on anything if she got up. I thought Crystal was drunk since we'd had wine with dinner. The bottle of wine on the table was nearly gone and the empty bottle near her hand was tequila."

"What made you think she was drunk, besides the evidence?" I was trying to form a mental picture of what the scene looked like through Tanya's eyes.

Tanya gave me a quizzical look. "Well, she lay on her right side, was all relaxed, like she'd flopped over on the couch and the bottle had slipped from her fingers."

I lowered my voice, putting as much care and concern as I could. "Did you know Crystal was dead?"

Tears spilled out of Tanya's eyes and she shook her head back and forth in short, jerky movements. "Not…not until…until I shook her…and…and she…she wouldn't wake up. I kept calling her name, louder and louder and that was…was when the shouting began."

My brows knitted. "Who shouted?"

"Some woman. She strode into the apartment with a man right behind her."

"Did you recognize either of them?"

"No," Tanya said. "The guy had a ring of keys in his hand and the woman was yelling. Then she whipped out her cell phone, said she was calling the police."

The man was probably the super but I wondered who the woman was. The murderer returning to the scene of the crime to establish an alibi?

"I kept trying to wake up Crystal but the woman pulled me off, telling me not to touch her. The man stepped in and blocked my view of Crystal until the police showed up."

I swallowed hard. Poor Tanya, she must have been going out of her mind. "What happened when the police came?"

Tanya hung her head as if defeated. "One officer took me into the kitchen and I told him everything I knew. I'm not sure about the other people but I presume they had to tell their stories as well."

She paused for a minute then continued. "It's important for you to understand, Sadie, that I didn't kill her. Crystal meant a great deal to me." She waited a second, her eyes darting around before she lowered her voice to a whisper. "You were so good at ferreting out who framed you for murder. Please help me. This is bad and I know the authorities look to a spouse or lover first. I'm just worried they won't search very hard for anyone else. We've been on shaky ground lately but I don't know who else to turn to. "

I brought my best friend's shackled hands to my lips, kissed them tenderly. "I'll do whatever it takes," I whispered in fierce determination.

The guard returned and clasped my friend's upper arm. As Tanya was walked away, our eyes connected and I gave her a look of more confidence than I felt.

Once out of the police station and back in my vehicle, I had to sit gripping the wheel so that my hands would stop shaking. Seeing Tanya in handcuffs had rocked me to the core, a slam in my solar plexus that had sucked the air out of my lungs. I had been where she was, feeling the same fear and panic hammering through her brain. It made me almost nauseous.

I considered texting Will with what I had learned but not until I had more. Instead, I headed to the house of an ex-con, someone that Tanya had helped put in jail and who had recently been released on parole after serving eight years.

Revenge was a powerful motive for murder.

I pulled into traffic and steeled myself. This would not be fun.

CHAPTER FOUR

On the stoop of a dilapidated house, staring at the business end of a handgun pointed in my face, perhaps it would have been better if Will had come along. However, considering who was holding the weapon, it was more prudent I was here alone.

Lewis Woods didn't trust anyone, including me.

"Hey, Lewis. How are you?"

Tanya's brother eyed me with contempt as the corner of his mouth lifted into a sneer. "Sadie Hawkins. What the hell do you want?"

"Just to talk, nothing else." When he didn't make any move to invite me in, I stared at the gun in his hand. "Maybe we shouldn't stand here for the whole world to see you violating your parole."

He waited for a heartbeat then shot a quick look left and right as if to check that no one had accompanied me, lowered his hand and walked away, leaving the open door as a signal to enter.

My stomach quivered like jellied salad as I stepped into the house. The Lewis I knew, the one who'd given Tanya and me the gears while at her house growing up one day then share his chocolate bar the next, wouldn't shoot me but that was before he'd been in jail. Did that person still reside under the black jeans and rumpled tee shirt? His dark hair was buzz cut to his head and a scar bisected his right eyebrow, which hadn't been there when he was young. He still had a handsome face, his skin tone lighter than Tanya's because he was her half-brother. A lean hardness took its place now, evidence of the road he'd traveled on.

Beer cans littered his living room. An odd mishmash of secondhand furniture and a pizza box with one slice left sat open on a beat up coffee table. An empty bottle of Tequila stood at the far end.

Lewis flopped down in an easy chair that looked like it belonged in the dumpster, laid the weapon on a TV stand beside it and pointed to a couch that sagged so much it would require a crane to get out of it. "Have a seat."

I perched on the edge to circumvent having to delouse my clothes not to mention the unladylike roll to the floor when it was time to get up. My gaze traveled around the room taking in the mustard yellow carpet in desperate need of cleaning, the ratty threadbare curtains that muted bright outdoor sunshine to washed-out beige, the lack of personal belongings and the bare off-white walls. This wasn't a home; it was a place to sleep.

He stared at me, waiting. Guess he wasn't offering sweet tea and cookies.

"Have you spoken to Tanya lately?"

His eyes narrowed and the sneer returned. "No. Have nothing to say to her."

I figured as much. Lewis was the eldest of the four Woods children, the product of Tanya's father's first marriage, and the only boy, which had put him in the unenviable position of having to watch over his other siblings. It had also made for a temperamental, cocksure young man, full of bravado who had become the perfect initiate into a life of petty crime.

After his mother had died, Lewis' father married again and Tanya came along nine months later. Despite the four-year gap, the two siblings had been close and Tanya had always been worried about him. We'd talked many times about how she tried to get him to drop his friends and focus on a career in sports journalism. But Tanya had said she felt he took her love and concern as meddling and retaliated by being withdrawn, sometimes even cruel. He had never struck his sister, yet wounds inflicted by words cut just as deep. She'd told me how tormented she was on how Lewis was throwing his life away and there was nothing she could do to help him.

Inevitably, the petty crime had blossomed into armed robbery of a convenience store and someone got shot. Lewis and another male, the shooter, were captured on store video in hoodies and caps that had covered their faces. When the local news network released the grainy video, Tanya recognized her brother by the specific patch on the shoulder of his hoodie. She'd sewn it on as a favor when he'd ripped the garment while helping her move into her apartment. She had come to my place in tears, not knowing what to do, her conscious unwilling to let her sleep. As much as she loved her brother, she knew he had done something illegal and if he wasn't stopped, the path he tread could lead to more serious crimes. In the end she called the police and turned in her brother.

She'd confessed to me that decision was the hardest thing she had ever done and it caused considerable friction between Tanya and the rest of her family. Although she hadn't regretted it, I could see she still carried the pain and grief like a cloak of armor around her heart.

"Why are you here?" Lewis asked again, pulling me back to the present.

"Tanya has been arrested and charged with manslaughter."

I paused, hoping for some type of emotion from him, some indication that brotherly love still hid underneath his stony façade.

The cool, expressionless gaze of his dark brown eyes held mine. "Who'd she off?"

My heart sank at his lack of concern, as if we were talking about a character in a television crime series and not his flesh and blood. "Her lover, Crystal Sherridan."

He snorted. "Oh yeah? Huh. She caught the dike in someone else's bed?"

He murmured something else that might have been 'serves her right' but I couldn't be sure. The urge to slap his face for the derogatory slur and his nonchalance almost engulfed me but that wouldn't do any good and probably earn me a black eye. To tamp down my fiery temper, I silently counted down from ten. I understood he was angry and knew he had a bone to pick with Tanya but she hadn't committed a crime. I was almost sure of it.

Almost.

Tanya and her lover had been fighting. Love and money were the two top motivations for murder and people did stupid things when they got mad. Tanya meant to talk to Crystal but had things got out of hand and she'd lied to me?

No. I saw the truth in Tanya's eyes and I believed she didn't murder Crystal. I needed to find out what Lewis knew about Crystal.

"Did you know Crystal?"

His eyes flicked to mine before he reached for an open beer can on the coffee table. "Maybe."

The hold on my temper stretched to a thin wire. "What's that supposed to mean? Did you know her or not?"

"It means," he ground out with a glare, "that I don't have to tell you anything."

Was the guy baiting me, hoping to get some type of reaction?

Although my inner voice was almost yelling to be careful of what I said, I shoved a sock in its mouth. "For goodness' sake, Lewis, she's my best friend and your sister!"

"So what!" He slammed the beer can down, which resulted in an arc of foamy liquid spewing over the lip, grabbed the gun, stood abruptly and paced back and forth. "I was her brother but that didn't stop her from squealing to the cops. I did eight years because of her!"

Was. Was her brother. Did he no longer think of her as family? As someone he loved?

"You did eight years because you broke the law, not because of Tanya."

Lewis spun around and whipped the gun up to point it at me. "Think it's time for you to leave."

My heart catapulted into my throat. *Geesus Sadie, put brain in gear before engaging mouth.* I brought my hands up, rose from the couch and left the room. At the door, I turned and was relieved to see he had lowered the weapon to his side. "She loves you, you know. Despite all that you've done, Tanya loves you."

"Fat lot of good that did me in jail."

"Did you ever think where you'd be if she hadn't stepped in? If she hadn't seen where you were heading and with whom and decided it was the only way to help you?"

His eyes collided with mine. "I've thought of nothing else for eight long years. I'd be living a hell of a lot better than this shit hole."

With a glance around, I brought my attention back to him. "You sure about that?"

His nostrils flared. "She's getting what she deserves." He turned and walked away.

Outside, the fear I'd held in check finally bubbled over. My legs shook to the point it hampered the trip to my brother's van. I'd known Lewis for years, had seen him grow from a boy who used to tease his sisters to a young adult and now to this bitter, angry man who blamed his incarceration on Tanya. *She's getting what she deserves.* Could he hate Tanya so much that he would frame his own sister for a crime she didn't commit?

I hopped into the vehicle, turned the key and headed to Blaine's house where I was staying until they came home and could make a plan to find out what, if anything Lewis knew about Crystal Sherridan.

CHAPTER FIVE

I was at the office early the next day having spent a fitful night sleeping because thoughts of Tanya kept going through my brain. The only way for my mind to focus was to give it a hit of Live Wire; a double shot espresso, four teaspoons of sugar in a mug of cola with a healthy dose of chocolate syrup made from eighty-five percent dark chocolate. The drink was from my college days to help me cram for exams and it was potent enough to wake the dead.

The pen in my fingers tapped against a sheet of notes, detailed scribbling of what I could remember about Lewis and any of his friends. A long shot, since he was released on parole a little over six months ago. His comment *she's getting what she deserves* made the hairs on the back of my neck twitch. Ramblings of a disgruntled brother or words of satisfaction?

On the Internet, I found the convenience store robbery story with Lewis and his accomplice's name, Jason Cullman, which I added to my notes. Maybe Will could find info on him and anyone else Tanya's brother used to hang around with. Did Lewis turn to his former pals to help enact retribution? Or maybe he enlisted someone he was chummy with now?

And what about Crystal? Did she know her killer? Was it someone with an axe to grind or was it just random?

I compiled a to-do list; go to Crystal's apartment, talk to people on the street and those who lived in the building, the superintendent and perhaps the cop first on the scene. I knew I wouldn't have access to Crystal's apartment so for those details I had to obtain a copy of the police report using Will's superpowers.

Will's prowess with computers and all things technical fell into the same category as the female character from the dragon tattoo books, awe-inspiring and slightly creepy for a non-tech person like me. He had taken me to where he worked and I remembered gaping at the racks of equipment, monitors and wires, grateful to have him as a friend. Tanya would be appreciative too only she could never know the depth of his role because that would mean she'd failed at making sure Will didn't violate his parole by hacking into computer databases, which would mean he'd go back to jail.

All the unanswered questions regarding Tanya's predicament made my brain do its best square dance imitation of the Virginia Reel so I returned the messages from my cell and contacted some potential new clients. After that I took my four-legged nephew,

Moose, who I had brought with me to the shop because I couldn't bear to leave him alone in an empty house all day, for a nice long walk.

As we were on our walk, a text came through from Will. *Bail hearing today at four. Courthouse on Franklin.* The man didn't mince words.

I'll be there.

Back at Hawkins Freight, I hustled Moose into the van and drove him back to the house. I didn't want to leave him at the office and with the late summer heat, keeping him locked in a vehicle was out of the question.

After a quick sandwich, washed down with a high octane cola, it was time to head downtown. A traffic snarl because of a fender-bender took some time and as I pulled into a parking lot near my destination my phone dinged with a message from Will.

"Where are you?"

I sent a quick reply to meet me out front and high-tailed it toward the entrance.

The Harris County Criminal Court building was a twenty storied concrete and glass edifice, its wide strip of three steps leading to a set of glass double doors. A large disc with the justice scales symbol sat above the entrance beneath a domed archway that jutted out of the building, breaking up the vertical monotonous framework and lending a more academic feel than a criminal institutional one. It sat across from Quebedeaux Park where someone could sit among the trees or stroll around. Did friends or loved ones of the guilty visit here to ponder life without them?

Hopefully, that wouldn't be the case for Tanya's friends and family.

Will paced back and forth at the doors, impatiently glancing at his watch when I jogged up the steps.

"You're cutting it fine," he grumbled, opening the door and ushering me in.

Will was usually mild-mannered and had only been this tense when he'd escorted me from a crime scene before the cops could find me there so I didn't take his complaint personally.

Our conversation ceased when we entered the elevator amidst a throng of people and watched the numbers climb, my anxiousness increasing with each passing digit until we came out on the correct floor. A carpeted hallway greeted us and we went into a wood paneled room, complete with a judge's chair on a raised dais, two tables facing the front of the room and the gallery behind. A few people sat at various spots in the seating area but I didn't recognize anyone.

Both counsel tables were occupied, although the one on the right held only one person. Tanya sat on the left with her lawyer, a shorter woman, their backs to me. My friend must have heard the door close because she turned around, caught my gaze and the mixture of gratitude and fear in her eyes ripped through me like barbed wire. I forced myself to portray support and confidence through that connection, yet felt anything but. How in the hell could this be happening?

An eerie sense of déjà vu settled like a shroud, transporting me back to when I was in the same position as Tanya. Only there was one big difference; I would almost stake my life that Tanya hadn't committed her crime.

That wasn't true for me.

While attending HCC, Houston Community College, my mom, Jolene had come from Amarillo for a visit and we'd gone to a block party where we'd ran into her off-again boyfriend, Ricky Best. He'd learned my mom visited, and since he knew I attended college there, had followed us to the party, hoping a drink and some dancing would put him back in her good books. It didn't. Later that night, noises woke me and when I went to investigate, Ricky attacked me. I came to moments later and found him violating my mother with enough force to kill her. I'd grabbed a baseball bat and beat him to unconsciousness.

I was charged with the possibility of murdering Ricky based on a statement from the neighbor who went to my apartment and thought he saw a dead body. But when the police finally arrived, there was no body. Even the bat was missing. Subsequently, the charges were dropped.

Ricky was not who he claimed. When authorities went to Amarillo for more information, they found his business shut, his house vacant, his bank accounts and assets cleaned out and all his documentation falsified. Basically Ricky Best did not exist. With no one to file charges, the lack of evidence and a straightforward case of having to use the force necessary to prevent further harm, my case was dismissed.

Since that day, the harbinger of vengeance from the man hasn't left me. He must still be alive. Why else pull a Houdini act? But I'd deduced he hadn't surfaced because the truth would come out as to the premeditation of his attack on my mother. I have wondered if I could have reacted differently, somehow come to a better resolution than trying to beat a man to death. But after seeing how the vital person my widowed mother had been and now was nothing but a hollowed-out shell existing in the self-protected world of her mind, I had no regrets.

Will nudged his knee against me, bringing me back to the present. "You okay?"

I pulled back from the mental nightmare and focused on the room before me. "Yeah, I'm fine."

The bailiff stood and announced the judge who entered from a side door on the left and everyone rose then returned to their seats. My heart smacked double time against my chest, making the blood pulse loud in my ears. Would the judge grant bail or would Tanya have to spend the rest of the time before her trial in jail? My breath started heaving. I'd been in those cells, knew what the atmosphere was like and it changed you. I clenched my hands and prayed my best friend wouldn't have to experience that.

The robed figure presiding over the proceedings was a woman, perhaps making things easier on Tanya. After hearing from both sides, she deliberated for a moment, then announced bail to be set at fifty thousand dollars, banged her gavel and asked for the next case.

Tanya rose, hands trembling as handcuffs were slipped around her wrists and she shot a quick panicked look at both Will and me before being led out by an officer of the court.

Will inhaled deeply through his nose, as if he'd been sucker punched. "Crap."

I let out a gasp. "Fifty thousand dollars."

"You think Tanya might have that kind of money?"

"No way. She doesn't even own her apartment."

He glanced around, searching for someone. "What about her family?"

"They're not here. They didn't even bother to show up." I'd hoped my best friend's sister who still lived in Houston or their parents would show some type of support for their daughter. Apparently, when Tanya had turned her brother in eight years ago a line was drawn.

Tanya's lawyer was already out the door and Will and I followed at a slower pace. My feet dragged, as if walking through waist high water, each step a trial of effort. We left the room and stepped to one side in the hallway.

"What now?"

"I don't know." The set of Will's jaw, his hardened gaze spoke of his anger. "I can try to get a loan from my father but don't hold your breath."

Will and his father had a falling out several years back because he'd helped his sister escape from the overbearing parent. Since then Stockwell Ellington gave his son an allowance and paid for his essentials but that was the extent of Will's finances.

He gazed down the hall. "I'll speak with her lawyer, see what options are open. Maybe she can suggest a bail bondsman."

We went farther down the hall, away from the throng of people clustered near the courtroom door. "I met with Tanya's brother yesterday, after our drinks. Has she ever spoken to you about him?"

"No. Do you think he needs checking out?"

I told him about my meeting with Lewis, the motive he might have against Tanya and also gave him the name of Lewis' accomplice in the robbery. I filled him in on what Tanya had told me about that night. Then I asked him to use his magic and get a copy of the police report.

"Give me some time to see what I can dig up. I'll call you when I find out anything. What are you going to do?"

"I'll talk to the officer first on the scene, if they will even tell me anything. Are you going to see Tanya?"

"If I can, yes."

"Tell her to hang in there. We'll figure something out."

"Okay." He gave my hand a light squeeze. "You hang in there too."

We parted and I threaded my way through people to hit the elevators. Before leaving the courthouse, I was directed to three different places before finally acquiring the name of the cop who was lead investigator at Crystal's murder. She was unavailable when I called so I left a message to contact me.

While driving home, Will texted me.

Found a bondsman. Requires ten percent down and collateral for the rest.

I pulled to the curb. Crap. There was a possibility Tanya may have the five thousand for the down payment but since she didn't own property and her car was an older model she'd have to spend the time before her trial in jail. My hands ached from gripping the steering wheel so hard. Tanya would not stay in jail. I wouldn't let that happen.

Am going to raise Tanya's bail money I texted back.

How are you going to do that?

Connections

There was a pause before he sent, *Good luck*

I went to feed and let Moose out before heading to my condo to change into more appropriate clothing. And since my plan could take most of the evening if not the entire night, I had to cancel my date with Wayne.

The call went to his voice mail. The reluctance in my voice was genuine but Tanya's future took precedent over a nice evening with a handsome man.

"Hey Wayne, it's me. Listen, I'm really sorry but I'm going to have to cancel our date tonight. Something has come up which can't be put off." I paused. "Umm, maybe we can reschedule?" Another brief pause. "Call me." A sigh of resignation pushed past my lips.

At my condo, I hit the shower. I'd have to come up with some type of excuse to tell him once Wayne called, if he called, because I sure couldn't tell him the truth about tonight.

Standing in front of my open closet after my shower, I inspected my collection. There were the few occasions when getting dressed up was fun and although this would be business the little black number and a pair of lacy, deep red panties with matching bra from Victoria Secret was just the ticket. The lingerie, my one vice besides high octane cola, slipped like silk over my skin, infusing me with a brief surge of feminine power. I'd take whatever boosts of confidence I could get, and pulled the black dress over top. My feet were wedged into sleek black heels

that weren't the four-inch torture devices from my
dating days.

A quick trip into the washroom to smooth a hint
of foundation on my face, add mascara to my eyes,
mix some gel into my hair, style it with my fingers and
with a last turn in the mirror to check for anything
amiss, the black clutch purse went under my arm and
I was out the door.

CHAPTER SIX

I held my black purse against my chest and knocked three times on a nondescript door above Frank's Diner. It opened a crack and a man who could have passed for a mastodon, minus the tusks, eyed me with suspicion but the round plastic disc in my fingers granted me access. I'd used the disc, a ticket to get in, the first and only other time a couple of years ago. Each person kept it with them until Freddy Mack, the silent partner of Frank's Diner and head of the establishment before me, demanded it back because of unpaid debt or it passed on through inheritance.

Trepidation swirled in my gut like acid, and I almost turned around and left. The room was richly decorated in dark paneling, a stark contrast to the cheap diner below. A few paintings of unknown origin adorned the walls, while even-spaced black sconces emitted warm lighting, an accompaniment to the hanging ceiling fixtures of black and gold. No windows, yet the air was not stuffy, an indication of a decent air flow system. Three round wooden tables sat within ten feet of one another, each with five or six occupants, both men and women. My stomach clenched as I crossed the deep maroon carpet of the proverbial lion's den to the gaming tables. An elegant woman dressed in dark blue approached me with a tray of cocktails but I declined, opting for cola instead. Focus was of utmost importance.

I needed my wits about me to utilize my familial talent.

My Uncle Stan had taught me to play cards as a child and eventually introduced me to poker. Although a wheeler-dealer, he was a decent man with a warm heart despite his penchant for gambling. That weakness had eventually made him lose Hawkins Freight in a card game. The habit plus the accidental death of my father during a move had led Stan to take his own life.

Sweet irony resulted in me gaining the business in the same manner my uncle had lost it. The money from my amicable divorce from Clayton gave me the capitol I needed to have Hawkins Freight up and running again within the family.

Standing off to one side, watching the players, assessing the dealers, deciding which table would provide me with the best outcome, I had the same temptation as one would get after quitting smoking. You want to try it again, knew it was a bad idea, but the lure of winning gave overconfidence you could handle it. After I'd won the business back, the challenge of bigger pots, of higher stakes, whispered its evil song in my brain for a long time. That voice had made Stan squander everything and he'd ended up in a drunken stupor, living in squalor, clutching his disc as if it held the key to his future. It had, in a sense, just not how he'd envisioned. Freddie Mack hadn't recouped the plastic pass because he didn't have a marker on my uncle so when I saw Stan the last time before he killed himself, I pocketed the disc.

Now the same road my uncle had traveled lay before me. Once I took that first step, would my outcome be identical? Thinking back to the last time I saw him, my reasoning for pocketing the disc was because I didn't want Stan to try his luck again and go into debt with Freddie. But was that the whole truth? The plastic unit itched in my hands. With Stan's image foremost in my mind, my fingers squeezed the round orb and it went back into my purse. I had come here for a specific purpose, to get enough money for Tanya's bail, and that was it.

I took a deep, steadying breath. My mission would not happen if I stayed on the sidelines.

One player at a table, a man, threw down his cards and rose not saying a word. He stalked out of the room, giving me the opportunity to take his place. The vacant wooden chair was comfortable with a leather padded seat, and I forced my fingers to stop trembling as they pulled the short stack of bills from my purse. With the small stash from my place and what I took out of my account at an ATM, my stake was minimal and I'd have to work hard to produce results.

The other opponents, three men and one woman, eyed me as if assessing the newest competitor but gave no greeting. This wasn't your friendly Friday night poker game with friends. It was one step below high stakes in places like Monaco or Malta. The big difference was they had legalized gambling; Texas only allowed some methods of gambling, but nothing like this. If this limited operation got raided, we'd all be arrested and I could kiss my business goodbye.

The dealer, a man, collected the cards, put them on a shelf below where he sat and retrieved a fresh deck. "New player, new deck," he said, removing the clear plastic wrapping. He weeded the two jokers, which he showed the group, then spread the rest of the cards face up. You'd have to be pretty quick to calculate if they were all there but no one called foul so he scooped the cards and began shuffling. "The game is five-card draw, aces high, deuces wild. Ante up. Betting starts at five hundred."

I stifled a groan and added the cash to the pot. With the loss of a few hands, at this rate, I'd be leaving in less than an hour.

The croupier, dressed in black pants, white shirt and black vest, passed out the cards from the deck and I brought mine together, eased them up just to see their denominations. Two tens, a five, a three and a deuce. Not bad. A three of a kind with the tens and deuce as a wildcard.

The person to the left of the dealer, a blonde woman in a low cut plum colored blouse began the betting, raising an extra fifty to the pot. If her plan on showing that much cleavage was to distract the men at the table, she needn't have bothered. They focused on their cards. The guy beside her with horn-rimmed glasses saw the bet, his dark eyes darting from player to player. On my turn, I tossed the cash onto the pile. The man next to me who smelled of cheap cologne folded. The last player, a man wearing a cowboy hat and pressed shirt tossed in his fifty, the dealer anted up and the play went back to the woman. She smiled like a cat and asked for one card, glasses guy got two, eyes still bouncing everywhere. I discarded the three and the five and received two new cards. The last player discarded three and the dealer gave himself one. The female at the table raised a couple hundred. Glasses guy folded, eyes shuttered in defeat. The cards dealt me failed to improve my hand higher than three of a kind so called with the two hundred. The dealer and cowboy both called. When we all revealed our cards I won the pot but only because of a wild card. I gathered my winnings, making sure not to change my expression and another round of play began.

Hours passed and time became irrelevant. At one point, I thought my phone buzzed. I had put it on vibrate before arriving, and wondered if it was Wayne calling me back. The thought got conveyed to the recesses of my brain because I couldn't lose focus. As the evening wore on, stakes rose and I immersed myself in the game's flow, the hushed murmurs of dealer and players, the hits and misses of hands. My world revolved around the table, the rest of the room faded. During the evening, my winnings amassed to almost thirty thousand, then went down to ten. I didn't dare look at my watch but continued on, a single-minded determination to win as much as possible. Players at my table came and went; cheap cologne lasted a few hours and the woman left later. My drink was constantly replenished and cowboy guy belted back shots of something amber.

My money stack had grown slowly when the next hand made my heart go pitter-patter—four of a kind with a kicker. Betting was heavy now and on the first round I raised five grand, which made one player fold. The second round didn't give me the golden card, a deuce, but I hedged my bets and raised another five. Two more players dropped out. The cowboy eyed me shrewdly, assessing what was in my hand, possibly because I called his bluff earlier in the game and he lost a hefty amount of cash. Eventually, he called and we both laid our cards on the table. My four sevens topped his full house.

By loose calculations, my winnings from the course of the evening were over forty thousand. The long day wore on me. My focus kept wavering and I was worried I'd lose my edge.

Three players left the table, no one else came to sit down. The other tables were empty, which meant only cowboy guy and I were left playing. Since I won the last round, the dealer gave me a questioning lift of his eyebrows to continue. I was so close to what I needed so that Tanya wouldn't have to spend another day in jail. I nodded my assent and he turned to my opponent. The cowboy took off his hat, ran fingers through short dirty blond hair and gave a quick jerk of his head. The dealer passed out the cards. I checked mine, placed a bet of five thousand. The hand was strong, a straight flush in diamonds with king high. If this round went to me, it would be enough.

My opponent checked his cards, the corner of his mouth lifting ever so slightly. "I'll see your five and raise you another ten."

I swallowed. What did he have? The only other hand that could beat mine was four of the same card with a deuce to make five of a kind. I couldn't calculate the odds because we weren't playing a type of poker to count cards even if I knew how to do that trick. Losing this hand would take my earnings and I'd need to play hours longer to win it back if cowboy even decided he wanted to keep playing. My heart hammered against my ribcage and my throat went dry. An image of Uncle Stan rose in my head, bringing a flash of indecision streaking right after it. Fold and walk away with thirty plus thousand. Return tomorrow and hope to win more? I pictured Tanya and the look in her eyes as they held mine in the courtroom—fear and hope. Maybe Tanya's parents might cough up the difference. But I knew deep down they wouldn't. If you didn't even come to your daughter's hearing, you didn't care enough to get her out on bail.

I passed on the option of another card, selected the bills from the stack in front of me and slid them to the middle with trembling fingers. "Call."

Cowboy quirked a brow and asked for a single card. The uplift of his lips happened again. Crap. Since I called and he didn't raise, I laid my cards first watched for the other player's reaction. His face was impassive but a flicker of disappointment sparked in his eyes. He leaned forward and spread his cards on the table. Four queens stared up at me with a nine holding them back from a five of a kind.

The breath left me in a soft gasp before my eyes closed in relief.

"You are one hell of a card player lady," he said with a sardonic grin.

"You had me going there for a minute." And he had.

The high of winning was almost like shooting back three Live-Wires but it was fleeting. I'd come here for a purpose, a job and having accomplished that I rose, gathered the money and extended my hand. "Good game."

He shook it, hung on for a second longer. "I'd like to try winning some of that back."

"Maybe another time."

A couple of hundred went to the dealer who nodded his thanks. The woman who had provided me with beverages also received monetary appreciation from me and then I made my way toward the door on shaky legs. Mastodon man was still there.

He opened the portal. "You be careful now. That's a lot of cash to be carrying."

On the other side of the open doorway stood a tall, slim man in a black suit and deep, green shirt that matched his eyes. Black hair slicked back off his face from a widow's peak while the sides were short but not buzz cut. Thick eyebrows almost met above a straight nose and a tiny black tattoo of a lightning bolt rested on the right cheekbone near the corner of his eye. A short, neatly trimmed beard covered his jaw and upper lip. Freddy Mack was in his mid forties, devilishly handsome and exuded an almost untouchable air. He pulled at the cuffs of his shirt, his mouth pressed in a thin smile of respect and resignation.

"My assistant tells me you did well tonight."

"Girl's gotta make a living." My chest tightened as I stopped breathing for an instant. The snark was supposed to stay in my head and not come out of my mouth.

His eyes ventured down my body then returned to my face where they stayed, assessing me. After a heartbeat he said, "Something tells me you have more intelligence than that."

The sincerity in his voice and unwavering level gaze surprised me considering we had never met. It also sent a slight tingle through me.

"Thank you."

"However, you cost me over twenty grand tonight."

He wore slash-toed leather shoes, which had to be Italian, based on the rest of his clothing because it was a fair bet he wouldn't be caught dead wearing anything else.

"One less pair of designer footwear for you then," I quipped lightly and inwardly groaned at my lack of restraint. It wasn't wise to speak in such a way to someone who ran an illegal gambling operation but exhaustion made me punchy.

Mastodon man inhaled in a quick gasp. Apparently, few people made that type of comment to his boss.

Freddy's eyes held my gaze for so long without blinking he'd have won a staring contest with a cat. People vanished from time to time if you pissed off men like him. Uneasy trepidation tiptoed up my along my nerve endings and I silently cursed my big dang mouth.

After what felt like the longest moment in history, a spark of what might be humor briefly flickered in his eyes and a corner of his mouth gave just the slightest hint of lifting. "My valet will be ever so grateful."

He stepped aside and said to his bouncer. "Make sure the lady gets to her car safely."

The hulk beside me nodded, ushered me across the threshold. I kept silent the whole time, not wanting to push my luck but a part of me was itching to glance over my shoulder and give my host a saucy grin before I hit the stairs that led to the street.

When the door opened to the outside, dawn had already splashed its golden yellow greeting to the day. I shielded my eyes from the brightness and stumbled. Freddy's employee steadied me with a hand to my lower back and escorted me to Blaine's van parked around the corner. He made sure I got inside and locked the doors then watched as I drove down the street.

I don't remember making the drive to Blaine's house, grateful the morning commuter traffic hadn't started yet. As I inched open the front door, Moose let out an angry woof and came barreling down the stairs to the entranceway.

"Hey boy, it's me." I leaned down and rubbed his head. "Sorry for being this late. You're probably hungry and need to go outside."

While the dog was out in the backyard, I put some kibble in his dish and fresh water in his bowl. With a fling of my feet, shoes bounced to the floor, and I rubbed my aching toes, wishing I could have worn my boots. A glance at the clock on the stove read six thirty. I had to be at the shop for nine.

Great, just great.

CHAPTER SEVEN

After standing in line to pay Tanya's bail at the courthouse, I dragged my sorry butt into the office around half past ten, pulling a reluctant Moose behind me. I didn't have the heart to leave him at home alone all day again. The need for sleep was almost more than I could stand but there was a minor job slated for the late afternoon. I also needed to get over to Crystal's apartment complex and ask questions.

The phone was already ringing when I opened the door and leaped at the instrument before the person hung up.

"Hawkins Freight."

The caller inquired about the cost of a move and I gave him a rough quote before settling on a date. A few more calls came in; the end of summer challenged parents to get kids off to college. Before long, the rest of the morning vanished with booking jobs and rearranging schedules.

When I caught my breath, I texted Will about posting Tanya's bail.

Within seconds, he replied. *What?? How?*

With money, silly. Even portraying the female version of Snow White's dwarf named Sleepy, I could still be a smartass. Had to yank the guy's chain sometime. *Clerk said Tanya won't be out till this afternoon. Have a moving gig. Maybe you could go pick her up at courthouse on Franklin?*

Will do.

Okay, was that pun on purpose? Even though he couldn't see me, I shook my head. *Tell her I'll come by to see her soon. Also, can you look into Crystal's background?*

For what?

Any motive for someone to kill her.

Will do. And a laughing emoji followed. Now he was the smartass.

My stomach growled louder than a tractor pulling contest; it had been hours since I ate breakfast. Because of the job later, best to grab something quick to eat while taking Moose to the park for a walk, then drop him off at the house. I tossed the dog's leash onto the floor after he jumped up into the passenger seat of the moving van and got in the other side.

A turn of the ignition key produced a few sputters, a cough, wheeze and a grind from beneath the hood. Another attempt brought the same result. After the third try with the same result, continuing would only drain the battery. I thumped my head against the steering wheel and let out a groan. Of course, this would happen while Blaine was gone and I had a load to pick up. Checking under the hood would be fruitless, since I had no clue what to look for. Blaine was the mechanic in the family so we had never used a garage. The stories I heard about being ripped off made me reach for my phone to see if any of my friends knew someone who could look at the van.

My fingers hovered over the phone keypad when the realization came with a dismaying clarity that I didn't have an extensive list to call. When I was married to Clayton, we associated within his social circles, the upper middle class, and since our divorce I'd been afflicted with 'third-wheel' syndrome. All our friends had been couples—doctors, psychiatrists, fellow lawyers from Clayton's firm, not a single mechanic in any of them. They were happily married partners who attended elite establishments and went on vacations four times a year with their children. No single entities allowed.

After my husband and I parted ways, my life had been too busy trying to get Hawkins Freight off the ground to cultivate any type of social calendar. Besides Tanya and Wayne, my pals numbered few. That needed to change soon. I dialed up Clayton in case he knew of a reliable person to help me but he was in court and would be for the rest of the day. Wayne was working and after asking for the favor the other day, not to mention canceling our date, he might not be that receptive. And Tanya was unreachable. There was only one other person I could think of.

"Hey Will."

"Hi Sadie. Something come up?"

"Sort of."

I paused and sighed. The job that afternoon was doable using Blaine's personal vehicle; it would just take me longer because I'd have to make more trips. But the moving van needed to be fixed immediately, which was sure to cost me an arm, a leg or some other body part.

"Do you know of someone who would come to the shop and have a look at the van? It won't start."

"I'm pretty sure my father's mechanic might be out of your price range and he won't make house calls." He resumed speaking after a moment of silence. "However, I have a solution to your problem. Remember Jessie Montgomery, the girl who helped with the antiques move?"

My memory turned back to picture a young woman in her early twenties. She drove the forklift to move a sarcophagus and at the time I'd mentioned to Tanya how uncommon to see a woman maneuver a piece of equipment with such efficiency. Tanya had commented that Jessie was a whiz with cars as well.

A spark of hope kindled. "Yes, vaguely. Do you think she'd mind coming over and checking it out?"

"I can ask."

"I can't pay her a lot." Although my finances were not even close to being healthy, I would give her some type of compensation.

"She could use it as part of her community time served," he explained and then tacked on. "I also have to check with the new manager."

"New manager? Thought you'd be filling in temporarily until Tanya came back to work?"

Will gave a short bark of laughter. "Are you kidding? I have a record. No, the new manager came in from another StreetSmart in Austin."

"What's he like?"

"He is a she. So far okay but she only started today."

"The woman's probably swamped and the last thing I want to do is bother her with something as trivial as sending one of her crew to help me."

"Don't worry, Sadie. I'll take care of it. Call you in a bit," he said and hung up.

Moose whined and his big brown eyes pleaded at me. When I let him out, he zipped to the door, back to me and paced frantically around in a circle.

"Oh, no you don't. Not here."

Once his leash was clipped on, he literally me out the door. First stop was to water a hydrant, then we both went for a walk. With no parks in this part of town, it was the sidewalk or nothing. At least the dog didn't demand a patch of green.

While I walked the dog, I scrolled through my phone log. Wayne called me back but didn't leave a message, however the officer from Tanya's case did.

"Hello, Ms. Hawkins, this is Officer Aquila Ramerez returning your call. If you'd like to phone me, we can arrange a meeting to discuss Ms. Woods' case."

I called her and although she was busy at the moment we set up a time later in the day to chat.

After a half hour later, we stopped at a food truck on the way back and I bought a loaded hot dog for me and a plain wiener for Moosie.

I broke the frank in halves. "If this gives you gas, I'm going to lose all respect for you."

He gazed at the links in my hands and answered with a woof and a whine. I took that as a promise to keep his bowels in check but he'd say anything to get food.

A motorcycle and an older model compact car stood near the rolling door of my shop, and agitated voices almost drowned out the ringing phone on my desk. My quickened pace took me inside to see a senior citizen brandishing a Taser at two young women, each of whom held a wrench in their hands.

And all three of them were yelling.

"Either of you make one more move and I'll zap you into next week," barked the eldest woman as she glared at the other two while moving the small black unit between them.

"You're crazy lady!"

"I thought you said you came here to help someone."

"Who you calling crazy?"

"Hey!" I roared above the din. "What the Sam-hell is going on here?"

Three people stared at me for a heartbeat, then explained. Simultaneously.

And then Moose chimed in too.

The senior put two fingers between her lips and gave an ear-piercing whistle. All clamor stopped, including the phone.

I closed my eyes, took a deep breath, and turned to the elderly woman. "Sylvia? What are you doing here? And what happened?"

"Why did you start with her?" snapped the sullen faced young woman with black lipstick and heavily painted eye shadow.

"Age before beauty," Sylvia defended. "Although I'm not too sure about the beauty part. Who are you trying to be, Elvira? Ease up on the clippers."

"You'll get your turn." I interrupted before the female with spiky black hair could respond and focused back on the hippie senior.

Sylvia Brady was the client with her six dogs that I had moved from Amarillo the other day. A pair of funky blue harem pants decorated with a white peacock feather and elongated gold diamond design replaced her flowing denim skirt from the other day. The material came to rest in an elastic cuff above soft blue suede Birkenstock sandals. A thin, light leather jacket covered her white peasant blouse.

"I stopped by to pay you for the moving job." She nodded to the two who were still within her Taser range. "Good thing too, because I found these two digging through your toolbox." She picked up some papers from the desk. "Oh, and I answered your phone. Here are your messages."

"I'll deal with those in a minute."

I recognized the last of the trio. She and the others at StreetSmart had helped with a move a few months back. Even though we hadn't been introduced then, I nodded to her. "Jessie, right?"

"Hi." Dark brown hair cut in a bob sat behind dainty ears and although soft spoken, her brown eyes were sharp as they peered at me. "I thought you knew I was coming."

"Yes, but I expected Will to call me back. He said nothing about you bringing company."

Jessie turned to her companion. "Erie gave me a ride."

Sylvia snorted. "You adopt that name to go with your look?"

"It's short for Erianna, not that it's any business of yours," Erie shot back.

"Okay, let's all just calm down. Hang on, how did you get in?"

"Door was open," everyone said in unison.

"Well, we got here first," offered Jessie. "I assumed you were around and looked to see what tools there were to work on your van."

"When I arrived the phone was ringing and recalled our conversation during the drive about having someone manning the lines. I figured might as well answer it. When the banging started and these two began talking, I knew I wasn't alone," added Sylvia.

To stop Moose from making a mess in the garage, I'd forgotten to lock the door on the way out. I felt pulled in five different directions at the same time.

I paused, sniffed the air and waved a hand in front of my face. We all stepped back from the dog. I glared down at the culprit at my side. "You promised."

The phone rang again.

"You deal with these two and I'll get that," Sylvia said.

"Great, thanks."

While the two young women followed me to the van in the loading bay, I explained the noises it made. Jessie asked me to try starting the vehicle again and after one attempt, made a slicing motion across her neck.

"Pop the hood," she said. She secured it before leaning in to examine the engine.

I stood beside Erie. "You with StreetSmart too?"

She shook her head. "Not as a client. I volunteer on occasion and was there when Will asked Jessie to come and give you a hand."

Guess he figured since they were on their way over it would be redundant to call me. "It was nice of you to give her a ride."

"Jessie doesn't have her license back yet so she depends on friends to get her around," Erie explained.

"How long have you been helping at StreetSmart?"

"Not long. I work part time at a coffee shop too and take night classes."

I nodded to her jacket. "At HCC? That's where I got my degree."

"Yeah. I'm hoping to get into social work, which is why I offered to help Ms. Woods."

I raised my brows. "You know Tanya?"

She shot me a quick glare. "She comes into the Beanery from time to time. We got to talking," she stated defensively.

I was a little taken aback by her tone but didn't show it. Some people just have a fun-loving personality. I hadn't seen this young woman the few times Will and I had gone into the coffee establishment we'd used as a meeting place. "I'll leave you to it. Keys are in the ignition."

In the office, Sylvia hung up the phone and added another message to the others on the desk.

She spied me in the doorway. "You really need an office manager, you know."

I thought about the jobs lined up over the next few days, the messages on my desk, my lack of focus in not locking the door to take Moose for a walk, how distracted I was worrying about Tanya and what I needed to do to help her.

"Are you offering to do the job?"

She quirked a brow and waved at the bits of paper. "You, ah…you've worked in an office before?"

"It's been a while."

Like before computers, when they still did things with pen and paper? Or an abacus?

"It…can be confusing, you know, figuring costs and giving quotes. You may have to deal with irate customers." For the life of me, I couldn't see this laid back hippie woman taking phone messages and filing. She seemed more of a commune type soul, sitting in the lotus position, toking on a hookah pipe and extolling the virtues of universal love.

She leaned in conspiratorially. "My aunt used to work in the White House during Nixon's term. She taught me everything she knew about dealing with people and a few other things, if you get my meaning." She gave me a look with lifted brows.

Oookaay.

"When can you start?"

Sylvia smiled. "Think I already have."

"So it would seem."

We settled on pay and hours and I left her with instructions to call those who had placed messages we would follow up with quotes, then ventured back to check how Jessie was making out.

"Well?"

The young woman straightened from under the hood, wiped her hands on a rag. An almost unearthly shift in reality sprung up in my head at seeing her do the same gestures Blaine did when he worked on vehicles, and it left me missing my brother even more.

"Good news and bad news," she said. "The good news is I can fix it and as long as we can get what I need today, should be able to get it running for tomorrow."

I thought about what the client had told me they wanted moved and knew I'd have to reschedule them. Damn. On the plus side, if Jessie could get my vehicle fixed right now, I wouldn't have to rent another cube van on my dime for the rest of my hauls until Blaine returned. "And the bad news?"

Her lips pursed and she waved me over to look under the hood. I dragged over a step stool we kept along the wall near the bench and clambered up to peer at an engine.

Erie also stuck her head in to see. "Do you know anything about engines?"

"No. Only that it needs gas and oil to work."

Jessie pointed. "See this? It's called a cylinder head. All cars have them, except if the unit is electric. Anyway, without them, the engine won't work. This one is cracked."

"Is that common?" This was out of my depth.

"It can happen. When was the last time you took out the van?"

"Last week."

"And you noticed nothing wrong at the time? No lack of power, leaking oil, engine light, things like that?"

"No."

The young woman nodded. "Will explained to me your brother was a mechanic and I would assume he kept up some type of regular maintenance on your vehicles."

"Absolutely."

"Then that makes this all the weirder." Jessie's pursed lips turned into a frown. "See the crack there?"

"Yes."

"The marks right near it shouldn't be there."

Erie spoke up. "What do you mean?"

Jessie's gaze went between her friend and me. "The marks are too clean. There's no oil or engine residue, which means they are very new."

I gazed at her, not understanding.

She moved back to stand upright, her arms crossed against her chest. "Those marks are deliberate; you can tell by the indentation. It actually looks like someone used a chisel and a hammer, maybe even a mallet. Someone has sabotaged your engine."

CHAPTER EIGHT

The familiar sense of a target painted on my back itched between my shoulder blades. The last time was when I found a dead body amongst the haul to Pampa and my lawyer ex-husband Clayton had commented about how the whole thing appeared as a set-up. For a short time, I worried someone had manipulated me to take the blame for the murder but that hadn't been the case.

But this, this was personal. "Someone monkeyed with my engine on purpose?"

"Yes," Jessie said. "The only thing is when?"

The van was in perfect running order last week when Blaine and I did a job. He usually did a quick inspection once a week and would have noticed the straight, short, sharp marks on the cylinder head. So, whoever made my life a living hell had done it within the last few days. Or maybe even the other day? The scratches on the front door made sense now and although no one spray painted obscenities on my walls, whoever had done this vandalized me.

I remembered the blob of pinkish substance on the floor. "Will the engine leak coolant with a cracked cylinder?"

"Yes," confirmed Jessie.

"Are you able to get the part you need to fix it now?"

She nodded. "I can pin it but suggest your brother check it when he comes back. I just need someone to take me to a parts store."

"Since I'll have to cut a check from the business, I'll take you."

"I don't feel like waiting around." Erie turned to her friend. "Call me when you need a ride. I'll come get you and we can hit that place on Rice we want to try. Maybe we'll see the musician."

Jessie knitted her brows. "Which one was that again?"

Erie tried to smother an eye roll. "You know. The one in Braeswood that was closed for a party and we ended up going to the movie night with everyone instead."

"Oh, yeah," she said distractedly.

"No need for that. I can take Jessie there," I suggested.

Erie narrowed her eyes like she wanted to argue, then turned and left.

I went into the office where my new manager was tidying up the desk. "Would you mind calling the client set up for this afternoon and reschedule maybe for tomorrow if there is room? I'm taking Jessie with me to the parts store."

"Sure."

I signaled to Jessie that we were leaving and grabbed the check ledger from the drawer of my desk. "Keep an eye on Moose for me will you? He may need to go out again, especially after he ate the wiener."

"That will cost you extra," Sylvia yelled as I walked out the door.

Jessie slid into the passenger seat and buckled her seatbelt as I drove out of the lot. "Thanks for the ride."

The ride wouldn't have been necessary except some a-hole tried to ruin my van, something best left unsaid considering my passenger barely knew me and it wouldn't be appropriate.

Twenty minutes later we were back at the shop. I parked near the doors. "How long will it take you to fix the van?"

"Not long," Jessie replied.

"Okay. Start and I'll let Sylvia know she can go home."

My office manager sat in the chair using Moose as a footstool, but the dog didn't seem to mind.

"Everything working out okay?" she asked.

I nodded.

"By the way, you look like hell," she said with a mix of concern and mirth.

I leaned against the doorway. "My eyes feel like a pair of eagle's butt-holes in a power dive–puckered up and about ready to close."

The rest of me wasn't in any great shape either. I was exhausted but the two Live Wires this morning helped. At lease I didn't drink last night. For all my complaints, I was happy and proud of myself for what was accomplished. I'd won more than enough money to pay for Tanya's bail and Will would pick up my best friend soon.

"Do I even want to know the cause of that metaphor?"

"The less you know the better."

"Your client didn't want to reschedule and said he'd get someone else. I couldn't change his mind."

Dammit! Whoever had sabotaged the van now lost me a client. Was that their purpose? To ruin me? "Thanks for trying. Fixing the van will take time, so you might as well go home early. Sorry for the confusion."

Sylvia eased away from the sleeping form on the floor. "That's okay. My neighbor Erick, that's with a *ck* as he keeps reminding me, has been trying to get me out on a date so this will be an excuse to hit Mojito Mondays at Wings and Things."

"But it's Tuesday."

She wiggled her eyebrows. "Any day is good for a Mojito with a guy who looks like Robert DeNiro."

She reached down to scoop up a round black object from behind the desk.

A helmet.

My eyes widened. "Is that your motorcycle parked outside?"

"Yes." She grinned from ear to ear. "A black heritage classic Harley Davidson. Movers dropped it off yesterday. Smooth ride. I could take you for a spin sometime. Even have an extra helmet, though it's not as cool as mine."

She showed me the helmet with Brady Lady stenciled in white above the face shield.

"I may take you up on that." I could picture Sylvia zipping down the highway and a grin split my face. "Have a good time with Erick."

She gave me a wink before donning the protective gear. "Plan on it."

I went to where Jessie was working. "Need any help?"

"No, I've got this," she replied, keeping her head under the hood.

Although there was always paperwork to do, I never talked with Jessie when we first met and I was interested in getting to know her. "Mind if we talk while you're working?"

She glanced at me, shrugged and returned her focus to the engine.

"You lived in Houston all your life?"

"Yes."

"What got you interested in cars?"

She flicked her eyes my way, as if assessing whether she wanted to reveal anything private. "I grew up with three brothers. It was the only way to spend time with them."

"They must be pretty proud of you."

The look again, this time a bit more guarded. "Yeah."

"And your parents?"

Her gaze shuttered. "They're not in the picture."

Her tone left no doubt that the subject was closed. I remained silent, hoping I hadn't overstepped a boundary.

"What about you? Were you born in Houston?" she eventually asked.

I shook my head. "Alabama. Moved to Amarillo with my family when I was younger, then came to Houston for college. You still live with your family?"

Silence.

"No." Jessie replied finally.

Obviously, that was a touchy subject so I let it go.

My phone pinged with a text from Will.

Have police report. Can we meet?

I replied I couldn't leave right now and asked if he would just text me info to which he replied with emoji with an 'as-if' expression.

Come to shop to discuss? Jessie working on van.

On my way.

"Will's coming here," I said to Jessie. "If it's okay with you, I might ask him to give you a ride back when you're done. I've got things to be taken care of."

"Sure. Will's great. He's like the glue that holds us all together at StreetSmart. Wish he was taking over instead of the new person." She added the last a hint of annoyance.

"Why? What's she like?"

Jessie pursed her lips. "Pushy. And bossy. She doesn't seem to give a crap about us. Not like Tanya."

I heard the loyalty in her tone. "Maybe she needs some time to settle in."

She gave a shrug, tinkered some more on the engine. "Maybe. But she seems…I don't know…sort of glad she's had to step in."

"What do you mean?"

She waited a beat before explaining. "I walked by Tanya's office yesterday and Ms. Bromskey, that's her name, was sitting back in Tanya's chair, swiveling it from side to side, all smiles but staring at nothing."

To someone who cared for their manager that could be construed as cold. "There could be a perfectly reasonable explanation. Perhaps it was good news not related to work?"

"I guess," Jessie mumbled.

My brain went down numerous mental avenues. Maybe she won the lottery? Or got a call for a date? Or elated to get a job? But then Will said the director was a transfer from another StreetSmart facility so she'd already have to be working.

"She's really secretive too."

I raised my eyebrows. "In what way?"

The girl straightened from under the hood. "While she was smiling in her chair, she had this book, like a notebook, black, and she kept tapping it to her chest while she looked at the ceiling. She must have caught me glancing in because she sat up real fast, slammed the book into a drawer, locked it and just glared at me. Like I'd done something wrong."

"Has she made any changes?"

Jessie wiped her hands on a rag. "Not yet, but she hasn't been there long. Sure hope Tanya will come back soon."

Not until she's proven innocent.

The office door opened and Will called out.

"Sadie?"

"Coming." I nodded to the van. "Almost done?"

"Shortly," Jessie said and resumed her position under the hood.

I strode to the office, leaving the connecting door to the garage ajar and sat at my desk.

Will held out a sheaf of papers and perched on the corner. "Cops already questioned our group; what we knew about Tanya's and Crystals' relationship; did we notice anything off about our boss? where were we on the night of the murder. Myself, Jessie, Erie, and a bunch more were at the all-night Indie Movie Festival until about three in the morning. Tanya was there with Crystal but they left early. According to her statement in the report, they left not long after it started."

I scanned the police report. Crystal Sherridan was killed by blunt force trauma at the right temple. Time of death was between midnight and two am. Copies of the crime scene photos showed items Tanya had mentioned when I spoke with her, all sitting on a glass coffee table; a wine bottle, less than half full, an empty Tequila bottle, and a triangular sculpture. No glasses anywhere. Either the killer never drank, chugged from the bottle or cleaned up after themselves. The last option was unlikely.

The murder weapon was the piece of medium-sized triangular quartz and when I peered closer at the pictures of it, I read the engraved base. It had Crystal's name and the word winner.

"This is the marketing award Tanya told me about that she picked up, among other things off the floor that night. She thought Crystal had passed out drunk and was worried Crystal would trip if she got up during the night. Damn."

Will's mouth pressed into a hard line. "It was wiped clean of any prints other than Tanya's."

This was bad.

"It shows the murderer had presence of mind," he ground out.

I continued reading. The police canvassed the neighbors on Crystal's floor. Nothing was heard until the superintendent arrived and the shouting started. He was in his unit the whole evening, playing cards, that was corroborated by the other three players. The woman who found Tanya in the apartment was Stephanie Waxton, a friend of Crystals. Victim's phone records showed a phone call placed to Stephanie close to eleven-thirty.

I tapped the paper. "Stephanie Waxton. What do we know about her?"

"I haven't had time to check into her yet," Will said. "I wanted to get this to you first."

"If she spoke with Crystal at eleven-thirty, and Tanya arrived around twelve-thirty, why did it take Stephanie an hour to get there?"

"Might be a good idea to speak with her and find out why. You want to take a stab at that?" I asked.

The corner of his mouth lifted. "I think that's more your purview than mine."

I nodded. "Okay."

The rest of the report provided little info. No security cameras inside the building, although there was one at both the front and back entrance. Unfortunately, the one at the back wasn't working.

I put the papers on the desk. "Any chance to getting copies of the security cameras from the building?"

A hint of a smile spread across his face. "Already working on it. And yes, before you ask I thought about traffic cams and other cameras in the area. It will just take a while."

I handed back the report but Will shook his head. "Keep it. I have copies."

The clang of something metal hitting the floor brought my attention to the shop for a second and a comment Jessie had made gave me a thought.

"What do you know about Elaine Bromskey?"

He shrugged. "Other than she transferred in from the StreetSmart branch in Austin, not much. Why?"

"Might be nothing but would you be able to check into her background as far as you can?"

"Sure."

Although acceptable for a movie script, would someone kill for a better-paying position within a company? Jessie's impression of her current boss could be nothing more than an objection to change. I was grasping at straws but wasn't about to rule anyone out in trying to find other suspects in Crystal's murder.

My finger tapped on the desk and I lowered my voice. "How far are you willing to go to help Tanya?"

Will quirked his brow in a 'what-do-you-think' look.

"Can you do a deep dive?"

He stiffened. He'd done this type of thing before, for me, but it was always risky. After a brief pause, he nodded. "Give me some time."

I took the slam of a hood as a signal that Jessie had finished. Will and I walked into the shop and met her at the vehicle.

"It's fixed for now but only temporarily. When you take it out, don't go crazy on the speed," she cautioned.

I beamed. "Awesome. What do I owe you?"

"Nothing."

I wouldn't let her go without some type of remuneration. "How about I buy you a drink or coffee?"

Her face hardened briefly. "I don't drink." When I didn't respond, she added with a tight smile. "I can use this as community service so we're good."

"If you're finished here, I can take you home," Will offered.

"Actually, I'm supposed to meet Erie. Can you drop me off?" Jessie asked hopefully.

"Sure," Will nodded.

"Thanks. I'll clean up first." She went to the bathroom at the back.

I watched her go and turned to Will. "Did I overstep?"

He just shook his head and motioned with his chin that Jessie was coming back and they both left.

I locked up the shop and took Moose back to Blaine's before I drove to Crystal's area of Houston. She lived in a moderate eight story building with no balconies. Since I didn't know the exact apartment number, I buzzed the Superintendent's unit.

The garbled response came from a speaker by the door. "Yeah."

"Hi. Were you the one who was a witness to the death of a young woman in her apartment earlier this week?"

"Police said not to speak to any reporters," a man growled.

"I'm not a reporter. I swear."

"Well, who are ya, then?" The voice said in an agitated tone.

The man sure wasn't making it easy for me. I considered lying but other than the press who else would inquire about something as macabre as manslaughter? "I'm a friend to the woman who's being charged with the crime."

A long, drawn out pause. *Please don't let me strike out before I even had a chance at bat.*

"Stay there. I'll be out."

Minutes later, a portly middle-aged bald man came to the glass inside door of the building. He eyed me, as if assessing whether I was worthy of his time and not some two-bit wanna-be looking for her fifteen seconds of fame on the nightly news. Apparently, I passed inspection because he opened the door.

"We can talk here," he instructed in a voice that meant the topic wasn't up for discussion.

"I gather that means I can't go up and see Crystal's apartment?"

"No."

Well, it was worth a shot.

"My name is Sadie Hawkins. Like I'd said, my friend is charged with Crystal's death. Can you please tell me anything about that night?"

He folded his arms across his chest. "I already told the police everything I saw."

Which was not much according to his statement in the police report. Since I knew all that, I was more interested in his impression.

"How about what you felt?"

The man's brows bunched together in confusion. "Huh?"

"What was your first impression? Was it grisly or did it hardly look like a crime scene at all? What about the person you saw standing over the body?" My throat tightened on the last sentence, making the words sound strained.

The building manager stared at me. "What kind of questions are those? You're a reporter, aren't you?"

I met his gaze straight on. "No. I'm not. I'm just trying to figure out what happened."

He remained silent for a moment and then his shoulders relaxed. "Looked kind of strange when I got there."

"Strange how?"

He shrugged. "Like Ms. Sherridan was sleeping. Or passed out. No sign of a break in or a fight."

So Crystal had to have known her assailant. That ruled out a random attack but it didn't ease my mind any. "And the woman who found her? How was she?"

The man pursed his fleshy lips. "She was really scared, shaking Ms. Sherridan and yelling, her voice getting louder and more urgent." He waited a beat before adding, "Either she's the best actress I've ever seen or she was scared out of her mind."

Although that didn't help me, the information might prove helpful to Tanya if the case ever went to trial.

"The woman with you at Crystal's apartment? What can you tell me about her?"

The Superintendent lifted one shoulder. "Not much. Never seen her before. Seemed genuinely concerned for her friend."

I ruminated over that for a second. "Concerned how?"

He narrowed his eyes at me. "You sure ask weird questions. I dunno. Her hands were shaking pretty bad when she called the cops and her voice got all quivery when she spoke."

Before I thanked him for his time, he said, "And her eyes kept jumping all over the place."

That snapped me to attention. "Like she was looking for someone?" Or something.

"Could be. Maybe she thought the killer was still there," he said.

Was that the reason or something else? I held out my hand, which he shook. "Thank you for your time. I really appreciate it."

I turned to leave but faced him again. "One other thing. The woman who came and got you, did she ever leave and go into another room before the police arrived?"

He shook his head. "No, but I think she wanted to. She went to step out of the living room but I seen enough TV to know that once a crime's been committed you're supposed to stay put. Might disturb evidence. So I didn't let her out of my sight."

I gave him a smile. "And who says you can't learn anything from prime time television?"

My phone rang as I exited the building. It was Wayne.

I brightened. "Hi."

"Hey," he said.

No warmth, no chuckle. Dang.

"Wayne, I'm really sorry—"

"Listen, Sadie. I…" he paused and exhaled slowly. "I'm wondering if…this is really meant to be."

No, no, no, I wanted to yell but that would make me sound pathetic. It's not like we had a deep relationship but I liked him. In fact, we'd been trying to go out for a nice dinner since we'd met but our schedules hadn't meshed.

I chose my words with care and whispered. "Perhaps it's not a question of meant to be but of worth pursuing."

He didn't answer me right away and I pictured him running his hand through his hair, on the edge of decision.

"Okay," he said after a minute.

The breath trapped in my lungs let go. "I'm glad."

"You free tonight?"

I had planned to check in on Tanya. "No, but I'm all yours tomorrow."

"Pick you up at seven?" he asked.

"Looking forward to it." And I was.

"Me too," he said and signed off.

I hadn't heard anticipation in his words but hoped there was some. My eyes went skyward in a thank you to the gods for second chances.

Tanya would have just gotten home by now so I text her and asked if she wanted me to stop over. She thanked me but said she needed some time alone. Despite being disappointed that I'd postponed my date with Wayne, I understood Tanya's decision for some alone time. After you've been in jail, it's like you had to ground yourself back into reality. Plus, my friend hadn't had time to grieve for losing someone she'd cared deeply about. I sent her a heart and hug emoji and said I'd touch base maybe tomorrow.

Now that I had time, I sent a quick text to Will. I felt guilty at always turning to him for favors but he could provide the information I needed much faster than me. The quicker I got answers the better for Tanya.

Sorry to bug you but did report have contact info on S.

I didn't use Stephanie's name because I knew Will would frown upon it in communications.

Within fifteen seconds, he responded with an address on Bellaire Boulevard and instructed me to write it down then delete the message.

Did I know him or what.

I memorized the address, sent thumbs up and did as he instructed. What was Stephanie so nervous about in Crystal's apartment that night?

* * *

After three knocks, I concluded Stephanie was not at home. With a defeated air, I turned and saw a slight figure walking my way in gray leggings and bright purple crop-top. Long hair swung from a ponytail that was threaded through the back of a black baseball cap. The woman's steps slowed as she approached and she plucked out small white buds from her ears.

She stopped a few feet away. "Can I help you?"

"I'm looking for Stephanie Waxton."

A wariness filled her eyes. "Why?"

"I was hoping to speak with her. Is that you?" I put on a hopeful smile.

Her flushed face lost a bit of its color. She didn't reply nor did she come closer. Was she going to bolt?

"My name is Sadie Hawkins and I just wanted to talk with you about what happened at Crystal Sherridan's."

She tensed. "I have nothing to say."

She brushed by me and stepped to her door, pulling a key from a tiny pocket of her leggings.

So she was Stephanie. "Please, I only want to find out what happened."

"Why?"

"Tanya Woods is my friend."

Stephanie's eyes widened. "Go away."

She wouldn't speak with me let alone invite me in so why not throw a comment her way and see her reaction. "What was the *real* reason you went to Crystal's apartment?"

Her gaze hardened to where her light blue eyes turned as cold as ice. "You're just like those vapid reporters. Leave or I'm calling the police." The woman yanked open her door and shut it with a firm click behind her.

Don't know why she felt insulted. She was the one who called me vapid.

Stephanie had something to hide because the look she gave me was not one of pain or indignation.

It was the flinty eyed glare of someone who had secrets she didn't want revealed.

CHAPTER NINE

The next day there was a moving job scheduled for midmorning and hopefully the van would behave. I did not relish the thought of it grinding to a halt in the middle of driving through town so, erring on the side of caution, considered asking Jessie to ride along, both as hired help and my on-the-spot mechanic. Only trouble was, I didn't have any other way to reach her except through StreetSmart and didn't know if the new manager would grant me privileges despite Jessie using her time toward community service.

At the office, with Moose dozing at my feet, I dialed StreetSmart and asked to speak with Tanya's interim replacement.

"StreetSmart, Elaine Bromskey speaking," the manager said when she picked up the phone.

"Hello. My name is Sadie Hawkins, I am a friend of—"

"I know who you are," Elaine remarked, cutting me off.

Ahh, okay.

"Jessie aided you regarding a vehicle matter. Are you reporting a problem?"

"No. Not at all."

Her voice wasn't curt, but an undertone of impatience carried in the statement. Maybe this was an inconvenient time. The woman was probably busier than a moonshine runner on Independence Day.

"I was hoping, if it wasn't inconvenient, that I might hire Jessie again to help with a hauling job."

"I see." A pause. "That would be up to Ms. Montgomery. I can bring up the subject with her if you like."

"Yes, that would be great."

"All right. When do you require her assistance?"

"Today. In a few hours."

Silence.

"I see," Elaine repeated, this time with an edge. "I will do my best to convey the message." After a heartbeat, she continued. "As much as the personnel at StreetSmart are required to do community service, we prefer they cast a wide net instead of directing their time to one or two individuals."

In other words, my free-pass ticket just got punched for the last time.

"I understand completely," I offered in my most humble tone.

"It's a good thing I got here when I did."

Elaine may not have actually meant to say that out loud because it was almost inaudible, but there was no mistaking her assertion. She sure wasn't sitting idle in her new position, which lent credence to Jessie's opinion about the new manager being pushy.

"Thank you for everything and if you wouldn't mind asking Jessie to phone me as soon as possible I would really appreciate it. If she can't help me, then I need to make more calls."

She said she would and hung up.

It wasn't long before Jessie phoned and we set a time to pick her up.

I was making sure we had enough blankets in the back of the van to use as protection for fragile pieces when a motorcycle's deep rumble announced Sylvia's arrival. She walked into the office wearing another eclectic outfit, this time a long tie-dyed dark green and black dress with billowy sleeves to her elbows and a brown suede leather vest.

I quirked a brow at her attire. "Isn't it difficult to wear a dress on a bike?"

"No. You just hike the material to your waist."

She must have seen my complexion pale at the idea of someone her age showing that much leg and more when she let out a howl of laughter. "I have a pair of shorts on underneath."

Sylvia deposited her helmet, gave Moose an affectionate pat and sat down. "What's on the books for today?"

"Before I forget," I pointed to the desk. "Here's a key. I'm on my way out to pick up Jessie to help with a haul. Should be done by mid afternoon." I hoped because I didn't want to cancel my date with Wayne. Again.

"I wanted to run something by you. Do you have a slogan for the business?"

"No."

"Ever considered one?"

I shrugged. "I'm not against it, just haven't given it any thought. Why?"

Sylvia smiled. "Well, since I'm now the office manager I thought I could help, you know, drum up business."

A grin formed on my mouth. "Okay. What did you come up with?"

"How about 'Hawkins Freight—we're packin' the heat to get the job done.'"

Ummm…what?

"It sounds like a company that deals in weapons."

"Oh. Maybe you're right," she conceded. "Need to work on that one."

I headed toward the van. "Keep at it. Call me if anything arises."

When I arrived, Jessie was just leaving the StreetSmart building accompanied by another young woman, shorter and with long blonde hair. I didn't recognize her but then Tanya had mentioned the clients came and went, sometimes only lasting a week.

The two young women parted on the sidewalk and my hired help gave a brief smile accompanied by a hello once she buckled in and we headed toward the waiting client.

"Thanks so much for giving me a hand. Really appreciate it. I'm hoping to get this job done quickly because then it's back to the office, get Moose and get home before seven."

"Don't forget about taking it easy on the motor," Jessie mentioned. "Why seven?"

I zipped around a corner. "I have a date tonight."

A quick, knowing smile appeared on her pretty face. "A hot one?"

"That remains to be seen."

I could almost guarantee my date with Wayne wouldn't enter the smoldering gazes and tangled sheets' zone. At least not yet. However, a passionate lip lock instead of the usual kiss on the forehead would be nice.

We arrived in the Eastwood district, which had a large assortment of Craftsman, Arts & Crafts, Foursquare and Mission style architecture. Developed in the early 1900s, the area was unique in its placement of oak and sycamore trees. Howard Hughes was believed to have lived with his aunt on McKinney Street while he was building an airplane in a garage at another nearby location.

The job was at a white brick, traditional style single house on Clay Street. A dozen small shrubs were evenly divided on either side of the decorative stone steps that preceded the wooden front door. The driveway led under a carport and carried on to the backyard.

I jumped out of the van and hurried up to an older couple waiting on the steps. "Hi, I'm Sadie Hawkins of Hawkins Freight for your move."

The man gave me a skeptical look. "You sure you can do the job?"

"Absolutely," I beamed, tamping down my ire and waved for Jessie to come forward. "Even brought extra help."

This time it was the woman who gave my companion a skeptical once-over but said nothing.

"Bring your van up the driveway. We have most of our stuff near the back of the house," the male said with a jerk of his thumb.

After I maneuvered the vehicle, Jessie waited while I assessed what needed to be taken and compared it to the rough quote given upon scheduling the move. After the contract got signed, the clients seemed appeased and left us alone.

My helper knew the job needed to be done fast and we hustled butt, concentrating on packing the van the best way instead of idle chitchat. I considered her suggestions for protecting a huge metal sculpture of a matador and a bull during the ride. Thank god it was made of aluminum and not cast iron or we'd never be able to lift it. We worked well together and a couple of hours later, with sweat pouring down our faces, I closed the back of the van and sat for a moment on the bumper to catch my breath.

The owner of the house came outside, paid me and gave directions of where to drop off the load. At least it wasn't far out of my way. My passenger monitored street names once I pulled away from the curb and slid into traffic.

Everything was running on time until we got sidelined by a chipmunk that had gotten into the cab, because I'd forgotten to close the doors earlier after grabbing some granola bars. It must have been looking for food because there was a torn and gnawed wrapper lay near my feet. We did our best imitation of stop-light-fire-drill before finally getting underway again.

"Well, at least the past half hour gave me something to laugh about," Jessie said softly when we were underway.

I pondered how to engage her in conversation without prying. "Bet you'll be glad to drive again."

"Yes, only a couple of more months." She paused and continued as an afterthought. "As long as Tim gives me back my car."

"Tim, your boyfriend?"

"Older brother."

"I have one of those too, can be a real pain in the ass sometimes, but he looks out for me."

Jessie's gaze drifted out to the passing sidewalk. "Bet he doesn't blame you for killing a member of your family," she said in a bleak voice so softly I barely heard it.

"Losing someone you love, no matter the circumstances, is hard," I counseled after a time.

My passenger sighed. "Unfortunately, he's right."

When she remained silent, I steered the conversation to a different topic. "Things must be different with Tanya being gone."

"Yeah, it sucks."

"I know what you mean. It was mentioned to me the StreetSmart crew can't favor particular places to contribute their time for community hours."

"I was told the same thing. What difference does it make how we do our service? It's not like we have a long list of organizations begging to hire people with a record." My passenger's mouth pinched. "Bromskey is making so many changes it won't ever be like it was before."

"Once Tanya is cleared and comes back she'll make it right again."

"If she comes back."

I glanced at Jessie, noticed the sullen expression. "Tanya is going to beat the murder charge." I'd do my damndest to make sure of that.

A forlorn look entered the young woman's eyes. "Okay, but that doesn't mean she'll be able to come back, especially if Bromskey has something to say about it."

Apprehension pressed against my chest. "What do you mean?"

Jessie shook her head. "I don't know. I don't trust her and sure as hell don't like her."

"Maybe you're worried because she's not who you're used to," I posed. "Is it possible you would feel the same no matter who the new director of StreetSmart was?"

"Maybe," she conceded, then added, "It's just…something isn't right with her."

I made a left turn onto the street, located the store, and parked at the curb.

As I reached into the door pocket for the clipboard that had the current contract, Jessie burst out, "I want to help Tanya."

I straightened at the determination in her voice. "We all do."

"No. I mean I want to spy on Bromskey."

I gaped at her. "What? Why?"

"Because something is off with her and I'm not making it up."

"No one is saying you're imagining things, Jessie."

She braced her hand against the dash, squared her body to me. "Then let me do this. I need to do this."

I thought about what she'd said to me before. Of how the new director seemed overjoyed at the position and now this new information. Will was checking into the woman's background, something he could achieve from a distance. What Jessie was proposing could put her in danger.

"I don't know…"

"Please, Sadie."

"Why? I get Tanya is your director and you probably feel some type of loyalty and maybe even friendship but you could jeopardize everything, like your parole or if not that you might be placed in another StreetSmart location."

Jessie's eyes filled with tears and I witnessed her force them back by sheer will alone. "Tanya is like the big sister I never had. I would do anything to help her. Please let me."

I paused, understood where that emotion stemmed from. With how strongly she felt about Tanya, the girl would do some snooping on her own just to appease her gut feeling not to mention wanting to contribute. Hopefully, she wouldn't take too many risks. Since she asked me, perhaps she could relay any info and, who knows, maybe there was something to her claims.

"I don't like that you're willing to put yourself in harm's way but since you are technically an adult, I can't tell you what or what not to do."

Relief loosened her shoulders and with a small smile she went to open her door.

"Jessie."

She paused.

"Are you really willing to risk your future if you get caught?"

"Yes," she said without hesitation and jumped out of the van.

* * *

When Jessie and I finished unloading everything, including the sculpture of the matador and a bull, I checked my watch and groaned. "Come on. I need to get you home."

"It might be easier and save time to get Moose first, then you can drop me off on your way to dinner?"

Oh yeah. The dog. Totally forgot about my babysitting duties with all the subterfuge going on in my brain. "Good idea."

I put my cell on hands free and called the office to hear a new slogan "Hawkins Freight—the movers and shakers of Houston?"

"Better but keep working at it," I replied to Sylvia. "Listen, I'm on my way to come get Moose off your hands. If you want to call it a day, head home but make sure you reroute calls to my cell." I rattled off my number as I sped through a yellow light. "I'll lock the door after I pick up the dog."

"Sounds good," Sylvia said. "See you tomorrow at ten."

I disconnected and bit back a smile. Movers and shakers. Catchy but that wasn't the reason for my grin. It was the same phrase a certain disc jockey had

111

labeled me with when we were chatting over the phone while passing the time one night in Pampa. Jackson Steel worked late at night at KRDL, a classic rock station and had saved my life. He'd called the police after assailants robbed and knocked me unconscious while we were on the phone and because I hadn't ended the call, the authorities could pinpoint my location. I'd been trying to get together with him for coffee or a drink but he'd shied away from face-to-face contact. He did, however, want me to call him while he was on the air. I missed hearing that incredibly sexy voice because the radio in my truck and Blaine's van didn't get reception from Pampa. Hmmm. Something to ask tech guru, Will.

The following call was to Wayne because I couldn't ready by seven.

"Hi Sadie," he greeted. "Please don't tell me you have to cancel."

"Hi. No, we're still on for tonight but I'm behind and I also have an errand to run. Can we meet at the restaurant say seven-thirty instead of you picking me up?"

"Oh. Okay." I sensed a hint of disappointment in his tone. Perhaps he was hoping for a continuation after the meal and the taking separate vehicles could be a sign that I wasn't interested. I was game for romantic involvement but if he wasn't, and for convenience's sake, I needed a means of transportation to check something out.

He gave me the name and address of the restaurant and I promised to meet him there.

Jessie took a long drink of water. "So, what are you wearing tonight?"

I blinked, surprised. With all the chaos in my life, I hadn't thought that far. Since we'd met, I'd wanted to have a nice dinner with Wayne. Now that it was finally happening my thoughts scattered like ducks flushed out by a hunting dog.

"Clothes?"

"That's a necessity," she smirked. At the nearest intersection, she said. "Why don't we just get you ready. You can drop me off downtown or wherever you're headed and I can call Erie to come get me."

As much as I felt obligated to ensure my helper got home, dropping her off first would make me even later. "I really should make sure you get home okay."

"I am over the age of majority," she pointed out.

True. "You're sure?"

"Yes. Don't worry about it."

"Thanks. I really appreciate the gesture," I said with relief.

At the shop, we swapped vehicles, gathered Moose, went home to let him out and put food down then careened to my place.

When we got there, I rushed toward the bathroom. "Can you pull out something for me to wear from my closet? Then while I'm dressing you can grab a shower."

"Where is he taking you?"

I told her the name of the restaurant and she nodded. "You're okay with me going through your clothes?"

"Yep."

I shut the door, peeled off my sticky clothes and hopped into the shower. Although I would have preferred to select my attire for the evening, there wasn't enough time because I would inevitably hem and haw about what to wear. Besides, there was nothing in my closet that would shock the girl.

After the quickest washing in history, I leaped out of the shower, toweled off fast enough to give me fabric burn, threw on the robe hanging on the back of the door, pulled out a fresh towel for Jessie and headed to my bedroom.

"Fresh towel on the counter! Next!"

"Got it," she called, running from the kitchen.

I stuttered when I saw the sleek, deep emerald green dress lying on the bed beside a set of black Victoria Secret lingerie. The dress was one I had worn on my first anniversary dinner with Clayton and a tidal wave of memories swam over me, making my hands shake. It had been a lovely evening, full of promises and a happy future. Wearing it for my first official date with Wayne would almost be like a betrayal even though Clayton and I divorced. I picked up the garment and turned to the closet to retrieve something else when I realized each piece of material would have some sort of connection to my former life with my ex-husband. I didn't regret closing that door of my life; it had been the right thing to do, for both of us. Inhaling a deep breath, I stowed those memories away, slipped on the lingerie and dress then wedged my feet into the sleek black heels Jessie had placed at the foot of the bed. This was the first romantic evening, hopefully, since my divorce and it felt kind of surreal.

When I passed the young woman in the hall on my way to the bathroom, which she'd vacated, she gave me a devilish smile and a wink. "That will get his attention."

"Don't start." At the doorway, I stopped. "Jessie."

She turned from her path down the hall. "Yeah?"

"Thanks. For…for today. With helping and…this." I fingered the dress.

Pleasure and surprise flitted through her eyes before she said, "You're welcome" and continued to the living room.

I applied the barest hint of makeup, some gel into my hair and styled it with my fingers. The same black clutch purse from my gambling evening went under my arm and I headed to my date with Wayne.

* * *

Jessie hid her face when I dropped her off at a cafe on Shepherd Drive, with payment in hand, but from her parting shot that she would drive next time,

115

regardless of a license suspension, I got a sense she was relieved to have arrived in one piece.

Showing up a few minutes late at the restaurant, I smoothed my dress before walking across the half-moon patterned sidewalk that led under a circular portico supported by three black slim wedge-shaped pillars. Light landscaping and a low wrought-iron fence surrounded an outdoor dining patio on the right complete with a working water feature. The setting sun bathed the building's white cement walls with a pinkish hue, a significant disparity to the dark gray tiles lining the bottom face.

When I entered, my eyes jumped from one spectacle to another; the gray, black and yellow patterned carpet at my feet covered the entire eating space that held tables with brown wooden chairs and yellow seats; a rotisserie spit and pizza oven embedded in one mosaic tiled wall; mosaic columns that supported walls painted with dynamic murals. The establishment vibrated an eclectic mix of tasteful old world and playful modern.

Wayne stood from a table off to one side and aromas of oregano and garlic tingled in my nose as I threaded around patrons on my way toward him. His eyes widened at my approach, then lowered in heated appreciation as he scanned me from head to toe. He'd never seen me in a dress.

"Wow," he smiled as he pulled out a chair for me.

Dressed in a dark blue sport coat, dove gray shirt, black tie and black pants, the man looked very handsome.

"I could say the same about you."

"You look fabulous."

My cheeks heated. "Not used to seeing me all dressed up are you?" I teased.

Whether the noise from other diners mixed with the upbeat Italian themed music made it difficult to be heard or he wanted to get closer, Wayne leaned in and murmured in my ear, "I like it."

A flush of pleasure added to the warmth in my face and I scanned our surroundings once more. "Cool place. Have you been here before?"

He moved back a bit and shook his head. "I asked around at work and this restaurant was highly mentioned. And I love Italian."

"Me too."

A waiter arrived and inquired if we cared for something to drink.

"Want to split a bottle of wine?" Wayne reached for the liquor menu.

I usually drank Wild Turkey but considering the location and type of food, wine would be the better choice.

"Sure. You choose. Red, but not too dry for me."

He scanned the list and opted for a Cabernet.

The waiter left and another server brought over a basket of crusty rolls with garlic butter and my stomach let out a loud growl.

"Didn't have time to eat today?" my date laughed, passing the basket to me.

My fingers pulled out a warm roll. I slathered it with butter and took a huge bite. I was starving. "A couple of granola bars and that was it. Crazy day. Speaking of, I'm really sorry for pushing back our time and being late."

"The wait was worth it." He held my gaze for a moment then retrieved a roll for himself.

The waiter returned with the wine, which saved me from blushing again. Although we had been on a few dates in a more casual environment, Wayne hadn't displayed this amount of interest before and I became flustered at the attention. The waiter showed the wine, uncorked the bottle and splashed a bit of the dark burgundy liquid into Wayne's glass for a taste. At his nod, the server filled both glasses, placed the open bottle on the table and straightened, indicating the menus sitting on the table in front of us.

"Would you care to order?"

"Ahhh…"

"I checked out the menu while waiting," my dinner companion interrupted. "Do you trust me?"

"Sure."

"We'll start off with the Carciofi, then the Caesar salad followed by Rigatoni Peperonata."

"Very good." The waiter removed the menus and we were alone once more.

"Seems like a lot of food."

Wayne winked at me. "You sounded hungry and besides you can always take some home."

"There is that." I took a sip of my wine. Full-bodied. Nice choice.

"So, anything new?"

"Remember the break in the other day I called you about?" At his nod I continued. "They did some damage. They sabotaged the motor in the van, cracked a cylinder head."

His eyebrows went straight up. "You're sure?"

"Yes. The van wouldn't start so a friend came over and they spotted the cracked head."

"Okay but that happens, Sadie."

"Not with noticeable marks from a chisel."

Anger and a flash of something else flared in his eyes and he muttered, "Sonofabitch."

"Yeah."

"Any idea who would do that?"

"Not anyone specifically. Could be the competition, a random act, who knows. Maybe it was a goon from the gang that stole my haul of the antiques and since the pack never got their money they wanted payback. I have no clue."

Or maybe your past is sneaking up on you, the dark side of my nature whispered. Had Ricky Best finally come slithering out from hiding and planned on bringing about my demise, one incident at a time? I ground my teeth. Would I ever stop hypothesizing every rotten thing that happened to me was Ricky's fault?

Wayne said nothing. He sat there studying me for the longest time.

Why was he staring at me with such intensity? "What?"

He shook his head as if he didn't want to answer. "You should get an alarm system," he said gruffly.

"You've mentioned that before," I reminded him with a grin.

"And?" he pressed.

"I'll check into it."

Our appetizers arrived, artichokes stuffed with a mixture of parsley, lesser calamint, garlic, salt and pepper and braised in water with white wine.

Wayne's eyes held mine, veered away. "Listen, Sadie…"

When he didn't continue, I prodded. "What?"

Another beat passed before he cut into his food, not looking back at me. "Never mind. Make sure you follow up on that alarm system."

I didn't comment but was curious what he had wanted to say. With a shrug, I took a bite out of my artichoke. It tasted amazing.

A burst of loud laughter grabbed my attention. The target was a group of ten snickering at one of their members as she pulled a tee shirt from its wrapping and displayed it to the other diners at her table. Assorted bags and tissue littered the surrounding area from some type of celebration.

The table of revelers was near the door and had they not triggered my focus I wouldn't have seen the next two people enter the restaurant. My eyes widened and my breath hitched as the maitre-d escorted my ex-husband, Clayton, and a stunningly beautiful blonde to a table near the windows. A deep blue dress encased the woman's model-like figure, coming to rest at a respectable mid-thigh length. Three-inch heels brought her almost eye level with her date and by the look she gave Clayton, she was thrilled to be in his company.

I remembered those feelings.

A whirlwind of emotions galloped through my brain; surprise, envy, hurt, happiness, they all danced around and around. My divorce from Clayton had been amicable and we were still on very good speaking terms. Hell, he'd represented me at no expense when I was charged with theft and probable murder but that didn't negate the shock of seeing him with another woman. I knew he would start dating, same with me, and I was happy for him but it was still weird. Perhaps odder than the situation was how I still felt about him. Something I was still trying to determine.

I must have lost track of the conversation when Wayne spoke up. "Hey, are you okay? You're awfully quiet."

"Sorry. Just thinking of work." I wasn't about to point out my ex was in the room. Or an idea that formed that afternoon, which had absolutely nothing to do with work or my dinner companion but refused to sit other than front and center in my brain.

Our main course arrived and we dug in. We talked about the day, but I still felt disconnected, maybe because of what could happen later, with or without Wayne, or maybe because Clayton was here with someone else. I didn't fix my gaze in my ex's direction for any length of time, instead doing my best to pay attention to the handsome man across the table from me. If Clayton had noticed me sitting in the same restaurant, how bizarre, he gave no sign. And every once in a while, when Wayne would catch me pausing, a slight frown would pull his brows together but he said nothing.

Over dessert, we touched on our predictions of the Astros and the local baseball leagues.

"You going to play again?" Wayne asked. He'd paid our bill and now sipped on coffee.

"I'd like to, just haven't found the time to check into it." We'd caught a few minor local games and one with the Astros. He also enjoyed playing ball as much as watching teams play. "But you should. They have some superb teams here."

A shadow passed over his face. Now he lost the flow of conversation. "Maybe," he said abstractedly.

I gazed into his eyes. We'd touched on the subject before and he'd been open to the possibility. What had changed? "There are dozens of leagues and just as many levels if you're worried about where you might fit in."

He averted my gaze. "I'm…I'm not sure. We'll see."

The space separating us at the table seemed to widen, as if the atmosphere between him and me ebbed and flowed like the tide—close then receding, near then distant. I knew the reasons for the existential void this evening on my end but what about him? Was he reacting to my reticence or was he afraid of getting too close? He never had this subtle edge in his voice and we'd always been able to talk easily before. What was bothering him? Why was he pulling away from me?

A thought slammed into my head with the force of a freight train and my eyes darted to his left hand, which sat on the table, fingers playing with the teaspoon of his place setting.

During his move from Pampa to Houston, we'd stopped and talked over burgers and fries. He'd asked about my life but now that I thought about it, he revealed little about his, only that he grew up on a farm in Iowa with three sisters. Nothing else.

I swallowed, my mouth dry. "You're married, aren't you?"

He looked at me but with confusion. "What?"

"Just tell me. It's not like we're in the middle of a serious relationship so no big deal." My heart plummeted to my stomach. Was that the reason he'd never gotten closer to me than a kiss on the cheek?

"Sadie."

I felt the flush of embarrassment heat my skin. I've been such a fool?

"Sadie." Wayne grasped my hand, held it tight and stared deep into my eyes. "I'm not married."

But maybe there was someone else. We had no parameters. He had every right to date other people. "Are you seeing another woman?"

His eyes softened. "The only woman I am seeing is the one across from me."

"Oh. Okay." I felt like an idiot.

He gave my hand another squeeze. "It's late and I have to work early in the morning. Maybe we should go."

The bubble of excitement that had buoyed my spirits at the onset of the date diminished. What started as a wonderful evening was now ending, not in ruins, but it seemed like we were on opposite sides of a chasm. Wayne stood and pulled out my chair. I forced myself not to turn and check out the table near the windows with the striking lawyer and the gorgeous blonde.

With a light clasp at my elbow, my date accompanied me out the door and into the warm Texas night. The evening breeze floated by, bringing laughter from a few diners sitting on the outside patio of the restaurant. A part of me wished to join in their frivolity. Wayne asked where I parked and we strolled in silence toward my vehicle a short distance away.

At Blaine's van, I turned. "I had a wonderful time, thank you for dinner. It was a lovely restaurant."

"I did too," he agreed, stepped back.

His retreat signaled there wouldn't even be a kiss on the forehead. A twinge of disappointment squeezed my chest.

"Hopefully we can do it again," he added.

That made my heart lighter. I smiled and nodded. "Have a good night."

"You too."

I dug into my purse for keys, unlocked the door but the desolate note in Wayne's voice, spoken in a rough, almost raw tone, stopped me from stepping inside.

"Sadie."

I turned.

He closed the gap between us in a heartbeat, captured my face in his hands, leaned down and brought his lips to mine. The kiss was deep, warm, with an edge of yearning that wound itself through my body, spiraling deep until it penetrated every part of me and went on long enough to leave me almost breathless. Wayne was trembling when he broke off, put his forehead to mine for the briefest moment then turned and walked away.

I watched him leave, hoping he would turn around and wave, but he didn't. I stepped into the van, closed the door and sat, waiting for my heart to resume a regular rhythm. With hesitant fingers, I touched my lips to hold the sensation of his contact. The kiss had caught me off guard at first but when it ended with his hands still cradling my face, I could almost sense a struggle within him.

I had hoped this evening wouldn't end right after dinner but since it had and Wayne walked away, did my distraction through the meal sabotaged the date? Or, based on my impression of some inner battle I detected in Wayne's eyes, was it his decision to keep the date from going to the next level?

Regardless, since the evening between us was over I might as well explore the idea I'd hatched earlier today. With the restaurant in my rear-view mirror, I drove through town and into the lower residential district of Houston to park down the block of Lewis Wood's house. I didn't know if my surveillance- move over *Cagney & Lacey*—of Tanya's older brother would amount to anything but it was a place to start.

Unfortunately, it got boring, fast.

Another car sat parked out front of his house. Lights were on in the structure but the threadbare curtains were closed and from my vantage point down the street I couldn't see into the window. I chewed on my lower lip, contemplating if it would be safe to venture out of my hiding spot, creep up and peek in another window or listen near the door. A scan of the area showed a neighborhood with no pedestrians. Most of the inhabitants inside watched television, as evidenced by the blue glow coming from their homes. I waited another fifteen minutes, then got out of the vehicle. I closed the door with a soft click, tiptoed across the street and keeping as much to the shadows as the streetlights allowed, made my way to Lewis' house.

Circumventing the front door, I ventured to the side and spotted an open window but it was too far off the ground. Maybe I could find something in the back to stand on. Sometimes, my lack of height was a definite deterrent. A few old wooden crates rested in a semi-circle and I hauled one back to the window, hefted my dress up a bit and climbed on top. Not the most stable platform to stand on, especially in my heels, but the crate brought me high enough to peer inside the room. I kicked myself for not having the foresight to bring a change of clothes with me.

My viewpoint turned out to be the kitchen, which was empty but conversation flowed from the front room. I could hear two possibly three different voices.

The men talked about events and people I didn't know. My legs burned at trying to hold my balance when patience finally paid off.

"So what do you think, man.? Do we let her in now or not?" a male said.

"Not my call." Lewis' voice was unmistakable.

"Didn't think she'd do it. Woman's got balls," the first male joked.

A different voiced chimed in. "Price to pay."

My heart sank. It appeared Lewis was back to his old tricks but who was the female and what exactly did she do?

"You better pray your sister doesn't find out or she'll kill you."

"She won't fucking find out," Lewis spat. "Not unless one of you assholes spouts off."

I gasped. Tanya. Was Lewis talking about Tanya? He had two other sisters but only one of them, Theresa, lived in Houston. Was he estranged from her too and the person they were talking about was connected to her? Or had Theresa done something against Tanya? My heart beat so fast it made my hands shake. What requirement gave you passage into a gang? My experience with this sort of thing came strictly from television but it was conceivable some type of serious crime was a requisite for getting in. Robbery or maybe even murder?

"Hey chill man," the third man said. "No worries. I'm getting another beer; you guys want any?"

A shadow loomed down the hall, came to the doorway and I ducked below the window, balancing precariously on the wooden crate. My heart thundered against my ribs as the sound of a fridge door opened then bottles clinked.

"We're getting low on beer," the voice in the kitchen bellowed. "Someone needs to go for a run."

"I went last time," Lewis retorted. "One of you guys go."

Crap. I needed to get out of there. The driver could spot me at the side of the house once he stood at the car parked out front. The ping of bottle caps hitting the sink, footsteps then the slam of the front door announced I was out of time. Launching off the crate, I took two leaping steps and dove over the neighbor's hedge, tucking to a roll at the last second. I landed on my right shoulder and a jolt of pain whipped down my arm but I gritted my teeth against crying out. I scrambled closer to the bushes, breath heaving in and out and waited for the car to drive off. Once it rounded the corner, I high-tailed it to my truck and drove off.

CHAPTER TEN

I called Sylvia the next morning after my late night stakeout of Lewis' place and told her not to expect me until later. There was nothing scheduled, so it gave me time to do some running around. My next call was to Tanya to tell her I'd stop by a little later.

Luckily, when I phoned the police station, I caught Officer Aquila Ramerez before she was heading to a scene.

"I'm sorry, ma'am, but I cannot comment on an ongoing investigation," she said in response to my query about details.

My teeth gnashed together and I pleaded. "Just a hint. Something. Anything. Tanya's my best friend."

Her voice softened eased. "I understand but my hands are tied."

"Can you at least tell me if there are any other suspects?" Should Tanya worry more than she already does? I was getting frustrated.

"It's still early and we are pursuing all avenues in this case," she responded.

"Have you checked into Stephanie Waxton's background?" I pressed.

"Again, Ms. Hawkins, we are pursuing avenues in this case. I really must get going," she stressed.

To her credit, the woman remained professional and polite despite receiving, I'm sure, the same type of pressure from some of her other cases.

"What about Elaine Bromskey?" I added.

Pause

"Who?"

"Elaine Bromskey has been brought in to fill Tanya Woods' position at StreetSmart."

"Does she have ties to the deceased?" Officer Ramerez asked.

"I don't know. She was transferred from Austin," I supplied.

A hint of a sigh. The officer's patience was wearing thin. "I don't see the relevance, Ms. Hawkins."

Okay, from her point of view I could understand that. "It could be relevant if she wanted the position and framed Tanya for murder."

Another pause, this one more pronounced. I think the woman's tolerance had ended. "I will take it under advisement. Now I really have to go. Thank you for calling, Ms. Hawkins."

With the connection severed, I stared at my phone. At least I put a bug in her ear.

My next stop was to see my mother.

Jolene Hawkins lived at Windhaven, an extended care facility where she was well looked after and a place I could afford because of the settlement from my divorce from Clayton. Although I was not to blame for my mother's condition, which was Ricky Best's fault, a part of me still harbored some guilt about how the situation evolved.

Knowing it wasn't my fault didn't make it any easier but at least my mother was alive.

I parked outside the facility and let myself into the front doors using the code. I nodded to the staff, made my way to the second floor and to my mother's room.

She was lying peacefully in bed, her strawberry blonde hair fanned out on the pillowcase. At times my mother was lucid. She would look at me with such clarity it took my breath but those incidences were getting farther and farther apart. I tiptoed in and stood by her bedside, hearing her laughter in my head, reliving all the pleasant memories we shared. A bittersweet ache squeezed my heart, rose to my throat and brought the prickle of tears to my eyes. I missed her so much, so very much.

Mom must have sensed my presence because she opened her eyes, blinked to focus and then smiled.

"There's my little girl," she said, her voice scratchy as if from lack of use. "What are you doing home from school, Sadie?"

She was in the past again. The bittersweet ache turned into a vise in my chest and I bit the inside of my mouth to focus on the pain to stem the onset of tears.

"Early afternoon off, momma. How you feeling?"

Her soft Alabama accent flowed over me like warm summer rain. "I'm just fine. Must have dozed off on the couch waiting for your father." She patted the bed beside her. "Tell me about your day."

And so I did, exchanging reality with fiction to keep her calm and engaged. It served no purpose to correct my mother on the notion her husband was never coming home, that he had died while helping his brother, my Uncle Stan, on a moving job. She would only get upset, tell me I was making up stories, that any minute Jerrald Hawkins was going to walk right in the door after being away on a convention, take her in his arms and sweep her off her feet.

We chatted and when her eyes drooped, I bent down, kissed my mother's brow and let my hand trail along her hair. "Rest now, momma."

Her smile was serene as I folded the blanket across her chest and left the room. In the hall I stood against the wall, breathed deep and slow, tried to regain my emotional balance. I thought again of the guilt plaguing me over my mother's condition, how the dark side of my soul came out to protect her, and dreaded it would arise again. A minute later I straightened from the wall, shot a quick glance at my mother lying in her bed, in this type of facility. A small part of me wished I would see Ricky Best again just to finish the job.

I planned on heading to Tanya's when Will called.

"What did you do?" His tone was brisk almost menacing.

Oh-oh. Someone was irate. I exited the building.

Trying to mitigate his unease, I responded with a snort. "Which time? I need some point of reference." Since he hadn't pulled my butt out of the fire recently, I didn't understand where the attitude came from.

"How could you have involved Jessie in Tanya's case!" he ground out.

Ahh. Papa bear has roared. Instead of defending myself, which would only antagonize him I asked, "What did she have you do?"

He sucked in a sharp breath. "So, you admit it."

"No Will, I'm not 'admitting' anything. Jessie approached me, demanding she wanted to help Tanya. She seems to think the new manager of StreetSmart is up to no good, to what extent I don't know. She is an adult and I have no legal right to say she can't get involved."

"How about a moral right?"

Ouch. "That's not fair. I told her I didn't want her in the thick of this but she would have spied on Elaine regardless. Her asking me reveals she wants to keep me apprised of what she finds out and we can guide her. She obviously trusts you enough to confide in as well." Despite Jessie being an adult, there was still a concern for her.

A moment of silence, then a grunt. Guess that was his way of conceding defeat.

"She didn't actually confide in me. I had to worm it out of her."

"Water boarding?"

"Hardly," he sighed. "She casually asked if I knew any background on Elaine."

"What did you say?" I was curious how he'd handled being put in that position.

"I didn't mention that you had asked me to do that already, in case you're wondering. Although she tried to be nonchalant, I could see the gleam in her eyes. I didn't want to burst her bubble," he admitted with affection.

"How very noble of you," I quipped. "Do you have anything?"

"Just surface stuff."

I dangled the proverbial carrot. "I may have info, though."

"Good or bad?" he asked, as if reluctant to know either way.

I took a page from his book. "You know I never discuss these things over the phone. Up for a coffee at the Beanery?"

He couldn't quite smother the chuckle. Guess I was forgiven. "Sure, meet you there soon."

* * *

On the way to meet Will, I stopped at the dry cleaners in hopes they could somehow get the dirt and grass stains out of the dress from my stunt-girl imitation last night. The clerk lifted an eyebrow at the marks, probably using his imagination on how they got there. I kept him guessing.

At the Beanery, I sat down across the table from Will and he gave me a lopsided apologetic grin. My eyes softened and our recent misunderstanding about Jessie was resolved.

"If anyone wanted to find us, they'd come here first. Most undercover operatives mix things up in case they're being followed," I joked.

Will snorted and took a sip of his coffee. "This is your party. What have you got?"

First, I told him about what I'd learned at Lewis' last night; of how he was in a gang and whatever some female did to get in had ties to either Tanya or her sister Theresa, who still lived in Houston.

Will hung his head before stabbing me with a glare. "The next time you want to put your life in jeopardy *please* text me the location so I at least know where to find your body?"

"Har-har."

"I'm serious."

"Me too. I don't always get in trouble you know."

His eyebrows skyrocketed. "Oh, really?"

Mollified, I grumbled, "It was late and I didn't feel like justifying myself."

He reached across the table and placed his hand over mine. "You never have to justify yourself to me, Sadie." Waiting a heartbeat he added in a lighter tone, "Think of it like letting the dispatcher know when the police go on location."

"Well, since you put it that way," I laughed.

"Since we're on the topic of Lewis, you asked about his robbery buddies. His accomplice in the robbery, Jason Cullman, is still in jail since he was the one who shot the store owner. No evidence came up that Tanya's brother was part of a gang at the time so there are no other leads to follow. I'll see what I can flesh out regarding this new info."

"Okay. Oh, and I spoke, or rather tried to speak, with Stephanie."

His face tightened but remained silent.

I relayed the Superintendent's impression that Stephanie was nervous, jumpy and my theory she might have wanted something from the apartment. "She was not forthcoming. In fact, she shut me down," I admitted. "But I riled her. She got down-right snippy when I questioned her real reason for seeing Tanya."

"Think there's something there?" Will asked.

"She's definitely hiding something. Do you want to see what you can dredge up?"

He nodded.

My hand went across the table and was placed on his arm. "Will, I hope you don't think I'm taking advantage of you." I paused and the corner of my mouth lifted ruefully. "Well, I guess I am. But I hope you don't think that's how I see you. It's just that…"

He placed a finger on my lips to still the outpouring of words. "Sadie, stop. That's not what I think at all. I told you when we first met and I'm repeating it now. Out of friendship, support and because I care, what I do is not because I owe you and your family."

My heart swelled at his words. When Will was much younger, my Uncle Stan had helped move his sister, Lissa, away from their suppressive family home. Years later, unbeknownst to me, I had helped her move for free, to leave an abusive boyfriend. That connection brought Will into my life.

"Besides, we all have superpowers," he added jovially.

I grinned. "Oh yeah? What's mine?"

He snorted. "Getting into trouble. What else?"

I conceded his point with a laugh and checked my watch. "Before I leave, is there some way to listen to radio on my phone?"

"Sure, that's easy." He motioned for my phone and started tapping. "I've loaded an app where you tap on it and scroll through the stations. Are you looking for something specific?"

He handed back the device.

"Thanks. Nope, just general stuff." No way would I gush about Jackson Steel from KRDL. "I have to go. I'm seeing Tanya, hoping to find out more about Crystal. We didn't discuss that in jail and I'm sure she needed some time. The police probably already asked her everything but she may give me more intimate details than the authorities."

Will rose. "Good idea. Keep me in the loop and I'll start investigating Elaine but truthfully I think it's a long shot."

"Agreed."

Will departed while I stopped at the counter and ordered coffee and bagels to go.

Driving to Tanya's, Sylvia called.

"Hello."

"Hey boss," she replied. "Two calls you should know about. One is from a client that needs heavy stuff moved. They're boxes of books, lots of them."

"For when?"

"That's why I'm calling. He needs it done tomorrow and it's from one end of the city to the other. I told him it would be extra because of the short notice," my office manager added.

"I don't give commission," I teased. "Anything scheduled for tomorrow?"

"No."

"Get the details and tell him we'll quote a flat rate because books are so heavy." I'd need help with this one. A few boxes of books were no big deal but if a client says lots they usually underestimate. "What's the other call?"

"Your brother. He didn't recognize my voice, said he thought it was the wrong number until he heard the slogan."

Of course. I had been so busy I hadn't called to let him know. I frowned, thought of the date. He was due to come home today so why was he calling?

"What catchphrase did you come up with now?"

"'Hawkins Freight–we'll hawk your wares to anywhere,'" she announced.

"Closer but don't you think it sounds like we're going to sell a client's things?"

"That could be why your brother said 'I don't think so' before he even introduced himself. And he didn't leave a message, just said for you to call him."

"Don't give up; the idea of a slogan is good. Thanks for the messages. Let me know a time for tomorrow so I can find a few people."

"Right on. Later, gater," my employee hung up.

I shook my head, smirking. Sylvia has a cool personality and I could see we'd work well together.

"Hey Bro, what's up?" I said when he picked up before the second ring.

"Sadie."

It wasn't the lack of greeting, but that one emotionless word made me sit up and clutch the phone. I pulled over, cut the engine. "What's wrong?"

"It's Karen. She went into labor last night."

"But she wasn't due for almost another month." Trepidation snaked through my gut. "Is she okay?"

"Yes, she's resting but there were…are…complications." He paused and choked out "The baby was born with the cord around his neck, he was almost blue."

"Oh god, Blaine. Is he…" I couldn't say it, couldn't vocalize the scream in my head.

"He's in the neo-natal intensive care unit right now. The doctors have assured us he'll live but will have to wait and see what effects arise from the lack of oxygen."

I closed tear-filled eyes, dropped a shaking hand with the phone to my lap. Breath shuddered in and out of my lungs, the pain in my chest like an anvil on my heart.

I brought the phone back up. "I'm so sorry, Blaine. God, I wish I could be there."

"Nothing you can do, sis," he said, his voice hollow and muted.

"How is Karen?"

"She's handling it. It all happened so fast, Sadie. Thank god it was last night and not on our way home."

After a moment of silence, I said, "A boy. Congratulations. Have you named him yet?"

Blaine's voice softened, filled with warmth. "Jerrald Matthew."

My throat hitched. "Jerrald. After dad."

"Yeah."

Another moment of silent communion and my brother spoke again. "Listen, I don't know how long we're going to stay here. Karen's parents are very supportive and with the doctors here knowing what's going on…"

"Of course. Stay as long as you need to. There's nothing that requires your attention. All is good." My brother didn't need to know about the curve balls thrown at me. He had enough to deal with. Before he could inquire about the business, I went on, "I'll let you go. Give Karen a hug and kiss for me."

"I will. Once we have more details, I'll phone you. I love you, Sadie."

"Love you too, Blaine."

I disconnected, leaned my head back and smothered the sob in my throat. I sat there thinking about those curve balls; friendships lost, potential lovers becoming distant, divorce, defending those you love against monsters, starting anew, death and…life, in whatever form it took. Events that changed your path made you stop, take notice, get perspective. I had a nephew; he was alive and so were his parents. Whatever came from the difficult birth we would deal with it. Together.

* * *

Tanya was waiting at the door of her apartment after she buzzed me in, dressed in loose light-colored pants and short-sleeved top. Her face wasn't as haggard as a few days ago but the tightness around her mouth spoke of the stress she was under.

I handed her a coffee and the bag. "Maple cinnamon French toast bagels."

A solemn thank you replaced the comeback I expected.

"How are you holding out?"

She shrugged, walked into the kitchen, plated the bagels, brought them into the living room and set everything on the coffee table. "All right."

"Do you need anything?"

"No, I'm fine." She gazed at me. "I found out you posted my bail. Why?"

I blinked. "You really need to ask?"

She flushed. Presumably her question was based on the tenuous state of our friendship of late. Perhaps this would be the first step toward uniting those threads again.

"Let me rephrase. How about thank you and how?"

"You're welcome," I replied and smiled. "Connections." Telling Tanya how the money for her bail was raised wouldn't be smart. We communicated for the first time in a while and I didn't want to turn this into an argument.

My friend took a sip of coffee, stared out the large picture window, her gaze troubled. "I had hoped my family…" That wistful whisper tore into me.

Wanting to pull her away from melancholia, I commented, "I met your temporary replacement, Elaine Bromskey. Well, not actually met. We spoke on the phone."

"Oh yeah? Heard she's made a few changes." At my inquisitive look, Tanya added, "I've been speaking with Will. He's kept me up to date."

I took a bite of bagel. So good. "Do you know her?"

"Met her at a few conferences. We went out for lunch once or twice."

"When was this?"

She thought back but couldn't give me exact dates.

My mind worked. "That was just before your promotion here."

She nodded.

"Tell me about her?"

Tanya lowered her brows. "Why?"

"The more I know the more I can stay on her good side, especially if I need a crew to give me a hand." Which I did.

"She seemed nice, worked out of Fort Worth. Had some ideas."

"Fort Worth? I thought she came from Austin."

"Actually, she's been in multiple locations." Tanya stopped for a second, finished her bagel. "In fact, she got the Austin posting just after I got promoted here."

"Do supervisors normally move from place to place?"

Tanya lifted a shoulder. "Don't know. Could be her contracts ran out or she was a troubleshooter or something."

"How about the clients? Do they relocate?"

My friend shook her head. "Hardly ever. Unless a person needed to get out of their city for safety reasons, most clients are already established and have support from friends or family. I don't know about our other locations but in the years I've been working I've only had one request from a young woman."

"Did it go through?"

My friend raised her eyebrow as if to say 'you-know-I-can't-tell-you-that.'

I raised a hand in apology. "Sorry, sorry. Force of habit to ask too many questions."

A theory formed in my brain. "Is your position the same as Elaine's? Do you have the same responsibility?"

"No. If memory serves, in Austin she was an executive assistant. I'm a manager." Tanya lowered her coffee, gave me a pointed look. "What are you getting at?"

I evaded her question. "Do you know if she applied for the same job you did?"

"Out with it, Sadie," she said tersely.

"I was just wondering, the changes she'd made and if she lost the job to you, if…you know…if she would be the type of person for retribution."

Tanya reared back, gaped at me. "Are you crazy?"

Well, admittedly, it was out there. What would be the odds that Elaine applied for the job, but Tanya beat her out of it and she knew Crystal and murdered her? The more I thought about it, the more outrageous it sounded.

"Sorry," I apologized after explaining my reasoning. "I'm grasping. It's just I'd accept anything if it meant proving your innocence in Crystal's murder."

Tanya grabbed my hand, squeezed it tight. "And I appreciate it, but do you honestly believe what you're saying?"

"No. But I was hoping."

She pressed my hand again and let it go. We sat in our own thoughts for a long time.

"I'm sorry about Crystal. Will there be some type of service?"

Her eyes filled with pain. "I haven't heard."

"How did you two meet again?" She'd told me once but I couldn't remember.

Bittersweet caring wiped away the pain in her eyes. "At Arthur Storey Park at a picnic fundraiser for StreetSmart. Her Frisbee landed in the potato salad."

I smiled. "Sounds like fate."

She did the same. "Maybe."

"Tell me more."

Crystal Sherridan's history lay out before me. Less than a year before they met, Crystal moved back to Houston from Montana to be nearer to her family and to start a new marketing job for a design firm. There had been an instant connection between the two women when they'd met that afternoon in the park. Crystal admired Tanya's work, had shown interest and appreciation for the StreetSmart organization. The young people under Tanya's care got to know the woman as Tanya's friend, nothing more. The two women were very discreet for fear Tanya's sexual preference would compromise her job. They both shared a love of music, especially blues with female leads.

"I'm sure the cops have asked this question, but can you think of anyone who would want to hurt Crystal?"

Tanya shook her head. "I've been over and over it. No, I can't. Things were fine at her work. Everyone got along well. She had her own place. No ex-lovers in town. She hadn't been here long enough."

"What about from Montana? Did she have a prior relationship that ended badly?"

My friend tucked her legs beneath her, nestled herself into the corner of the couch. "Not sure. Yes, she had a lover in Montana, but didn't provide details regarding the relationship, only that they parted ways.

I would think if it had been volatile, she might have mentioned it. Most people tend to dish on their ex's."

Difficult to verify that information and like Tanya said, the authorities had probably already probed into that avenue of the investigation.

"Was anyone following her, stalking her?"

Tanya looked down her nose. "Quit trying to imitate *Agatha Christie*." But that demand held a suppressed smile. It was the first positive sign from her since this nightmare started.

She stilled. "Come to think of it…"

"What?" Oh please give me someone, something to target.

"Crystal mentioned once she thought we were being followed to my place. We spotted no one, but she felt like eyes were being drilled into her back."

I leaned forward, closer. "Did you tell the police?"

"What was there to tell? There wasn't anyone there and it never happened again."

"How long ago?"

She thought for a second. "About six weeks after we started seeing each other but like I said, it never happened again and she forgot about it."

It was probably nothing. The same with any leads I had hoped to gain, a big fat nothing.

Tanya sagged back, weariness settling over her.

"I'm going to head out, but would you consider getting away from these four walls tomorrow for a few hours?"

She hesitated. "I don't know if I'm up to being around a lot of people."

"It wouldn't be many. I need help with a job. Jessie might lend a hand, too. Want to come along? Give your mind a break for a few hours."

"What about Blaine? Can't he help you?"

My gut twisted but I kept my expression neutral. "He and Karen are visiting the in-laws." I wouldn't burden Tanya with the news about my new nephew, not right now.

"Well…"

"Only your friends plus the client will be there. Jessie would love to see you."

Tanya's mouth lifted in a small smile. "I'd like to see her too. Sure, why not?"

"Great," I beamed. "I'll call you with a time and we'll coordinate. Thanks, Tanya, I appreciate the help."

We rose and hugged, the two of us clinging for a long moment. The friendship threads were getting stronger and I was relieved.

Out in the van, I called Jessie's cell. She had given me the number yesterday and left a message on voicemail. At least now we could avoid Elaine.

Instead of texting Jessie, what I wanted to say had to be face-to-face.

CHAPTER ELEVEN

After Tanya assured me she would help with moving a massive amount of books tomorrow, I went to Hawkins Freight to get the details and to check on my office manager.

When I walked in a strong, pungent odor wafted from a cloud of smoke circling the ceiling before drifting out the door.

I coughed. "What the hell is that smell? If you want to smoke pot, that's your business but since I personally can't stand the stuff would prefer you did it outside."

Sylvia was in the middle of doing some type of dance, waving smoldering sticks of…something…while she murmured words and hummed.

She stopped. "Oh, hey. There's some nasty karma around here so I'm smudging the place."

"You're what?"

Her head tilted. "Smudging. You know, giving those no-good vibes the boot."

Okaaay.

"I'm almost done."

I went into the shop, stood in the middle of the floor, and my eyes went to Blaine's toolbox. The unit drew me as I walked over and lovingly put a hand on the cabinet. My brother would return, of course he would, but until it was safe to bring the baby home with him, he would stay with his in-laws. Without him here, a part of me felt un-tethered, like I was alone in the world. With a shake of my head, I admitted my self-pity was shameful when compared to what he and Karen had to face.

"You okay?" Sylvia asked, coming closer.

I straightened my spine, pushed the loneliness and shame away and turned. "As good as winning the blue ribbon at the county fair."

She eyed me with speculation but decided not to comment. "Got those details for the job tomorrow." As she turned to head back to the office, she commented, "Considering you brought someone in to look at the van when it wouldn't start, I'm guessing your brother is the mechanic in the family?"

"How'd you know that?"

Sylvia jerked her thumb over her shoulder. "His name is on the tool cabinet and on some checks I came across while straightening the office. Do I get to meet him?"

I stiffened but shook it off. "He and his wife, Karen, are visiting her parents. Not sure when they're coming back."

Sylvia studied me for a long time. "Guess you'll temporarily have to take any repairs to a garage."

"Perhaps." I followed her back where she consulted a large calendar on the desk.

"Tomorrow, nine in the morning. The client's name is Professor Shamdi and the books are at Strayer University. They're going into storage--"

I was making a note of the info when Jessie called back.

"Hi, got your message," she said in a low tone.

"Thanks for calling back so soon." I paused, my eyebrows lowered. "Is this a bad time?"

"No, it's fine."

"Then why are you almost whispering?"

"Because I'm in Bromskey's office looking through files."

Jessie had said she would probe into the new StreetSmart office manager, but I still felt a sense of nervousness quiver through my bloodstream.

"Gees, be careful."

Sylvia gave an odd look at my warning and spoke with a hush. "Why are you whispering? Did you want me to leave?"

I shook my head and waved her off, turned my attention back to the phone. Jessie agreed to help with the move and said she'd try to get Erie to assist as well.

With another word of caution, I disconnected, turned and found my employee appraising me. "What?"

"Do I really want to know?"

Sylvia's directness was charming, another reason I liked her, but what was going on, trying to prove Tanya's innocence, wasn't something she needed to be aware of. At least not right now.

"Nothing to know," I said with a false grin.

"Okay," she winked. "I'm heading home. Good luck with the move. Talk to you tomorrow."

I rerouted the phone, locked up and went to Blaine's place. I entered the house, gave Moose a big hug and surveyed the surroundings differently. How it would change with a new inhabitant, one that might require special needs. I traversed the rooms, felt the warm atmosphere emanating from photos and various elements of my brother's family battle against the loneliness cloaking me.

Moose approached, nudged my hand and his deep brown eyes gazed up as if in support. I squatted down, slung an arm around his shoulders, leaned my head against his. "I know. They'll be home soon. And with someone new to protect."

He huffed a reply.

I straightened, went to the door. "Come on, Moosie. Let's go for a walk."

The walk ended up being a four-mile trek around the neighborhood, through the park, where the Saint

Bernard rolled around in the grass doing his best bear-stretching-in-the-sun imitation, and circled not one but three fire hydrants, leaving us in a laughing tangled mess. By the time we got back home, I was tired but my funk had lifted.

I fed the dog, and myself, then set my alarm for ten and took a nap. Tonight, I'd head over to Lewis' again to see what else I could learn.

* * *

I donned more appropriate attire than the last time I watched Lewis Woods' house. Stopping short of smearing black camouflage paint on my face, I dressed in dark clothes and a black baseball cap. ID, debit card and some cash went into my pockets. Moose eyed me at the door.

I ruffled his ears. "Not this time, buddy. Sorry. I'll bring you a treat instead?"

Monitoring the traffic from the van, I watched for anyone coming and going from Tanya's brother's place. The past hour had been uneventful; only one car arrived, parked at the curb and had remained. Listening at the kitchen window again was an option but twice in a couple of days would push it. It would be preferable if Lewis left so I could follow him, maybe to where he and his gang hung out.

A text pinged on my phone from Will.

Anything yet?

As promised, I had notified him of where he could send the hearse. He didn't think that was funny.

No. What about on your end?

Still checking.

Nothing more from him after that.

Time dragged. No movement at the house.

To ease boredom, I opened the radio app Will had installed on my phone and scrolled through the station names in search of KRDL, which was listed and I tapped onto it. Seconds later, classic rock music sprang from my phone and I waited to hear *the voice*. Before long Jackson's baritone, like a mixture of James Earl Jones and Sam Elliot, slid over me like satin, imbued my blood, made me close my eyes and sigh in a long, low moan. Lordy, a gal could get in serious trouble having someone who spoke like that in her bed, murmuring terms of endearment or other naughty things.

A station break cut in, pulling me away from the dream with a shake of my head. My fingers scrolled through my contacts and hovered over the number Jackson had given me when he asked me to call him.

I hadn't reached out to him yet. My hesitancy could be because of everything that was going on or maybe once that step was taken and we communicated on a deeper level, he would no longer be a figure of mystery. My illusion of the fantasy would cease to exist and the person behind the silky, sexy voice would take shape, form and become real.

Or maybe I was just scared.

Scared of allowing another man into my life, in whatever capacity that entailed, across the miles between Houston and Pampa. It would require letting down my guard, opening up, exposing myself, regardless if it would be just friendship.

That had already been done with Wayne, with no regrets, yet the impressions I received from our last encounter were confusing me. I'd opted to give him some space, since he'd been evasive during dinner and had walked away, but there had been no communication from him since. Had he picked up on my distraction during our meal, coming to the false conclusion I preferred to be somewhere else and was now giving me the same space I thought he needed? The man could be busy; he had a life, and I clung to that reasoning. For now.

Then there was seeing Clayton with another woman. The logical part of my brain accepted we had divorced, something I didn't regret, however my emotional side wondered if I was entirely over him, or ever would be.

Around and around wove my thoughts, intersecting, branching into one another, like the waterways in the bayou.

Jackson spoke again and his words, like a siren song, wove their spell, pulled at me and before I knew it, my finger tapped the call button of KRDL's listing. The phone rang several times and I considered hanging up but refused to allow fear entrance, to grow, morph and invade some aspects of my life.

"KRDL, this is Jackson."

And with those words I was lifted, carried away and deposited back into the dream while the rest of the world only heard the classic rock he currently put on the air.

"Hi, Jackson. It's Sadie."

"Hey, you finally called." No admonishment, no hint of accusation. Just a sprinkling of relief.

"Yes, I did." A smile broke across my face.

"How've you been?"

"Fine. Busy. How about you?"

"Good," he paused. "I'm glad you phoned." There it was, that subtle undertone of pleasure, the one which had embedded itself into my memory when we had spoken last. The one that refused to let go.

"Me too."

Silence emerged, as if each waited for the other to begin the conversation, to be first to reach out, connect.

He took the initiative. "So, tell me what happened that night in Pampa with the bad guys."

I spent the next ten minutes filling him in on how I was knocked out and what had ensued; theft of the load, found by the police thanks to him, suspected of killing my supposed client, and how the woman, and her lover, the janitor, had executed the robbery and murder. Certain parts of the ordeal remained unspoken, of how I committed a break and enter to get evidence, how I'd seen a man shot before my eyes. Those details were for another time, if at all.

"That's quite the tale," he said with a bit of awe.

"Sounds like a movie or a novel, I know."

"And now you. Tell me all about yourself."

I started with my childhood in Alabama then the relocation to Amarillo and eventually Houston. How my father died, then later my uncle and the eventual acquisition of Hawkins Freight. I didn't elaborate on the method used to acquire the business; that was private and too sensitive. Instead, I mentioned the capital required came from my divorce and my hopes of eventually expanding to a fleet of trucks or long hauling.

Jackson told me he heralded from California and that his name was Morro Jackson, named after Morro Bay, California where he was conceived. He'd chosen Jackson Steel as his on-air personality because most people in his profession didn't use their real names. He had one brother, an architect, and his family still lived in California.

"Why would you leave California for Texas?" I asked with a laugh. "Everyone wants to live in California."

A long pause. "Different life path," he said.

We talked some more, sharing a hobby of reading but our tastes were different. Where I loved curling up with a mystery or thriller, Jackson leaned more toward non-fiction and poetry and had a soft spot for dog stories.

"Ah, a soul with depth," I teased.

"I think so," he agreed with humor.

"Did you always want to be a radio DJ?"

The silence on the other end of the line tugged my attention from something I spotted down the street. Jackson finally answered quietly. "No. It chose me."

My hopes for further explanation would have to wait. "Would you be angry with me if I told you I have to go?" I crossed my fingers because I enjoyed our conversation.

"Depends. Are you tired of talking with me?"

Without thinking, I said, "That would never happen."

His low intimate chuckled tickled my nerve endings.

"Okay then. Hopefully, we can talk again soon," he said. "I'm glad you called, Sadie. I really am."

A flush of warmth spread through me. "Me too. Have a good night."

Jackson said the same and disconnected.

The phone got tossed onto the passenger seat and my focus zeroed in on movement down the street.

Lewis was leaving.

CHAPTER TWELVE

The van's lights stayed off as I pulled away from the curb and followed the car that carried Lewis Woods away from his house. At night, in a residential neighborhood, a car following another, regardless if it sat half a block away, would be noticed. Once his vehicle rounded the corner, I gunned down the street in hopes of not losing him. My right turn let me see Lewis' car turn left at the next intersection. I stayed well back until the vehicle merged onto the expressway and proceeded after it, switching on my lights once I melded into traffic. My quarry seemed to be headed downtown, which was verified when they traversed down a primary thoroughfare that held an assortment of bars and pubs. The car eventually pulled over, the occupants vacated their mode of transport and Lewis, with three other males and a female, headed into a dive bar.

Hell. They were on a pub crawl.

I drove past and made a split decision to head to Crystal's neighborhood. Different people traverse the area later at night than during the day. Perhaps I would get lucky and glean new information about the night of Crystal's murder.

Traffic was thin and I had no problem finding a parking spot on Rice. I hesitated before leaving the safety of the van. A petite woman walking alone was not the smartest idea, but people would avoid talking to me if I carried my baseball bat. Observing from the vehicle would accomplish nothing.

Numerous apartment buildings lined the two blocks within the immediate area. A florist shop and a boutique were already closed. A bistro was still open although the hours on the sign stated they would lock their doors soon. I went in, spoke with the staff but learned they couldn't tell me anything of relevance and there was no security camera on the premises.

There was a busker nearby packing up his belongings.

"Hi," I said. "Do you usually play out here?"

He closed the lid of a well-used guitar in a hard-shelled case. The young man had long, brown hair which was neatly combed and wore faded jeans and a long-sleeved dark-colored tee.

He stood and shrugged, "Pretty much."

Supplying the date, I asked him if he was playing the night of Crystal's murder.

"Can't remember the exact date but if it's the one when the cops came just down the street with their lights flashing, then yeah, I was here." A slight wariness crossing his features. "Why?"

"For personal reasons, I'm trying to find out what happened. I'm not a reporter and I'm not a cop," I assured him. "Did the police already speak with you?"

He snorted. "I avoid them as much as possible."

I took that as a no. "Did you see anything odd that night?"

"Nope. Just the usual people," he replied.

"How about unusual people?" I asked hopefully.

His brows lifted a bit. "If you're thinking weird as in crazy, then no. Most people who come to the bistro live around here and act pretty normal. There might be the odd person not from this area but not very often. He lifted the guitar case, paused for a second. "Although there was this one chick, she definitely wasn't from around here."

That got my attention. "Why do you say that?"

"I've been busking here for the past year. Never seen her. In fact, at first I thought she was a guy because she had a black hoodie covering her face and was slim, not curvy like most women. She had her hands in the pockets and was hunched over but the leggings gave it away. Guys don't wear leggings. And I could smell perfume."

My heart sped up. "Did you see her face?"

He shook his head. "Nope. She walked by too fast." He went to leave. "I gotta go."

"Wait," I said with desperation. "What time was this?"

"Can't remember the exact time but it was late, well past midnight, maybe even one. Not sure," he said. "The bistro was closed for a private party. I provided some cheap entertainment, then stayed and came out here afterward. Make better coin when there's a party."

He turned to go, so I fished out a twenty. "Here. One last question, I swear."

The busker took the cash with a nod of thanks.

"Which direction did she come from?"

"Which time?"

I sucked in a breath. "She went by more than once?"

He nodded. "Yeah. Twice within roughly an hour. Both times from up the block. She parked over there. Drove a white Beetle." He pointed across the street about twenty feet away. "Look, lady, I really gotta go."

I grabbed another ten dollars from my purse and shoved it into his hand. "Thanks so much. You've been a great help."

He nodded his thanks again and left.

I trotted back to the van and hopped in, my pulse thrumming. According to the busker, a slight woman walked to and from Crystal's apartment close to the time of the murder. Could it have been Stephanie? She fit that description from what I saw when I tried to speak with her. And she also wore leggings. Granted that wasn't sufficient evidence, but if it was her, why had she lied to the police about coming to Crystal's only once? Did she commit the murder, then returns, playing the concerned friend to establish her alibi? And was she the person Tanya spotted coming out of the apartment complex's front door? Tanya admitted because of darkness she didn't get a good look at *him* but it could have been a woman.

Flush with the possibility of another suspect, I drove up and down the street. Traffic was sparse so I didn't have to worry about impatient drivers. Will was already checking into whatever traffic cams were in the area so I concentrated on alternate forms of surveillance. Bank machines have cameras but there were none close by.

I pulled into a convenience store parking lot two blocks down from Crystal's apartment, got out, went inside and scoped the ceiling and doors for telltale cameras. One mounted on the top shelf behind the counter captured the cash and the entrance of the store. Perfect.

I wrote the store's name and address on some paper. Back in the van, I used GPS to navigate the easiest route from Crystal's place to Tanya's apartment and drove the streets, one eye on the road, the other switching from sidewalk to buildings and traffic lights, searching for cameras. I spotted two but there were probably more.

A few blocks from Tanya's place I swung into a convenience store parking lot and slid into the last spot at the very end of the building. This sleuthing had given me the munchies. My eyes focused on a figure walking out of the store.

It was Lewis.

I hit the floor between the seats of the van. Odds were Tanya's brother didn't see me but I remained hunkered down, watching as he went to a car. There could be a lot of legitimate reasons for his appearance at this store, but it was a long way from his place, over half an hour. Coincidence?

Lewis slid behind the wheel of a black vehicle, reversed and drove out of the lot. I sat up and followed. Even though he didn't know Blaine's van, I kept far enough back so that I hoped Lewis didn't think he was being tailed. Fate was with me because the car eventually slowed, pulled to the curb and parked but the motor kept running.

Right outside Tanya's apartment building.

Lewis never got out, just sat there in the car while I parked down the block, my headlights off. Why was he here? Was he waiting for someone? From my vantage point and the darkened windows, distinguishing a passenger was difficult. Nor could I see what Lewis was doing. If I opened the driver's door, he might spot me in his rear-view mirror. Instead, I maneuvered into the back, exited the sliding door on the passenger side, slid the door slowly closed and prayed he didn't notice. I slunk as close to him as I dared, using shadowed doorways to conceal me. I made a mental note of his license plate number, make and model of his car. If Lewis was near Crystal's the night of the murder, maybe Will could spot the car on traffic cams in the area.

An orange glow flared, then died. Someone in the car, if there was another person besides Tanya's brother, was smoking. Time dragged. I shifted from foot to foot, antsy but unwilling to approach in case I was spotted. After about ten minutes, the car pulled away. What was that all about?

Remembering my promise of a treat for the dog, I circled back to the convenience store. While waiting in line to pay for the pepperoni sticks for Moose, my gaze spanned the store and I noticed a surveillance camera pointed toward the cash. My focus then went to watching people enter and exit and I pondered why Lewis had been in this store. Maybe he was the smoker from the car and needed to buy more cigarettes since he was in the neighborhood.

As I drove home, theories and questions sped through my brain. Why was Lewis in Crystal's area? Had he been there before? And why had he sat outside his sister's apartment complex? To visit but chickened out? Did he call up to Tanya and she didn't want to see him? Or was he keeping her under surveillance?

After giving Moosie his treat, I crawled into bed with a mental checklist. I had to give Will the locations of the two convenience stores; one near

Tanya's and one near Cyrstal's, to view footage of the night of the murder. Those were long shots but I didn't want to leave any avenue unexplored. Also, the traffic cams en route between Tanya and Crystal's place. And if he could get the ownership from the license plate on the white Volkswagen Beetle parked near the bistro, it might confirm Stephanie had been to Crystal's more than once that night.

That would bump her up on my suspect list.

CHAPTER THIRTEEN

Tanya sat beside me in the moving van bright and early the next morning.

"You're still pale."

She watched traffic out her side window. "Not sleeping that great."

Understanding all too well, I tentatively broached the subject. "Haven't thought of anything to tell me that might help?"

"No."

"Have you heard from your family?"

Her eyes flicked to mine, went back to gaze outside. "Tracy called to see how I was making out. Someone must have let her know what's going on."

"How are your sister and the boys?"

Tracey, her husband James and their twin boys, Cody and Caleb, lived in Northern Idaho.

"Fine. The boys are in little league. They love it." She added in a low tone, "Haven't heard from Theresa or my parents."

My lips compressed to prevent commenting. Family dynamics were a complicated thing, unraveling and reuniting, sometimes splitting apart. Apparently, those of Tanya's family that still lived in Houston hadn't buried the hatchet. The lack of support spoke volumes but could this bit of news have any connection to Lewis gang's newest female member?

"What about Lewis?" I was fishing, hoping to glean any insight that would help me help her.

Tanya faced me. "What about him?"

"Have you seen him since he was released on parole?"

My friend almost winced, as if whipped across the shoulders. "I tried. Once. It didn't go well."

I played stupid. "He still blames you?"

"Of course he still blames me," she snapped, refusing to keep my gaze any longer. "I put him in jail."

We were at Strayer University and I parked near the door of the building to meet the client. "He put himself in jail, Tanya. You merely saved him from someplace worse," I pointed out softly.

My friend had her hand on the door handle and when she looked at me, the agony radiating from her eyes punched into my heart. "Did I?" she asked and disembarked from the van.

We waited on the sidewalk for someone to appear from the building. A few minutes later, another vehicle came to a stop in the parking lot and Jessie and Erie came up to meet us. Without breaking stride, Erie walked up to Tanya and embraced her warmly.

My eyebrows hiked up a notch. Chummy way for a barista to greet a customer out of work.

Tanya must have noticed my surprise. "Erie is Crystal's sister," she explained once they broke apart, her arm resting across the other girl's shoulder.

I took in the young woman's features, trying to find some resemblance but couldn't see any.

"Crystal's parents adopted me when I was nine," Erie provided, witnessing my scrutiny.

"I'm sorry for your loss."

Erie solemnly nodded her thanks. She turned to Tanya. "Has there been anything new on the investigation? Has your lawyer updated you at all?"

A flicker of pain drifted across Tanya's face and she shook her head. I felt like smacking Erie. The whole point of getting Tanya out of her apartment and with other people was so that she wouldn't think about her case.

Jessie must have seen my hands briefly in irritation because she spoke up, "How's the van holding out?"

"So far so good." If something else happened to it or Blaine's van before he came back I'd be stuck. The notion sat like a stone in my gut, heavy, unyielding, and a flush of anxiety washed up into my brain. Not wanting to tempt fate by focusing on that outcome, I was grateful when a distinguished looking older gentleman came out the entrance and strode to our group.

"Hello. I'm Professor Shamdi. I gather you are here for the books." At my nod, he continued. "If you will follow me, please, I'll show you where they are and you can start loading."

We trailed after the professor, our footsteps echoing down hallways as silent as a crypt. Perhaps this part of the University must not be used as much. We entered a large room through paneled double doors filled with neatly stacked boxes.

I swallowed. "That's a lot of books. More than what was mentioned."

The man glanced away sheepishly. "Another shipment arrived after my phone call with you. I hope you don't mind. Is it a problem?"

I did mind because it could have cost me precious time in multiple loads but kept that comment to myself. "Not at all." I turned to Jessie and Erie. "Can you bring the two dollies from the back of the truck and start stacking?" As the young women left, I addressed my client. "Is there a closer exit where we can load from?"

He nodded. "Yes, this way."

Farther down the initial hallway was a set of outside doors. Once I discerned how to get to this part of the building, we retreated the way we came in, passing Erie and Jessie along the way and I let them know which door we would be using.

"I will leave you for now and check back later to see how you are making out," Mr. Shamdi said and strode away, a light swing in his step, since he wouldn't end up with sore muscles.

We worked in teams of two; Erie immediately partnered with Tanya to load boxes while Jessie and I unloaded and stacked them in the van. Jessie was silent, a firm set of her mouth whenever Erie brought her stack of books up the ramp into the truck. I had a feeling my companion was miffed that she wasn't able to spend more time with Tanya. Understandable considering how she felt about the StreetSmart leader but Erie and Tanya had a kinship through Crystal, and gathered they took solace in that link.

Before long, Tanya announced we were nearing the end of the load, so I ventured to find Professor Shamdi and bumped into him rounding a corner.

"Oh. Sorry." I stepped back. "We're done. I'll need the address of where to drop off the books and as per the conditions of the contract half payment now and the balance after we deliver."

The man continued walking as he spoke. "Here is the address." He reached into his jacket pocket and withdrew a piece of paper, which held the name of a storage facility in the city. He stopped outside the open back door of the van, leveling a critical eye over the cargo, counting the rows and stacks, like he was calculating the number of boxes. "All seems in order." He withdrew a check from the inside breast pocket of his jacket. "Full payment, as there is no receiver at the storage location. The unit number is

517. Inside, you will find a stack of pallets. Please make sure none of the boxes are set directly on the concrete floor. On the paper with the location, you will also see a set of numbers. That is the combination for the lock of the storage unit." He turned to stare at me. "It will be changed before end of day."

Okay. No mistaking the intent of that gaze.

"One other thing," he leaned closer and lowered his voice for my ears only. "Under no circumstances is the seal of the boxes to be broken. Is that clear?"

Ordinarily I would have been insulted at the insinuation that I would invade a client's privacy, and considered giving him a comeback saying as much, however his serious tone and level, piercing stare from his deep brown eyes told me he meant every word.

My gaze held calm professionalism. "Perfectly."

He held out his hand. "Then we have concluded our transaction."

As I went to seal the deal, he added, "However, may I call upon you in the future when these boxes need to be transported again?"

Again? My curiosity rose but I tried not to let it show. "Absolutely. And thank you for using Hawkins Freight."

He nodded, turned and entered the building, closing the propped open door behind him.

Tanya, Erie and Jessie stood beside me as I studied the boxes, the elder of the three noting my pensive expression. "What's wrong?"

"Mighty serious about his belongings."

"Anyone else notice all the boxes are the same?" Jessie said.

"And that they're sealed with no labels or writing," added Erie. "Whenever I've helped someone move they were lucky to get their hands on any type or size of box and always wrote what's inside."

"Did he say what was in them?" asked Tanya.

"He claimed it was books when he called Sylvia."

"I'm going to find out," commanded Erie as she went to get into the van.

I held her back. "No can do. First off, it's none of our business. Payment is to haul, not to pry and second, they're sealed and Professor Shamdi specifically said they were not to be opened."

"We re-tape them. What's the big deal?" she said, as if it was the simplest explanation in the world.

"His privacy," I said sternly.

"If they are books they must all be the same type because there are no bulging sides or misshapen boxes." Tanya paused for a moment. "Encyclopedias maybe?"

"In this day and age?" commented Jessie. "Do they still even print those?"

"Perhaps it's not books. Could be something illegal, like guns or contraband or something. Maybe stacks of counterfeit," opined Erie.

I arched my brows at her suggestion and glanced at my watch, noting the time. "The client has paid me and left instructions." I jumped up on the fender, pulled down the sliding door and secured the latch. "We need to get across town and unloaded before the combination will change."

Because of my love for classic mystery shows, my imagination ran rampant at the possibilities of what was in those boxes. I jumped into the driver's seat with Tanya riding shotgun and the girls followed in Erie's car.

"What do you think is in the boxes?" Tanya asked as we hit the freeway to circumvent the downtown traffic.

I shrugged. "Doesn't really matter to me," to which Tanya scoffed. She knew me better. "I can't break a client's confidence. Plus, if he found out, and how could he not since we'd cut the tape on the box, my reputation would be ruined."

My friend murmured in agreement.

But I was curious and nervous as I drove down the road, constantly checking my side mirrors for any sign of unmarked police vehicles following me.

I changed the subject, trying to pull Tanya into a conversation. "I didn't know Erie was related to Crystal."

The former StreetSmart manager's eyes softened. "Erie's a good kid. Wants to get into some type of social work."

"She mentioned that when we talked before. She's taking her sister's death in stride."

"Erie doesn't show emotion very well and can come across as sullen but she is hurting. Don't forget, Crystal lived in Montana for years before she returned, has been back less than a year and living in her own place." She paused, then spoke in a whisper as if she needed to remind herself. "*Had* been back and *lived* in her own place. Past tense."

We didn't speak for a few minutes until a small sigh escaped my friend's lips.

"You okay?" I asked, concerned.

Tanya remained silent.

"What is it? I know you're worried about the charges but you're innocent and the police are doing their best to find the killer."

They'd better be but knew from personal experience how overworked our law enforcement was and wondered how hard they were searching when they already had a prime suspect.

"It's not just the case, Sadie. I have to consider my future. Even if cleared of all charges, it's an almost guarantee I'll have to find another job now that me being gay has become public knowledge."

It almost slipped out that Will mentioned the same thing. Tanya didn't need to know that he and I were doing our own bit of investigating. It would only bring more stress onto my friend and speculation of Will's and my cooperative relationship.

She turned to me. "Seeing Jessie, having Will keep me posted on how things are at StreetSmart has got me thinking. I can't bury my head in hopes everything will turn out like roses and sunshine. Perhaps I should consider what other line of work is out there for me."

Although Tanya was being pragmatic, I still had a hard time with her outlook. "Cross that bridge if you need to. That's in the future and things might be different."

We fell into a comfortable silence until we reached the storage facility. I pulled off to the side of Professor Shamdi's unit so other drivers could get past, got out and lowered the ramp. Jessie and Erie arrived as I unlocked the storage unit. We set down the pallets that were stacked against the wall and worked in tandem unloading the boxes. The four of us chatted, easy superfluous conversation that didn't require too much thought or opinions and it seemed to lift Tanya's spirit.

In less than two hours, we were done. I offered to take Tanya back home, but Erie pushed to spend some time with her and my friend agreed. Jessie stood with her arms crossed near the car and mumbled something about getting dropped off along the way since I headed in a different direction back to the shop to exchange vehicles. It seemed Jessie was being labeled as a third wheel and my heart went out to her.

Tanya refused to accept any money so after paying Erie, I went to Jessie and leaned close, pressing some cash into her hand. "I know Tanya would love it if you called her maybe tomorrow and made plans."

The young woman's eyes jerked to mine but she said nothing.

I was speaking for Tanya, but Jessie may not have considered the boundaries required between her manager–former manager at the moment–and herself despite being away from work. The last thing my friend needed was any misconception of inappropriate behavior between her and her charges.

My hand rested on her arm. "Trust me, Jess."

A small smile of gratitude graced her pretty face and she nodded once before stepping into the back seat of Erie's car. With a light beep of the horn, the three of them drove off and after checking to make sure Mr. Shamdi's unit was secured, I drove back to Hawkins Freight.

The office was empty, Sylvia having already left for the day, so I checked for any jobs tomorrow, nope, left a note to my office manager to deposit the check from the professor that was locked up in the filing cabinet and left for Blaine's with visions of a long soak in a hot tub.

At a traffic light, something I overheard the other night kept poking me in the brain, demanding attention. It was the comment by one of Lewis' pals praising a girl for getting into their gang. Despite not knowing what the event actually was, it was a sure bet it had probably been illegal. What concerned me more was their assertion that Lewis' sister would not be happy if she ever found out. My gut told me the sister they were referring to was Tanya. I had nothing to corroborate the idea but there was one way to find out.

* * *

Moose gazed up at me with sad puppy-dog eyes as I was about to leave. I heaved a sigh, hung my head and relented. What could it hurt? The poor guy spent most of the past couple of days cooped up either in the house or at the shop.

"You can come as long as you also do guard duty."

He tilted his head to the side as if to ask, 'what's guard duty?'

"Never mind." Holding his collar in case he darted once the door opened, we got into the van and left.

I had parked the van down the street and was watching Tanya's brother's house. There was no car outside, yet a light shone in a downstairs window.

Ten minutes later I let out a low groan and turned to the dog. "This will not work, you know that. You shouldn't have talked me into this."

Moose remained silent and had the decency to hang his head.

My fingers ruffled his ears. "I forgive you."

Another fifteen minutes went by with no movement whatsoever. It was like waiting for a snail to cross the road. We could sit here all night and still be no closer to gaining any evidence to help Tanya's case. Maybe Wayne could make inquiries within the police force about Lewis and his gang. But it would mean answering questions and revealing my interest in Tanya's case that went beyond mere concern. We hadn't spoken since that night and I wondered how he would feel if the only contact I attempted would be to request a favor. However, this could be an opportunity to feel him out, to discern if the remoteness I sensed was my imagination.

Before I chickened out, I dialed his number on my phone. The call didn't complete a full second ring then disconnected. Odd. In the past, the connection usually went up to six rings and then his voicemail would kick in. The same result with another try. Okay, so his phone was probably off. No need to second guess his intention, like maybe he was avoiding me. He could be in bed. Or working on a case. Maybe undercover. But a tiny voice in the back of my brain whispered *He's a cop. Shouldn't they be available at all times in the event of an emergency? And why would he turn off his voicemail option?*

Before I could contemplate that new wrinkle, Moose let out a low growl. My driver's door flung open and I got yanked out of the van.

CHAPTER FOURTEEN

I twisted out of my oppressor's grasp, ready to reach into the van and retrieve Louis from under the seat when I was hauled back, thrown against the door which slammed it shut.

"I don't like being watched," Lewis growled at me.

My four-legged companion went berserk inside. His mad barking was accompanied by a row of snarling teeth as he lunged toward the door.

I mashed the hit of panic riding up and down my spine like a bucking bronco. Despite the murderous anger on Lewis' face, I shoved him. "Get your goddamn hands off me!"

He took a small step back, sneered. "Or what? You gonna stomp on my toes with those fancy boots of yours?"

The turquoise water snake part on my Dan Post's held a fait glow in the streetlight.

Instead of curling my fingers into a fist, I wrapped them around the driver's door handle. "No. I'll let loose the Moose and you can deal with him."

I didn't know if the dog would rip him to pieces but Lewis got the point. I hid the smirk of satisfaction at seeing his eyes widen in alarm while he took a step back.

"Hush, Moose," I called through the window to my furry buddy. "Lewis won't hurt me." I leveled my gaze at him. "Will you?"

"Friend of Tanya's or not, you got no business sitting out here watching me."

With no comment from me, the arrogant curl of his lip returned. "You're lucky it was me who caught you watching the house. Had it been one of my boys, things would have ended differently. Leave Sadie, now, while you still can."

A warning for my wellbeing. Or was he merely his muscle?

I wanted to argue but was busted and Lewis had a point. Nothing more would be gained tonight. I opened the door, holding Moose back with my hand and squeezed into the driver's seat.

Before the door closed, Lewis leaned in. "If I catch you here again it will be the last." He shut the door hard and stepped back, intent on watching me leave.

I turned over the engine and floored it, madder than a croc having its tail grabbed. I'd been lazy, watching other parts of the street, which was the only way Lewis could have snuck up on me. He must have spotted the van from a window, concluded it wasn't part of the neighborhood and came to investigate.

Moose sensed my anxiety because he squeezed his bulk between the two front seats and let out a soft whine.

"Thank you, sweetie, for being so brave. I didn't realize you had such a temper," I chuckled as my fingers gently framed his face and kissed his head. "You'll get extra treats when we get home."

A glance in the side mirror showed Lewis making his way to his house. My teeth ground in frustration. Coming to the intersection to make my turn, I veered toward the curb to avoid getting hit by a car that cut the corner and came into my lane. My head whipped around and when I shot a glare at the driver, my eyes widened.

She looked familiar.

I hit the brakes while the other car continued on, oblivious to the near collision. From the driver's side mirror, I watched the vehicle as it came to a stop halfway down the street, right in front of Lewis Wood's house. I zipped the van around the corner, slammed it into park and leaped out with the motor still going. I sped around the corner and hid behind the closest tree. Inching my head around the trunk, I spied Lewis as he waited by his door for the female walking up the pathway to the house. Once they were inside, I went back to the van and drove to Blaine's.

My mind jumped from incident to incident, trying to place the familiar young woman behind the driver's wheel of the car.

Once home, I walked absentmindedly into the house and closed the door when a loud woof broke into my fog. Dang, I forgot Moose in the vehicle.

"Sorry, boy." I held onto his collar as he leaped out and we went inside. He ran straight to the treat door, not letting me forget my promise to give him his reward for the show of bravery. With surprising gentleness, he took each of the half dozen biscuits one at a time, the loud snap and crunch of his chewing the only sound in the dimly lit kitchen. Before he got the last one, I brought it to my nose, inhaled, then thought what the hell, and bit off a tiny piece. The heavy artificial beef flavor tasted sour on my tongue. Apparently, he drew the line at eating someone's leftovers because he took one sniff of the offered biscuit, huffed and walked away from the half-eaten delight.

"Hey, no wasting. These are expensive." The last of the biscuit went on the floor near his water bowl.

Despite the late hour, I was too keyed up for bed. I considered calling Jackson again but thought that might appear desperate. Instead, I poured myself a bath. Letting the heat relax tense muscles, I closed my eyes and went over the events of the day; Mr. Shamdi and his mysterious boxes and Lewis' threat of retribution. I thought of Tanya's reticence, Erie's pushy exuberance at being able to work with us, and Jessie's concern. Notions of Jessie reminded me I needed to call Blaine tomorrow to see how he and the family were making out.

As a sigh escaped my lips and the desire for sleep called me to bed the elusive identity of the woman driver popped into my brain.

I remembered where I knew her from.

CHAPTER FIFTEEN

The next morning, tingling warmth flowed up my arm. It entwined my nerve endings in a soft cocoon of pleasure, made me shiver in anticipation and want. My breath caught in my throat, then escaped on a low moan as a tongue caressed my wrist with such sensual intensity it made my toes curl. My head pressed back against the bed, my hips shifting with a need I hadn't experienced in a long time. The tongue kept working its magic and before long a soft whimper reached my ears, low in tone.

"Jackson," I breathed huskily.

He made a chuffing sound in agreement, like a mixture of a chuckle and a huff.

I figured he'd be more of a sexy growl of desire guy.

And when the expected nibble on my skin just below my ear turned into a tongue that felt big enough to give the lead singer from *Kiss* a run for his money I knew something was off.

My lids sprang open to a hairy face so close to mine I stared cross-eyed into the fathomless deep brown eyes of Moose.

His mouth gaped open in a grin as he gave me a nudge with his wet nose.

"You know I love you, pal," I groaned, pushing up onto my elbows and shoving his nose away from my face. "But respect the personal space in bed, okay?" I sat up, rubbed his big floppy ears and kissed his broad head.

My feet swung over the side of the bed as Moose sat back; his tail wagged so fast on the floor it would have put one of those electronic vacuums out of business. "All right, all right. I know you're hungry. Come on."

It was kind of fun having him around, to have something else to focus on besides the difficulties of my life, which currently had more downs than ups. While Moose waited for me as I scooped a large quantity of kibble into his bowl, I wondered once Blaine and the family came back, if there would be room in my life for a pet. Not a huge one like this Saint Bernard, but something that would welcome me home instead of vacant silence. Some small creature I could share my troubles with and who would love me unconditionally. A consideration once dog-sitting duties were over.

I went into the backyard, left the door open for Moose to join me if he wanted, sat with a high octane cola and dialed my brother. It went unanswered before swinging into voicemail. Guess he was busy. I left him a message saying I was thinking of everyone and would try again later.

Moose brought me a mangled football and we played fetch. The sun warmed my skin, adding an extra layer of joy to the simple thing of playing with a dog, the peace of living in the moment, being grateful for what I had. Others were struggling; Tanya, with the loss of someone she cared deeply about and the looming charge of murder; Blaine with the unknown ramifications of a son born a month early with a cord wrapped around his neck; my mother whose hold on reality was slipping away.

For me, it was going to be an 'up' day.

My phone rang with a redirect from the office.

"Hawkins Freight."

"Boss. You need to get in here. Now."

The seriousness of Sylvia's tone had me standing and moving toward the house, calling Moose to follow.

"What's wrong?" A tense knot formed in my belly.

"Someone's broken in and trashed the place." Sylvia's voice held no panic but it had an edge. "Can you come?"

"Yes. Call the police, don't touch anything and stay outside."

"Okay," my office manager said and disconnected.

Dammit! Teach me to tempt fate. So much for my 'up' day.

I drove faster than was wise, considering getting there sooner wouldn't change anything. A police car stood parked outside next to Sylvia's motorcycle. She met me as I strode toward the building, putting a hand out to stop my progression.

"The cops asked us to wait outside until they were finished."

Frustration grated on my nerves, made me stamp my boot, not at the delay but because my procrastination for getting a security system could have avoided all this. It was like insurance. When you declined it, you always gave yourself a head smack afterwards when you needed it.

"How bad is it?"

Sylvia shrugged her shoulders. "Messy, but I don't know if anything was taken."

My hands clenched into fists.

"Hey, chill. It could have been worse. They could have torched the place."

"Did you see or hear anything?"

My office manager shook her head. "I found it like this when I got in. Then I called you right away." She paused a moment. "Have you stepped on anyone's toes lately?"

Lewis' face popped into my mind. Was this his warning to back off? Since he'd already done that, was this his way of making sure I listened?

The officer, a middle-aged Black woman, came out of my shop, walked toward us and gave a crisp nod. "I'm Officer Lorring. Are you the owner?"

"Yes, Sadie Hawkins."

"Would you come inside please and check to see if anything apparent is missing?"

Both Sylvia and I followed her. I didn't see any additional scratches and the door was still hanging normally. Was it the same culprit as before and they used the same method to get in only this time had left no marks? While Sylvia waited in the office, I ventured through the shop, cringing at the tools and other items Blaine used for keeping the moving van in top shape. His toolbox had been tipped over and a spike of red-hot anger flared at the almost desecration of something my brother cared about. My eyes swept the area but until I put everything back and conferred with my brother, I couldn't see anything of note missing.

The officer wrote that down, flipped the notepad closed and stuffed it into the breast pocket of her uniform. "Do you have issues with anyone at the moment?"

If I suggest Lewis, the cops would certainly head down to have a chat with him and possibly monitor his movements for the next day or so. If he didn't do this, he'd be furious that I fingered him as the culprit. Would he then contact Tanya to tell me to back off? She'd find out I'd been to see him, a few times, and hadn't told her. It would jeopardize everything. I couldn't take the risk.

When I shook my head, she continued. "If it was someone doing this for kicks, or if it was gang related they usually leave some type of colorful calling card." The woman motioned with her head. "There is, however, a fist-sized hole in the bathroom door. Was that there before?"

"No."

She paused, glanced around then focused back on me. "I could get a fingerprint team in, if you like. You and anyone else working here would have to provide a sample for elimination."

Blaine was gone so he couldn't provide any, I was pretty sure Sylvia didn't do this and because Jessie had fixed the van she would have to get involved and the last thing I wanted was any focus on her just because she had a record.

"No, that's okay." My gaze went to the van. "It surprises me they left the moving van alone."

The officer agreed with a nod. "And your office doesn't look touched, although you'll have to confirm that once you go through your files. My opinion, for what it's worth, this comes across as someone who was mad. Especially with the hole in the door. If they really wanted to hurt your business, they could easily have done much more damage. Even set fire to the place."

"My office manager said the same thing." My mind whirled.

"Is this the first time something like this has happened?"

Telling her about the jimmied door and the tampered van would inevitably bring up Wayne's name and since he'd come after hours and no official report was filed, I didn't want to get him into any trouble. If Wayne's identity was kept out of it, the explanation would become convoluted and then I'd have to lie and it just wasn't worth it. So I shook my head and said nothing.

The officer walked toward the office. "I will file a report because you called 911 but I've done all I can." She fished her card out of her pocket. "If you think of anything or find articles missing, call me."

I took her card, slid it into my back jeans pocket and thanked her for coming out.

As she stepped out the door, she turned back. "Consider getting some type of security system."

"Thank you, officer. I'll keep that in mind."

"What are you going to do?" Sylvia asked, sitting in the chair and typing on the keyboard.

"Talk with a few of the businesses to see if anyone else has had similar experiences in the last few weeks. While I'm doing that, would you mind checking the computer and the files for anything out of the ordinary?"

When I returned I told Sylvia we were the only establishment hit in the last few years.

"What now?" she said, eyeing me.

"Clean up the mess on the shop floor, put a poster over the hole in the bathroom door, then call a few security companies for quotes."

One break in was bad enough but twice in the course of a week couldn't be ignored.

Someone was targeting me specifically.

Over the next few hours I sorted Blaine's tools, righted his toolbox with the help of Sylvia and did a thorough examination of the moving van, including under the hood, checking for anything out of the ordinary. Nothing. No telltale puddle of fluid as evidence someone had tampered with the engine. During that time, Sylvia searched through all the files, both paper and electronic and saw nothing wrong. She phoned around and got quotes for a security system and I'd make my decision by tomorrow.

I did a small moving job in the afternoon by myself; a lovely elderly woman going to a nursing home. She'd been a world-renowned opera singer. After loading her few possessions, I took her to a tearoom, where we drank tea and she told her tale of defecting from Russia after one of her performances while touring. Her story of adventure was interesting but also enlightening. She spoke of her immigration to America, which she had planned well in advance as a young girl. It was an enjoyable few hours and allowed me to focus on other things.

At a stoplight on the way home, my gaze drifted to a cluster of people standing on the sidewalk waiting to cross. One was a young woman with blonde hair and all of a sudden I remembered where I had seen the mysterious female driver who almost ran into me the night before; the one who ended up on Lewis' doorstep. She was the girl who came out of the StreetSmart building with Jessie on the day she helped me with the move.

Too big a coincidence to ignore.

Time to call in reinforcements.

CHAPTER SIXTEEN

I stopped at home to check on Moose and the first person I called to get more information on Lewis' mystery female guest was Will. I didn't have a name to give him but I was sure he knew of her.

"Yes, I know you who mean," he acknowledged once I gave him a description. "Melinda Tanner. She arrived about a week before the new manager."

A week before Crystal's death. Did she have a direct connection to the murder? She *had* one to Tanya's brother and that may not go over well if it was discovered.

"Can you get me whatever you can on her? She has ties to Lewis Woods."

"I'll try to see what's in her file at StreetSmart."

"Okay." I paused, considered the probable reaction of what I was about to say and figured it couldn't be avoided. "Umm, since you are the only tech genius I know, can you give me a recommendation for a security system?" Although Sylvia had gotten quotes, it was prudent to speak with an outside source who understood systems and could give me what I needed, not what a company thought they should sell me.

There was a long, drawn-out moment of silence during which Will's even breathing came over the line before he inhaled sharply. "Why do you need that?"

His tone was flat, not angry necessarily, more of a 'what-haven't-you-told-me' mixed with 'are-you-okay.' At times, I thought having one brother was bad enough.

"I don't need it for Blaine's or my place. It's for the shop. There was another break-in."

"Another?"

"I didn't mention the first time because, well, I thought it was a onetime thing." Maybe my explanation would take the steel out of his voice. "But it happened again today."

"I see."

Two words. Measured, controlled. Yeah, he was angry.

"Was anyone hurt?"

"No."

Pause. "Would you tell me anyway?"

I sighed. "Yes, Will. I'm not stupid and I wouldn't lie to you."

Now it was his turn to release a rush of breath. "I'm not saying you're stupid, Sadie. Far from it. My concern is your tendency to brush aside things that are serious. What happened?"

I filled him in on both incidents, the first resulting in my need of a mechanic for the van, which turned out to be Jessie, and the escalation of the second.

"Can't say for sure the two are related but the other businesses in the area haven't been hit so I'm thinking they are. Hence the reason I called you."

Will agreed. "Thank you for trusting me. I know a few systems that could meet your needs and also a few companies. It all depends on your budget. Unless, of course you want me to set it up and monitor it?"

Ahhh, no. For one, that would ask too much from our friendship and the second reason, as crazy as it sounded, I'd rather have a stranger keeping tabs on things than a good friend. It would be too weird.

"No, Will, but thank you for your offer. Getting me the quotes will be more than sufficient."

"Okay. I'll make inquiries, compile a short list, perhaps see if I can get you a rate. I know some people in the business."

I'm sure he did but didn't comment. He said he'd get back to me and I thanked him again before disconnecting.

I called Blaine again and this time he answered.

"Hey Sadie."

Two words. Again. These were not edged in anger but with resignation.

"Blaine. What's wrong? Everything okay?"

"Yeah, everything's fine. As well as fine can be at the moment." He paused and in his tone I heard the worry, the fear and a hint of hopelessness he sometimes relayed when we were younger.

"Karen and I have been meeting with specialists regarding Jerrald. It's still early but it appears he may have some brain damage."

I couldn't hold back the gasp, the low moan of dismay. Tears filled my eyes and my throat tightened so much I had to wait and swallow before speaking so my brother wouldn't hear the sadness. He didn't need that right now.

"Okay. But like you said, it's still early. It could be nothing, right?"

Silence.

"No, Sadie. They've done brain scans and imaging and it shows signs of damage."

Oh God, oh God, oh God. The tears rolled down my cheeks and I pulled a shuddering breath into my lungs.

"How bad?" I choked out.

"Too early to tell…but from what the doctors are saying they don't think it's severe."

"That's good." The whispered words were all that I could think of to say.

"There's still tons of tests they have to run…and well…I…I just don't feel right leaving Shanty and Karen here regardless that we're staying with her parents." The last bit was rushed, as if he was trying to justify what he didn't want to say. As if he was asking my permission.

"Of course. Yes, Blaine, you need to stay there. For as long as it takes. They need you. Jerrald needs you."

His voice cracked, maybe from relief, the sharing of burden or our close bond. "What about the shop? What about you?"

"Honey, don't worry about me. The shop is doing just fine. Honest. If I need any help whether on the van or with a move, I've got it covered. There are a few people in Tanya's crew I can call upon. They've already helped me before, so it's all good."

"You're sure? You would tell me, right?"

Was that hope or hesitation in his voice?

"Yes. I would tell you if something came up I couldn't handle. Stay with your family, Blaine. Be there for them, for yourself. All is well here, even with Moose."

That brought a slight chuckle from him. "Is he behaving?"

"Absolutely. He comes into the shop now and then for a break. He and my office manager, Sylvia, have a thing." I laughed to help ease his mind.

"Okay. I'll…ah..I'll keep you updated when we know more. It's a day-by-day thing right now."

"Okay."

"And you'll call me if you need me, right? You promise?" he stressed.

"Yes, big brother. I promise." Which was a lie. He didn't need or deserve my drama.

A pause. "I love you Sadie," he said quietly.

"Love you too, bro. Give my love to the girls. Call if you need to. Bye."

I disconnected, sat at the kitchen table in Blaine's house, gave release to the pent-up tears and sobbed.

By the time my emotions were under control, Moosie had his head in my lap. He must have sensed my distress and I was grateful for his comfort. I patted his head, rubbed his ears.

"Looks like it's going to be you and me for a while, buddy. Mom, dad and Shanty have to stay away for a bit." My throat tightened again. "But you won't mind, will you?" The words sounded thick.

He gave a small whimper and wagged his tail. I patted his head again, gave him a kiss of thanks and stood. Since my stay could stretch out for possibly months, I needed to get more clothes and check on my place; thank goodness I owned it and didn't have to worry about rent. Then there was what to do about temporarily replacing Blaine at the shop. The van was running fine, for now, but to keep it that way required regular maintenance and my brother would have my head if things slipped. Not to mention it would jeopardize the business. The most logical thing was to hire Jessie if she wanted the job. Although she didn't have mechanic's papers, the way she'd dealt with the cracked cylinder head, it was clear she was more than capable of handling the general upkeep of a vehicle and she could also help with my hauls.

I gave her a quick call and asked if she could meet me at the Beanery. We made plans for after dinner. I then phoned the shop to speak with Sylvia, but she must have already left because there was no answer and it went to voicemail. I would let her know what was going on tomorrow. I fed Moose, made a quick sandwich, took the dog for a walk and drove to my place to gather more clothes and a few other things and then headed over to the coffee shop to meet with Jessie.

The place was hopping with the early evening crowd, an eclectic mix of students, urban professionals and the prosperous newly retired. Jessie sat near the back talking with Erie, who was dressed in black with a black half apron, hands latched on her hips. She was obviously working, and she'd toned down the Goth look. The young woman gave me a curt nod of acknowledgement, took our order and left to make our drinks.

"How's it going?" I asked, noting the pinched look in the girl's eyes.

She flicked her gaze to the barista. "Fine."

My eyes copied her movement. "You sure?"

"It's fine," she stated firmly, waited a beat then continued. "What did you want to talk about?"

Things were obviously not fine but if Jessie didn't want to talk about it that was her prerogative. Erie brought our beverages and set them down.

"Thanks," Jessie mumbled.

"Thank you, Erie." My focus settled on the person sitting across the table. "Did you want anything else Jess?"

"No, I'm good."

"That's it for now, Erie. Thanks. I'll settle up on the way out in case we want another."

She nodded once and left. No chit-chat, no 'I'll-talk-to-you-later' with Jessie. Something was definitely off. I could understand Erie not being overly friendly with me as we barely knew each other and her demeanor wasn't vivacious but there was a subtle tension between the two young women that wasn't there before.

"Thank you for the coffee," Jessie said. "What did you want to talk about?"

"I was wondering if you would consider coming to work for me part time."

She took a sip of her coffee, put the cup down. "Why?"

Okay, that wasn't what I expected her to say. "Because I need help."

"Yeah, I get that but why me?"

I studied the young woman, her quietness, how she was never front and center with the StreetSmart group when they had helped me and I wondered what or who had a hand in shaping her personality.

"Because you're a capable, talented person who could use a break."

She bristled. "I don't like charity or anyone feeling sorry for me."

I raised my hand as if to stop her. "I don't feel sorry for you, Jessie. If anything, I admire who you are. I'm offering you a job, not charity. You'll be earning the wage, especially with some hauls that come up. I also need a mechanic I can trust. And I do trust you, Jessie."

She stared at me. "You may not after what I have to tell you." She took a deep breath, looked away, fidgeted before meeting my gaze again. "I used to jack cars."

Although I never knew her background, her confession wasn't a stretch given she was with StreetSmart and was talented with a wrench. When I didn't react, merely waited for her to go on, Jessie continued.

"Remember when I said my ability with cars was because I grew up with three brothers? Well, I took that knowledge and used it to steal cars, take them to chop shops where they would be dismantled and sold." She fiddled with her cup, eyes on the table between us. "My mom died when I was young and later dad ended up in jail. Tim, the oldest, was working hard to provide for my other brothers and me. One day I heard some kids talking trash about how they made all this money stealing cars so I went along for the ride. When I gave Tim some money, he wanted to know where it came from so I lied, said it was from working odd jobs. I just wanted to help, take some of the pressure off him.

"One night, something went wrong. Guys were chasing me. I called my brother Scott in a panic, didn't know what to do. He told me to try to lose who was chasing me and we'd meet up at a warehouse. He never yelled, never swore, just told me to stay calm and we would figure it out once we got to the warehouse." Her hands shook as she sipped her coffee, put the cup back down, and raised her eyes to meet mine. "Only he never made it. He was hit by a drunk driver while trying to get to me." Her brown eyes held a soul-deep pain. "While I got nailed by the cops, Scott was in hospital. He died and I never got to say goodbye because I was in jail."

It was a long time before I responded. "Is that why you don't drink?"

"Yes."

I couldn't fault her reasoning. "It was an accident."

She tried to stifle the rough edge of anger in her voice but failed. "I know that but if I hadn't been stealing cars Scott would still be alive. And Tim wouldn't hate me." She leaned back a bit. "So, you sure you still trust me and want me working for you?"

That rough edge of anger and tinge of defiance Jessie was trying to portray could not overshadow her vulnerable, caring personality. She wasn't the type to welcome platitudes or gushing words of understanding and comfort.

"Yes," I said firmly.

She watched me, unblinking, as if to examine my intent and whether I was stringing her along. "What about your brother? Isn't he the mechanic in your business?"

"He is. But some things have come up in his personal life and I don't want him to divide his loyalty. The position is only part time and I can't tell you how long it will be for. At least a few months, if not more."

She considered this for a moment. "I can use his tools? Guys can get really protective of their tools."

"Yes, there's no problem."

"I may not be available all the time because I still have community service to do with StreetSmart," she noted.

"We'll work around that. Speaking of, do you have to run this by the manager of StreetSmart first?"

Jessie wrinkled her nose. "I don't think so. If I can show I'm meeting the conditions of my parole, I should be okay. Besides, Bromskey doesn't need to know. She'd spout regulations and procedures and if there wasn't a policy for this sort of thing, she'd make one."

The corner of my mouth lifted at the snark in her voice. "Things still rocky with her management style?"

My companion snorted. "She's making all these changes, as if Tanya won't be coming back. But she will, won't she? When the police find the actual killer, things will go back to the way they were."

I didn't have the heart to say Tanya had already considered a different future, one that didn't include StreetSmart but that could still change.

"We'll wait and see."

"When Tanya comes back, Bromskey won't be living the high life," Jessie muttered.

My brow frowned. "What do you mean?"

"It's like the first day she was dressed normal, you know, business clothes but nothing special. Now she's got these clothes that look like they were made for her, all sharp and in fashion. She even got a new haircut."

"That doesn't sound off. Maybe she needed to find her feet and she had those clothes all along. The haircut proves nothing."

Jessie leaned forward and lowered her voice. "Maybe not, but the new Porsche does."

My eyes grew wide. "Maybe it's used."

She raised one brow and gave me a look. Of course, she would know if the car was new or not.

"Could be a loaner."

Again with the look. "Who would loan out a brand new Porsche, and why are you defending her?" she accused.

"I'm not defending anyone. I'm trying to look at all the angles because from experience, what seems obvious to some is not necessarily true."

Mollified, Jessie sat back but her face still showed doubt. Me too. It did sound suspicious.

I inwardly winced at my next suggestion. "Well, we can always do a bit of digging." Will would tear a strip off me for sure.

That got her attention. "How?"

"If we can get access to her financials maybe something will pop up. In the meantime, can you keep track of her comings and goings? Perhaps keep a log of her daily routine, if she sees anyone regularly, anything out of the ordinary."

Jessie smiled for the first time since I sat down. "Sure. I can do that. How do you plan on getting her financial records?"

My gaze jumped away for a second. "I might know someone."

She smirked. "It's Will, isn't it?"

I feigned confusion. "Will? As in your Will, from StreetSmart? No."

She restrained her laugh. "Liar. Of course it's him. Who else would it be?"

"I know other people," I defended.

The young woman shook her head and grinned. "Give it up, Sadie. I know Will has helped you in the past. We're a small group. Even if he never told me, it was pretty obvious, at least to me."

I glowered at her. "You're too smart for your own good."

"Relax. It's not like I'm going to rat him out, especially to Bromskey."

We sat there both suppressing grins, drank our coffees and contemplated our next moves.

"You started watching Elaine a few days ago so keep at it. Also, get me the plate number for her car, just in case," I pressed when it looked like she was going to argue. "I'll see what Will can find in her DMV records to make sure the car belongs to her."

She nodded and it appeared our conversation was coming to a close. As she stood, I touched her arm. "Jessie. This is serious stuff. Be very careful." When she went to brush that off as nothing, I emphasized, "I'm not kidding. If Elaine is doing something illegal, she may take action not to get caught. Most criminals do. Always, and I can't stress this enough, always have a back-up plan or a way out of whatever situation you're going into. Whether it's at her desk or listening at her door, it doesn't matter. Have a reason in place for being there, okay?"

She nodded solemnly.

"Good. Now, would you like a ride home?"

"Sure. Thanks."

Jessie hung back while I went to pay for the coffees. Erie efficiently gave me back my change and moved to the espresso machine to finish another order. I motioned with my head as we neared the door. "Don't you want to say goodbye to Erie?"

Jessie glanced down to the floor. "No. I'm good."

Once outside, I pulled her to the side. "Jess, is something going on between you and Erie? If you don't want me to pry, it's okay, but it seems to me things are very strained between the two of you. You weren't like this in the shop when you helped fix my van. Is there anything I can do to help? Sometimes it's easier to talk about it."

She swiveled her head to peer into the window at the barista. Confusion and dismay flickered across her face, then was gone when she shrugged. "She hardly wants to spend time with me anymore. I know it sounds whiny, like I'm twelve or something, but ever since Crystal's death and Tanya got out of jail, all she wants to do is spend time with Tanya."

"Do you feel left out?"

"Sort of."

"They both lost someone they loved. Perhaps this is their way of dealing with the grief."

"I guess," she muttered and started walking in the direction to Blaine's van. "Seems whenever I want to talk to Tanya or visit, Erie's always there."

I felt for the girl. It was hard being on the outside of something. "Like I said, they are finding comfort with each other. It will pass."

Jessie remained silent and we got into the vehicle and drove off.

I got a text from Will when I returned to Blaine's.

Have info. Can we meet tomorrow to discuss?

We can talk now on the phone. I knew what the answer would be.

How long have you known me? Followed by a winking smiley face emoji.

Gees the man was paranoid.

Okay, fine. I'll check schedule in morning and text to set up time.

His response was a thumb up sign.

I got ready for bed, thinking what Will had unearthed. It could be quotes on a security system but he was also working on gathering backgrounds on my list of suspects; Elaine Bromskey, Melinda Tanner, Stephanie Waxton and Lewis Woods.

CHAPTER SEVENTEEN

Before I went to see Will and learn what info he had to share, I called the office to check in with my office manager.

"Hawkins Freight. Groovin' to do your movin'."

I burst out laughing. "You know I kind of like that. Let's stick with it for now."

"I am a woman of many talents," Sylvia commented.

"Anything new work wise?"

"Nothing on the books for today," she said with a hint of disappointment. "But it's still early. Wondering if we should make up some flyers or work on some advertising on social media."

"Knock yourself out but run it by me first before you put anything out there for the world to see. I should be in later but wanted to fill you in on a few things."

I explained about Jessie coming on board temporarily but didn't give any details why Blaine was AWOL.

"Please get the paperwork ready for her to sign when she comes in?"

"Sure," my office manager said. "You have a job booked for next week but no details. If it's a large one, maybe she will help you with it. Do you want me to contact the client?"

Wow, I forgot about that. "Yes, thanks." I was seeing how much my business needed someone like Sylvia to keep things running smoothly. "Do you have those quotes on the security system?"

She did and relayed them over the phone. These would be compared with Will's if he had that info ready for our meeting. I signed off with Sylvia, promised Moosie he'd get a long walk later and drove to meet Will at a new location; Andros' wouldn't be open yet and I didn't want to chance the Beanery in case Erie was working again. Having coffee there yesterday with Jessie appeared normal because we'd been together at the shop but coming in the same place with another StreetSmart member was too suspicious. The result was an out-of-the-way diner I'd never heard about.

Stepping into the place, the tantalizing aroma of maple bacon set my mouth to watering. My stomach reminded me it was empty. Will hadn't arrived yet, so I found a table at the back and sat facing the door. It was a typical diner set-up; tables along the window and across the back, a short counter with half a dozen chairs for overflow or quick eaters. No Formica tabletops like you would see in the fifties but easy to clean melamine that held an assortment of condiments and salt and pepper. The owners had forgone booths for sturdy wooden chairs. Although there was no sign the establishment came from the era of rock and roll, it maintained a ghostly retro feel, perhaps of days gone by before any renovations were done. The tiled floor was clean but not new as evidenced by the scuffed path down the center.

The waitress arrived with a menu; I mentioned waiting for someone and ordered coffee. A few minutes later, a tall, lean figure in a grey hoodie and jeans walked in and it wasn't until he removed the hood that I saw it was Will. My eyes widened as he approached.

"What?" he said as he sat down.

"I didn't think you even owned those types of clothes."

He gave me an eye roll and asked for coffee when the waitress put mine down. She returned with his brew and I ordered a large breakfast while Will stayed with coffee.

I put the mug to the side and leaned forward. "Okay, what have you got?"

"Don't you want to wait until after you eat?" he teased.

That earned him a glare.

He smiled, reached into the pocket of his hoodie and withdrew some papers. "First off, here's a list of security systems that will work depending on your budget. Below are a few reputable companies who won't try to extort you. Near the bottom is a name of a guy who can get you what you need, install and also monitor it."

I eyeballed him on that last comment. "He's not monitoring this from his jail cell is he?"

"No," he answered evasively. When my gaze continued to hold his, he relented. "All right, yes, he was in jail but strictly legit now. He's starting out in the business and could use a break."

"How'd you meet him?"

"In jail. We shared a cell together. He got caught breaking and entering."

My breakfast came and while I ate my eggs, toast and extra order of maple bacon I reminded myself that Will did a short stint for tech crime, hence his role in StreetSmart as part of his parole. However, Will had earned my trust. He had hauled my butt out of the fire a few times and if he was going to bat for this person from *You Won't See Me Security* then I would give him a shot.

"Okay. Let's give your man a try."

"Great. I'll get him to call you and set up a meeting. Next is Melinda. Like I said before, she arrived just before the new StreetSmart manager got here. In fact, both women came from Austin."

"I wonder if maybe Elaine was Melinda's supervisor. Tanya said this was a promotion for Elaine so it's feasible she followed Melinda if they had a close connection and the young woman had relocated." I paused, my brain working overtime. "Weird that the woman lands a job within a few weeks to the exact location where a former client transferred."

Will's brow darkened. "And that said job opening was unexpected. You think there might be a connection?"

"Don't you?"

"If it is a coincidence, it's dammed bizarre," he admitted.

"For arguments' sake, let's say Melinda had something to do with Crystal's death. Murdering someone just so your boss can get a job is extreme. And if that is the case, there would be some sort of pattern. Surely someone would have noticed if the managers at other locations suddenly had accidents."

"That's easy enough to check out. Leave it with me and let's move on." He leafed through the papers and pulled one to the top. "I went through Melinda's financials and there was nothing suspicious. She doesn't have a lot of money. There are the deposits between five hundred and a thousand but that could be a payment from a job but they're not consistent."

"Wouldn't a business do direct deposit?" It would make bookkeeping much easier.

"Depends on the business. A major company, yes, but something small, like yours for instance, wouldn't do direct deposit because it would mean having to pay a company for that service instead of writing a check directly to the employee. Or even paying cash."

"What about her record? What did she do to land with StreetSmart?"

"I don't know. I didn't want to hack into the police database unless it was for a good reason and she hasn't done anything other than meet up with Tanya's brother. If she did a major crime, I can't find any mention of that on the net."

"And StreetSmart's files?"

He winced. "You know the saying 'never steal from your own bank?' Hacking into StreetSmart's files is cutting it too close to home. I'm not saying I can't do it, but whatever we find out, we can't use as proof if it is remotely connected to Tanya's case."

Will had hacked into some pretty secure databases and he'd never been this hesitant. "Why not?"

"Because, Sadie, if there were questions about how the information was obtained, in any manner, they would know it came from me. No one else at StreetSmart has been convicted of tech crime. How else would you get the dirt on another person in the organization other than hacking?"

He had a point. "Still. We used the same type of data when you got into Back in Time Antiques files to help prove I didn't murder Lionel Stanton. And you made sure not to leave any cake behind."

He chuckled. "You mean cookies and that was different. There was no direct connection to Back in

Time Antiques, you or me other than they hired you for a haul. Also, you had an ace up your sleeve; your ex-husband who was also your lawyer. This time we don't have any players like that on our team."

I pushed my empty plate away. "True. Where does that leave us now?"

Will took another sip of his coffee. "For Melinda, that's it. On to Elaine."

We went over the current StreetSmart manager's financials together. She had direct deposit but there was nothing that stood out like a red flag on her primary account. She did, however, still have three active accounts at three different banks in other cities.

"Don't you think that's odd?" I suggested.

"Not really," Will said. "My father has accounts at multiple banks, some even in different cities."

"Yes, but your father is a millionaire. I wouldn't expect him to have all his chickens in one coop."

"Don't forget Elaine has moved around a lot and probably didn't remember to close off some of her accounts. There is one that hasn't seen activity for a few years."

He slipped out another piece of paper. "Stephanie Waxton owns a white Volkswagen Beetle and before you ask, I'm still checking on traffic cams."

"While you're at it, can you check for this plate? It belongs to Lewis. Maybe we'll get lucky and the car will be seen near Crystal's place at the time of the murder." I slid a piece of paper with the info to him.

He inhaled a deep breath. "I'll try."

I clenched my teeth in frustration.

Will sighed. "I still have to do community service, Sadie, so my 'free-time' is limited."

I hung my head. "You're right. I'm sorry. I know you're doing the best that you can."

He nodded. "I found out something rather interesting on Stephanie; she and Crystal used to work together at a company."

I wouldn't find that interesting. "What kind?"

"Marketing and design," he replied. "Strangely enough, they both left at the same time. The same day, actually."

Now that was interesting. My brows lifted. "Really? When was this?"

He scanned his notes. "Recently. Less than a year."

That's a bit too coincidental. "I wonder why?"

Will shrugged. "Could be a variety of reasons. There was nothing in their personnel files at the company."

An idea formed in my head. "Can you find out if Stephanie still works in that field and if so maybe approach her as a potential client? Perhaps try to find out why she and Crystal left their jobs."

"Me!" he croaked. "Why me?"

"Because Stephanie has already seen me and Jessie is busy watching Elaine. You can pull off the executive type looking for a creative design team to help upgrade his company image." When he paled, I kept going. "I know you prefer to be the 'behind-the-scenes' guy but there isn't anybody else."

"Okay," he grumbled, looking not at all pleased. "What are you going to do?"

"Some snooping. Do you have the addresses for both Elaine and Melinda?"

Will wrote them down on the back of the papers he brought. "Here, I don't need these."

We rose and went outside the diner.

I stepped back from the building and noted the establishment's name. "How did you find out about this place? The breakfast was terrific."

A wistful smile spread across his face. "Lissa and I would come here occasionally. Brings back fond memories."

I reached up and gave him a peck on the cheek. "Thank you for bringing me here."

He flushed. "Do I have to remind you to be careful?" Will asked before we parted.

I gave him a huge grin, winked and went to my vehicle. Inside, I zipped him a quick text.

Hey Dispatch. I still have the tracker active on my phone.

He replied with a warm smiley face emoji.

A girl could never be too careful.

* * *

I stopped by the office on my way home; it was odd thinking of Blaine's place as home despite it being temporary. Sylvia and I bounced around some advertising ideas before she left early for a hot date with Erick, and I went home to take Moosie for a walk. The autumn air in Houston was lovely, warm but not baked potato hot, and we played in the park near Blaine's house. It gave me time to think about my strategy, about what I hoped to learn about Elaine and Melinda. Jessie didn't trust them, but I *did* trust Jessie and her feelings. She was my eyes and ears at StreetSmart. Tanya's case seemed to be at a standstill as her lawyer had given no updates to Will and if unconventional thoughts and ideas would help prove my best friend's innocence, I would follow every lead.

It was nearing the end of the workday, so I headed to the StreeSmart office and parked across the street so I could watch the building. It felt odd and sort of sad, sitting at a distance and watching from the outside, when I used to waltz right in the front door any time and visit Tanya. I never abused that privilege, but periodically brought her coffee and toasted bagels to catch up on life. Our visits hadn't been the same since I had crossed the friendship line and asked her subtly investigate my murder charge. There was a disconnect in our relationship, one which I worried would never be rectified and sitting here in Blaine's van made me realize how much I truly missed her.

Less than half an hour later, a smartly dressed woman in professional attire exited the front doors. I trailed her progress across the parking lot until she slid into the only sleek, silver Porsche there and drove away. Elaine Bromskey. I pulled in behind another car, keeping my quarry in sight. The woman probably wouldn't recognize my mode of transportation. We hadn't even met, but there was no use taking any chances. I had her address from Will but wanted to watch her routine, what she did at the end of her day, where she went. She stopped on the way home to a quick mart and came out with one small bag. I was too far away to make out what was inside, maybe something from the deli counter. Next stop was the dry cleaners, understandable given her uptick in attire according to Jessie, and eventually continued on to her address.

When the sports car drove into an underground parking garage, I stayed on the street, shut off the engine and waited. Elaine's building was seventeen stories at my count, had a brightly lit foyer, manicured grounds, and a uniformed concierge doorman on duty at the front door.

There was no correlation between Tanya's apartment, which she rented, and this place. It was like night and day. Tanya's was nice; neat, within her price range, something a social services manager could afford. The high-rise Elaine's Porsche had turned into for underground parking was the total opposite. I double checked the address in case I had followed Elaine to somewhere other than where she lived. Nope, this was her address.

Interesting.

As this was only a preliminary scouting mission, I drove off in search of Melinda's street. This part of Houston was unfamiliar to me but at least the address didn't lead into the 'no drive zone' of the city, parts where it wasn't advisable to venture after dark. I located her house; a modest duplex with a vehicle on either side and parked down the street to observe. As with Elaine, I wasn't staking out the location, merely trying to get a feel for how the occupant was living. Melinda's car was nondescript, a basic older model Honda in decent condition. The yard was maintained, no derelict car or freezer on the front lawn.

All the other buildings up and down the street were the same, kept in relatively decent condition. In other words, nothing unusual.

After about fifteen minutes with no movement, I put the van in drive and left. I hadn't expected to learn anything monumental. That would have been a miracle, but it felt like I was missing something. What didn't I see? What didn't make sense? It would take another trip, possibly two, to put my finger on what was bothering me.

At a stop light, my thoughts ventured to Wayne. I hadn't heard from him. He didn't owe me a call but I was uneasy regarding our last time together, the unspoken words, that wonderful breathtaking kiss. And then nothing. Not even being able to leave a message on his cell phone when I called him made me apprehensive. When the light turned green, I passed a pizza place and before I could talk myself out of it, turned in and ordered a large pepperoni to go. While waiting for the pie to bake, I kept trying to talk myself out of where my thoughts were going. The guy had given me subtle hints, saying perhaps our relationship, in whatever context, wasn't meant to be but that was before dinner, before that *kiss.* Had I read something into it, something more than a mere goodnight?

The young man at the counter bellowed my order was ready and I grabbed the cardboard box and went to my vehicle. *It's no big deal. Just swing by Wayne's place, the house you helped move him into, knock on his door and display the pizza as a peace offering. What peace offering?* the other part of my brain clamored, *you did nothing wrong.*

"Shut up" I yelled at the silence and floored the gas pedal.

It was after nine in the evening when I came to the street that Wayne lived on, the roadway almost deserted. Blue glows of television screens permeated from living room windows with the occasional warm yellow light from an upper story bedroom. A man walked by with his dog but other than that no one else was out. The van slowed as I neared his bungalow where we'd laughed about having double rain-checks for dinner. It was dark.

No truck in the driveway.

I sat in front of his house a few minutes then gave in. I tried his cell. Again the abrupt disconnect with no option for leaving a message.

To hell with it.

I launched myself out of the van, pizza box in hand, marched up to the door and knocked.

Nothing.

Knocked again, this time with more emphasis.

Silence.

Okay, so the guy was out. Probably working.

I went back into the van and contemplated what to do next. A logical person would go home, crack open some type of beverage and enjoy the pizza while watching a movie. Instead, I looked up the nearest police detachment to Wayne's house and went there.

After pressing the buzzer at the door to the precinct, I was allowed entry only to be met by a burly officer in blue glaring down at me.

"State your business."

I thought about saying 'delivery' and twirling the pizza box on my index finger but figured that would get me booted out the door.

"I'm hoping you can tell me if Officer Wayne Timmins works out of this detachment."

The man stared down his nose, which looked like it had been broken once and not set correctly and said, "We don't give out that information."

Really?

"Why?"

He blinked. "Because it's a privacy issue."

"If it's a privacy issue why do cops hand out business cards?" I reached into my purse and pulled out Officer Ramerez's card where it had been placed before throwing my jeans in the wash.

The cautious part of my brain screamed 'you're pushing it' but I was hungry. Yes, the pizza was still all there because it was polite to share with someone instead of offering leftovers. And if I really wanted to admit it, I was hurt because it felt like Wayne had cut all ties with me.

My gaze dropped to the floor before I sighed and tried again. "Whether with this precinct or not, I just want to know if he's still with the police." On my phone, I scrolled through my contacts, located Wayne and showed him. "I've tried calling his cell but can't even leave a voicemail. At this point, I only want to know if the guy is still alive."

I think those last words and the tone in my voice must have struck a chord because he paused before saying "What was his name again?"

I told him, even giving the man Wayne's address.

"Wait here."

Just as I was about to leave because I thought the officer was yanking my chain, he returned but I couldn't read his expression.

"He wasn't with this precinct so it took a few minutes but Officer Timmins is no longer a member of the Houston Police."

I gaped at him as if he said he was from Mars. "Pardon?"

"He's no longer here, ma'am."

What the hell?

"Ahhh..can you tell me when he left?"

The man shifted from foot to foot, glanced around. "I'm really not supposed to."

My heart hadn't moved from where it lodged into my throat. I swallowed, cleared my throat. "Okay. Well, thank you…" I looked at his nametag "Officer Fletcher. I appreciate your time."

I was about to turn away when he placed a gentle hand on my arm. "He left last week. Handed in his resignation. No transfer on his file."

The air left my lungs and I gave a nod of thanks. After walking two steps, I swung back.

"Officer Fletcher?"

He faced me. "Yes?"

"You hungry?" I placed the still warm pizza box in his hands and walked out of the building.

CHAPTER EIGHTEEN

As dawn peeked into my bedroom window, bright pink followed by soft yellow, I was already sitting up in bed because I hadn't slept. My mind had refused to settle and my tumultuous thoughts barred me from entering dreamland. Even the Wild Turkey didn't help, however past practice kept me from finishing the bottle.

I stared out the window and thought about Wayne. How he wasn't even on the force when I'd called him the day of the first break-in at the shop and he said he was just getting off shift. And on the night we had dinner, he mentioned having to work early in the morning. Had Officer Fletcher lied when he said he checked and found Wayne had left the week prior, figuring the man could get me out the door faster? His regretful demeanor said otherwise. Or had Wayne lied about working? My mind tumbled back over the past few months, all the times we were together and realized I'd never once seen him in uniform. But he had been in uniform the first time we met, when he responded to the 9-1-1 call Jackson Steel had made when I was unconscious.

Wayne had been with the Pampa police force prior to his transfer to Houston. That wasn't a lie because Clayton had verified Wayne had been the responding officer. So why the deception now? Why did he resign and leave? Why would he throw away his career like that? Or a database glitch and Wayne was still employed with the Houston Police? Returning to his house and peeking in his windows would be too much like stalking but that wouldn't change anything. Wayne still hadn't contacted me and I could not reach him. Odds were the information given by Officer Fletcher was correct and Wayne had left. My psyche wrestled between equal parts concern and anger but eventually conceded there were no answers.

Wayne left without saying goodbye and life went on.

During the night when I wasn't ruminating over my lack of love life, I came up with a plan to monitor Melinda. She was the only one with a direct connection to Lewis Woods who sat at the top of my suspect list in Crystal Sherridan's murder. Melinda and I hadn't met so she wouldn't recognize me and she didn't even look at who she almost bashed into on her way to Lewis' house.

It was too early to call Tanya and see how she was doing, or Blaine for updates on Jerrald or my mother to check up on her. Instead, I grabbed Moose's leash and we went for a walk in the early morning sunshine. Afterward, I fed the dog, gave him extra treats because he'd be left for a long time, took a shower, and headed out the door to begin my mission.

At Melinda's place, I parked down the block, sipped on a cola and watched her house. The neighbors were already in motion, starting their day and I had to be aware not to stay too long and attract attention. The StreetSmart crew member eventually exited her house, got into her car and backed out of the driveway. I pulled Blaine's van away from the curb, kept back about half a block and followed the Honda. Her first stop was a coffee shop from a major chain and I had visions of nodding off while she chatted over lattes with her BFF. Melinda appeared moments later with a to-go cup and zoomed off again.

My eyebrows rose when the Honda eventually parked in front of a string of boutiques. The woman disembarked from her vehicle, used her fob to lock the door and entered an upscale hair salon. I didn't have to check the name to know this was not one of those places where beginner hairdressers learn their trade by offering reduced rates to potential clients. The establishment was middle to high end, more than what I could afford. I pondered this while I waited, speculating perhaps she was dropping off the coffee for someone, but when Melinda didn't appear after fifteen minutes, I gathered she was there to stay for a while. Was this where she worked, the place that provided the cash amounts Will and I saw deposited into her account?

I sat for a few minutes, got my story together of what to say to the receptionist upon entry and hopped out of the van. Although I was pretty sure Melinda wouldn't recognize me, I was still nervous going in. What if Lewis told her about me? But then, why would he? Tanya's brother did not know I was following this young woman. With a quick shake of my head, I opened the door to soft music greeting me and the light odor of chemicals. No peroxide in this place.

"Good morning," a slim girl with luscious black hair greeted me. "How can I help you?"

"A friend of mine mentioned this place and I came to check it out."

I made a point of examining everything; the half dozen chairs, four of which were occupied, three nail stations, currently empty and two specially designed chairs for pedicures where an older woman sat in one with a dress that probably cost more than the wage I cleared in a year from my business. A folded small white towel lay across her eyes. Yeah, I wouldn't even be able to afford a single toenail done here let alone a full pedicure.

"Our prices are listed on the board," the receptionist pointed to the wall above her head. "We're fully booked right now but take a pamphlet home. It has our website and phone number."

While I was surveying the room, I tried to keep my back to the salon chairs so Melinda wouldn't see me and remember when I attempted contact later. I needn't have worried; she was getting her hair washed at a sink, head back, eyes closed.

I swung back to the employee. "Thank you, I will take a brochure." And to make it sound like I legitimately wanted to be there, added "Are any of the stylists taking on new clients?"

She took back the pamphlet, made a notation beside a name on the back and returned it to me.

"Thanks very much," I said with a smile and left.

A perusal at the prices on the pamphlet made my eyes boggle. Will mentioned that Melinda had little money, so how in the heavens could Melinda afford a cut and color? While I sat back and waited for her primping to be finished, I surmised she received a gift certificate, had been saving for a once-a-year-treat or had a nice benefactor.

To pass time, I phoned Tanya.

"Hey, girl," she said in a quiet tone

"Hi Tanya. How you making out?"

"I'm okay." She paused and her voice dropped. "Crystal's funeral is tomorrow."

I waited a beat. "I'd like to go. Would that be all right?"

"Yes. I…I'd appreciate it if you could be there."

"Okay. What time?"

"Ten tomorrow morning at Forest Lawn cemetery."

"Did you want me to take you?"

She didn't answer right away and I filled in the silence. "I'm here for you, Tanya, in whatever way you want. I don't mind taking you but if you prefer to get there on your own that's fine too."

After a hiccup and a sniffle, she cleared her throat. "I'd like that."

"Is there anything else I can do for you? Anything else you need?"

"No." An almost strangled whisper. It sounded like she was struggling not to break down.

"Okay. I'll swing by at nine-thirty to get you. If you need anything else or there's a change in plans call or text me."

Another pause. "Thank you, Sadie."

"You're welcome, hon," I murmured and hung up.

The pain in her voice was so raw it twisted through my heart, burned my eyes with tears. I drew in two shuddered breaths, tipped my head back against the headrest and tried to calm my nerves. Three more deep breaths and my emotions were under control.

The wait for Melinda to finish whatever she was doing was endless. I texted Will and Jess about Crystal's funeral in case they wanted to attend. No response from Will but Jessie said she would like to go when I offered a ride. I thought about calling

Jackson Steel to talk but only had the station number and he worked the night shift. I phoned my mother and we chatted.

Melinda appeared from the salon so we ended our call. I now understood what took so long. Her long blonde hair was cut to a stylish bob with shimmering highlights. She fluffed her new quaff as if it felt foreign from the longer locks she had sported and entered her car. I waited for two cars to pass then slid into the same lane and followed from a discreet distance. After a couple of rights and a left, Melinda pulled to the side, parked and got out of her car, fluffing her hair again. I guessed she liked the new look.

Half a block from her vehicle I waited while she ventured into store after store, boutique after shop. Sometimes coming out with bags, sometimes empty handed. When the purchases became too much, she went back to her car and stowed them in the trunk. Despite going on a major shopping binge, the gal didn't appear all that eager. Maybe she was contemplating on what her credit card bill would be.

My phone pinged with a text from Jessie.

Bromskey leaving office. Want me to follow?

Jessie didn't have wheels yet so either she was biking it, which I couldn't see her doing, or she would deputize someone to help her and I didn't want anyone else involved.

No.

She replied with some type of emoji that could have passed for frustration but I didn't care. Melinda was on the move again and I couldn't split my focus. The young woman didn't go very far, only a few blocks, before she pulled into a lot beside a quaint bistro and entered, arms laden with her recent purchases. My stomach let out a rumbling growl, reminding me I had forgotten to eat breakfast. Again. Since Melinda didn't know who I was, I might as well treat myself to a tasty lunch and followed her inside after a moment.

The restaurant's robin's egg blue walls encompassed bistro-like tables on light gray flooring and white metal pendulum lights suspended from the ceiling. Most of the tables were already occupied. Funky, eclectic music played under the hum and bustle of conversation, beeps from cash machines and the occasional hiss of released steam from an espresso machine I would have given a body part to own. No table available near Melinda but one was close to the kitchen doors, and I settled in to observe.

The waiter was leaving Melinda's table when he spotted me and came over. I opted for another cola and asked to see a menu to which he pointed to a massive blackboard on the opposite wall. When the server returned with my drink, I ordered the daily soup and sandwich and settled back, pretending to be focused on my phone while watching Melinda. She texted on her phone and then sipped her yellow-orange beverage through a straw.

I took a swig of my drink just to quiet my stomach and wished for crackers or something to take the edge off because once my meal came, I would inhale it out of hunger.

The waiter passed my table with a plate and I debated about bribing him to leave it with me until I saw the small round of cheese drizzled with deep red sauce, probably raspberry, sitting on top of a single lettuce leaf and figured it wasn't worth the effort. Melinda sorted through her bags, checked her phone while I drummed my fingers in anticipation of food. When my order finally came, I forced myself to calmly, with decorum, eat my meal without appearing like I was raised by a pack of wild boars in Alabama, making grunting noises while I shoved my nose into my food.

The soup spoon was halfway to my mouth where it hovered because I'd spotted someone walking in. Although I'd been across the street the day before when I'd seen Elaine leaving StreetSmart, there was no mistake in recognizing it was her as she headed straight for Melinda's table and sat down. They exchanged idle chatter, no happy greetings, a business lunch perhaps?

The waiter took their orders. I continued eating, feigned texting and watched as Melinda brought out pieces of clothing from the bags, showing each to Elaine for inspection. Most passed with a nod of approval. One item, a blouse got a wavering opinion and one, a pencil thin black skirt, achieved a vehement shake of the head. Many of the articles could be dresses, but I couldn't quite tell because Melinda didn't take them completely out of the bags.

I was getting the feeling this lunch was more than professional, especially when Elaine reached across the table, fingered Melinda's new hairdo and nodded her approval. Maybe all this was something as simple as readying the young woman for a job interview and the StreetSmart manager was showing her support over the selections of purchased clothing.

Apparently, I wouldn't learn anything vital so I paid for my food and left, staring straight ahead and not making eye contact with any table. In the van, I called Sylvia and asked her to call Mike Lavinksi, Will's man, and set up a meeting regarding the new security system. Then she could close up and head home, rerouting calls to my cell. I sat in the vehicle and watched the door for Melinda's departure.

The two ladies came out together about half an hour later. They conversed, then parted. I opted to stay with Melinda, as she was my target for the day. She ended up going home. The remainder of the afternoon I watched for any movement at her place but it appeared she was staying in. At dinner, when I saw her silhouette in the kitchen window and what appeared to be her preparing food, I went to feed Moose and let him out into the backyard and spend the evening indoors watching TV.

Tomorrow was Elaine's turn for surveillance.

CHAPTER NINETEEN

Black wasn't the best color on me but more appropriate when attending a funeral. Although the morning dawned bright and sunny, the reason for my attire weighed heavy.

I wondered if Tanya got any sleep.

Jessie became my first passenger and the young woman stood waiting in front of the house where she rented a room, dressed in black dress pants and black blouse. Usually, she'd wear jeans or cargo pants and a variety of t-shirts. Practical pumps in black replaced her normal combat boots.

"Thank you for picking me up," she said, getting into the back seat behind me.

"You're welcome. And you look nice."

One shoulder lifted in acknowledgment.

We were silent on the drive to Tanya's apartment, the mood somber. When we arrived, Jessie stayed in the van and I rang the buzzer under Tanya's number.

"Hi. I'm here."

"Can you give me a minute?"

I heard the shakiness in her voice. "Do you need me to come up?"

"No," she said. "I'm okay. I'll be right down."

My best friend arrived a few minutes later in a black short-sleeved dress that stopped at her knees and she held a black clutch purse. Her eyes were red rimmed, puffy and I noticed she'd tried her best to cover the signs of grief with makeup. I took her hand, tucked it under my arm and we walked to the van.

Tanya's brows lifted at seeing Jessie and the corners of her mouth tilted up a bit. "Thank you for coming."

"You're welcome," the young woman said.

The three of us didn't talk on the way to Forest Lawn cemetery. From the parking lot, we walked to where the graveside service was held, meeting up with people along the way. A wreath of flowers rested on an easel, the white lilies and carnations a stark contrast to the green grass. Half a dozen rows of chairs lined one side of the burial plot, some already occupied. I glanced around, hoping this time Tanya's family would be here, to show their support but didn't see anyone I recognized. It took me a moment to register that Stephanie Waxton wasn't in attendance. I found that odd, considering she was the person Crystal called just before her death. Why wasn't she here?

My attention diverted to an older couple in the front row sitting beside Erie, which I assumed were Crystal's parents. The woman, whose expression held both compassion and devastation, raised a hand and beckoned Tanya to come sit beside her. I took Tanya's hand and squeezed. She kept her face impassive but by the firm set of her lips she was trying to keep herself together as she moved to take her place on the offered seat. Crystal's mother's obvious belief and endorsement of Tanya's innocence in her daughter's death was almost my undoing. Erie rose from next to her father, moved to sit on the other side of Tanya and held her hand. I sucked in a deep breath to steel my emotions and guided Jessie to a couple of seats a few rows back.

The service started and the Officiate positioned himself at the head of the casket, which was on a raised platform beside a hole, when a tall figure cut across the lawn and came nearer. My eyes widened and my heart clenched when my ex-husband, Clayton, drew up beside me and sat down.

"Hello, Sadie," he murmured, leaning closer.

"Clayton," my voice ragged with astonishment and gratitude. "What are you doing here?"

"I've known Tanya for as long as I've known you, and although she and I are not close, she is your best friend. I came to pay my respects." He took my hand in his. "And show my support."

If I thought Mrs. Sherridan having Tanya beside her as a sign she considered her daughter's lover part of the family would be my undoing, Clayton's compassionate deed pushed my composure. I blinked to dispel tears that threatened to fall and squeezed his hand tight before letting go. I gazed into his moss green eyes, grateful for his presence, for the love we had once shared, for his friendship and faced forward as the service began.

The congregation of mourners was small since Crystal hadn't lived here her whole life but a few people rose to make speeches, commenting on the woman's vivacious nature, her love of music and zest for life. None of her family, or Tanya, came forward, too wrapped in their grief of a loved one's life cut short. Before long, last words were spoken and the assembled went forward to convey their condolences to the family. I hung back until the group passed, went to Tanya who introduced me to Crystal's parents, expressed my sympathy and told my friend that Jessie and I would wait for her by the van.

"That's okay," Tanya said hoarsely. She worked to swallow. "Frank and Louise," she gestured to Crystal's parents, "said they'd give me a ride. I want to stay for a bit."

"That's fine," I said and addressed the older couple, taking each of their hands. "Again, I'm sorry for your loss."

"Thank you," they both replied.

I turned to Crystal's adopted sister. "I'm so sorry Erie. Never having a sister, I can't imagine what you're going through."

The young woman said nothing.

Erie was standing so close to Tanya that when I leaned forward something flashed in her eyes and she stiffened. Was that irritation? Maybe she thought I was planning to hug her but realized I meant to embrace my best friend and stepped aside.

"Call if you need me, no matter what time." I wrapped my arms around her tight.

"I will," her voice cracked and then she let go.

When Jessie held Tanya, I noticed Erie had the same reaction again, only stronger, and I realized that from the procession of people who stopped by the family, some clasping hands, some giving brief embraces, no one offered arms of comfort to Erie. Perhaps she was uncomfortable with public displays of that sort other than from direct family. Then I remembered what Tanya had said - *Erie doesn't show emotion very well.'*

A stranger approached me while Jessie and I walked back to the parking lot. "Excuse me. I know this is a difficult time but may I ask if you know the grieving family well?"

The young woman was about the same age as Jessie. She was petite, the black pants and blouse fitting loose on a thin frame and her blonde hair was held back with ornate combs. Her question flipped a warning switch in my brain and I wondered if she was from the press wanting to get some type of comment for a story.

"Why do you ask?"

"I was hoping you would pass along a message to Crystal's girlfriend. From appearances, it came across that you and she are close. I watched you when you arrived."

My gaze drifted over the stranger, looking for some type of recording device or earpiece. I glanced around the area, my focus resting at the gravesite before moving on and coming back to her. I was checking for cameras.

"Are you with the press?"

The woman's face paled. "God, no."

"You can go talk to her now." I was pretty sure Crystal's father would run interference if things got out of hand.

"No. I don't want to intrude on the family's grief and it's something that needs to be spoken in private. Please. Would you pass along a message?"

The earnestness of her expression and the sorrow reflected in her eyes made me nod my head. "Okay."

She gave a tenuous smile. "Thank you." The woman reached into her clutch purse, withdrew a pen and piece of paper, wrote on it and handed it to me. "That's my name and phone number. Would you please ask Crystal's girlfriend to call me?"

"I will." The name on the paper said Mandy Beckster.

Mandy nodded once, turned and veered off to a cluster of cars parked farther away.

"What was all that about?" Jessie asked, her eyes wide.

"No clue."

"You going to give Tanya the message?"

I thought about the sincerity of the stranger's gaze, the tone when she expressed her decision not to speak with Tanya at this difficult time. "Yes, but in a day or so." I stuffed the paper into my purse and continued walking.

Clayton was waiting when Jessie and I reached Blaine's van. He put his hands on my shoulders. "You okay?"

I gave a halfhearted shrug but nodded my head. "Thank you again for coming. It was very thoughtful."

"You're welcome," he said with a small smile. "When you have a moment, would you call, please?"

"I'm not on any schedule if you want to talk right now."

He checked his watch. "Unfortunately, I am. And it's also something that can wait. You've had a trying morning."

"All right. I'll call you later today."

He leaned down, gave a light kiss on my cheek. "No hurry. Tomorrow is fine. Take care, Sadie."

"You too," I answered and watched as he got into his car and drove away.

There was a glimmer of amusement in Jessie's eyes when I slid behind the wheel of the van.

I started the ignition. "What?"

"Nothing." She smiled.

I gave her a pointed glower, like I knew what she was thinking then gave up. "Would you like to be dropped off at home?"

Jessie shook her head. "Actually, if you don't mind, I have to go into StreetSmart for a while."

"Don't you want to change first? And by the way, you look very nice."

"Thank you," she replied sheepishly. "Bromskey wants me to help with some office work, filing and stuff, so what I'm wearing is fine. Besides, the faster I can finish with her the better."

I dropped Jessie off, went to Blaine's to change, took Moose and went to the shop. I was feeling like an absent, silent partner in my business because of how little time I spent there.

"Hello, stranger," my office manager said when I walked in.

"Yeah, I know. Sorry."

"And you brought company," Sylvia added when the dog flopped down at her feet. "What's up?"

"Nothing really. Just wanted to touch base, stop by and...I don't know."

Sylvia Brady watched me with wizened eyes. "Rough day?"

"Rough few weeks."

"Want to talk about it?"

I considered what had gone on in my life the last few weeks, how I hadn't been able to confide in anyone because the people I would normally turn to, the ones I had in the past, were all dealing with their own issues. The person sitting at my desk observing me was like a clean slate, had no preconceived notion of me or my past—sort of like a therapist.

I sat down, leaned back. "Not without some assistance."

"You mean the fifth hiding in the bottom drawer of the filing cabinet?" When my face heated, she laughed. "I spotted it my second day here. Personally, I like Tequila but whiskey will do in a pinch."

It had been my Uncle Stan's stash and I couldn't bring myself to get rid of it despite alcohol being a catalyst in his taking his life. To me, that bottle was my last connection to him, however warped that seemed. But these four walls, *they* were the connection I would always have.

"I'll get the glasses."

We sat and sipped while I splayed my soul, well most of it, some parts I just couldn't reveal even to a therapist, impromptu or not. Sylvia learned that my mother was in a facility just not how she got there. I told her about my nephew who would probably have struggles for the rest of his life, however long that would be. Next came the story about the man I'd like to start a relationship with but he had a different opinion. And lastly about the stranger who haunted my dreams with a voice so melodic, so alluring, he was probably a vampire–if you believed in that sort of thing.

As I poured us both another, the buzz in my head signaled I had better slow down or at least put some food in my stomach.

"I need to eat. You hungry?"

Sylvia shook her head. "Lightweight. No, I'm good."

I raided Blaine's stash of potato chips. "Okay, I've spilled my guts, your turn."

The senior flicked her hand as if the topic was unimportant. "Married twice. The first time was a mistake. At eighteen, went to Woodstock, fell in love, followed him to Vegas, got married, left there, settled into an Ashram and found regardless of living close to nature and having a lot less stress, I preferred modern conveniences. However, while I was there I met a fabulous Guru, learned all about crystals and now know the five worst diseases that could decimate a weed crop. Marriage number two was an even bigger mistake; met him in Mali, came back to the US, went to Vegas, got married, followed him to Texas and comprehended that although we met when we were both in the Peace Corps there was nothing *peaceful* about him.”

Although Sylvia recited her life in a tone of comical nonchalance, the last statement wasn’t funny. Far from it.

“What happened? You obviously left him since you said were married, as in past tense.”

“Well…more like he left me. I shot him.”

Whisky launched from my mouth although, thankfully, not onto Sylvia’s face.

She waved away my expression of horror. “Relax. He’s still alive, although some days I wished he wasn’t. We were on a safari and despite my vehemence of not wanting to go along, it wouldn’t have looked good to the guys he was schmoozing into investing in his new company. While we were out hunting, his idea not mine, I saw a lion charging. I yelled to Malcolm, my ex, but his rifle jammed so he screamed at me to shoot and I did. Only as I pulled the trigger, what I thought was a lion was actually a wild pygmy pony so I deflected the barrel and ended up hitting Malcolm instead.”

My eyes felt as round as saucers. “How bad?”

“A flesh wound in his leg, but to hear him tell it you’d think I’d nailed him with a musket ball in the gut.” She paused, took another sip of the amber liquid. “That was the beginning of the end. He never trusted me after that but in all honesty the marriage was doomed pretty much from the start.”

"And the pony?"

The slightest twinkle entered her eye. "Escaped without a scratch. Malcolm swears he saw nothing."

I couldn't suppress a chuckle. "I think there's a moral in there somewhere."

"Two actually. Not everything is as it seems." She raised her glass. "And stay away from Vegas."

Before I could comment further, my cell pinged with a text from Jessie.

Found something that might be interesting. Are you free to come get me?

I took stock in how I felt, inebriated wise, and figured with the potato chips and a burger I'd get along the way I should be okay.

Give me 30 minutes.

She sent a thumbs up and I pocketed my phone.

"I have to see Jessie about something. Do you have those papers for her to sign?"

Sylvia opened a desk drawer and handed me a file folder. "It's all in there."

I took the folder, tilted my head, and studied her. "Mali has had some tumultuous history. When you were part of the Corps, did they teach self defense, particularly the women?"

"Yes."

I narrowed my eyes. "Weapons training?"

She avoided my gaze. "The basics…and I don't hunt."

I walked to the door and threw the statement over my shoulder, "Who said anything about hunting?"

* * *

Jessie was waiting for me outside StreetSmart when I drove up with Moose in tow. She pushed him to the back seat and climbed in.

"What did you find out?"

She buckled up. "Pictures are on my phone. Might be better if we go somewhere. Take a look and tell me what you think."

We opted for a park where Moose could run around. We hit a quick mart, picked up drinks and bottled water for Moose and drove to Congressman Bill Archer Park. While Moose played fetch with a Frisbee I found under the driver's seat Jessie scrolled through her phone and showed me two pictures she had taken of what she'd found in Elaine's office.

"Explain what I'm looking at."

The young woman expanded one to reveal a list of numbers and letters, swiped to the left to show another very similar and returned to the first picture. "While I was filing, I found this small notebook."

"The woman is the manager so what's so special about this one?"

Jessie gave me a smug smile. "It was in a locked desk drawer."

My eyebrows rose to my hairline. "And you gained access…"

"One of the group gave me a few tips."

I gave her my best-'you-shouldn't-have-done-that' stare.

Her eyes widened. "What? I put it back exactly like I found it."

I shook my head and peered closer, trying to make heads or tails out of what appeared on the page. Each line started with a set of numbers with a period in between followed by a single letter and ended with another single number.

4.6.M2; 5.3.S4 and so on.

Moose dropped the Frisbee at Jessie's feet and she flung it for him to retrieve. "Any ideas?"

"No, you?"

"No."

I handed Jessie back her phone. "Were there only the two pages?"

She shook her head. "There was more but they had the same type of thing on them and I ran out of time."

I didn't want to pierce the girl's bubble, but I didn't see any importance to this. "Could be nothing."

She turned to me. "Then why keep it in a locked drawer?"

True.

"Was there anything else in there, something that required security?"

"Nope. A few pens, sticky notes, that sort of thing. And she had one of those caddies on her desk that already had pens, pencils, erasers, all that office stuff. Why keep the rest locked up?"

"Extra supplies?" I was grasping.

"Thought so too but the office has a supply cabinet for all of that, plus toiletries."

Moose came back, flopped on the grass, tongue hanging out. I opened the water bottle, poured some in my palm and gave him a drink.

"It's curious. I'll grant you that, but isn't considered suspicious." I waited, took a sip of my cola. "Is it possible you're seeing something that isn't there because of how you feel about the woman?"

Jessie didn't reply. A fleeting look of disappointment and something else came into her eyes before it was gone. She sipped her drink and was silent for so long I thought I'd hurt her feelings.

"It was a good idea you had, taking a picture," I said, hoping to assuage any ruffled feathers.

"I'd come across the locked drawer before, when I was in her office the first time. So when Bromskey asked me to do the filing while she went to Juvie court I had my chance."

We turned around, started back to the van, the dog trotting beside us.

"I didn't set out to hate her," Jessie said suddenly, breaking the silence. "Well, maybe a little but at least I'm not trying to be her best friend like Melinda."

The young woman who had lunch with Elaine yesterday.

"Melinda? Don't think I know her," I said innocently. "Is she new?"

"Yeah. I think she arrived just before Bromskey. Anyway, they like to have their little meetings often."

All of that could be explained but Jessie's enthusiasm shouldn't be deflated. She shouldn't think she was making something out of nothing.

"Might be something to check out. If you're able to, the next time they have one of their meetings, see if you can hear or learn anything."

"Okay."

"You ready to go home now?" I hadn't monitored Elaine today and was itching to get started. Although the StreetSmart manager and her charge spending time together, both in and out of the organization, could have a logical explanation, I wanted to make sure.

"That would be great, thanks."

During the drive, Jessie didn't talk and I got the feeling she was withdrawing, struggling to find her equilibrium with recent events. When I pulled to the curb in front of her place, I slipped the engine into park and faced her.

"Here's an idea. How do you feel about going to a movie with Tanya and me? I know you've wanted to spend time with her but am wondering if maybe getting out, seeing something light and funny will help her forget things, even for a few hours."

Jessie's eyes brightened. "I'd like that."

"Great. I'll give her a day or two, then set something up."

"Okay." She exited the van.

"Jessie." I didn't want her leaving thinking what she found while snooping was inconsequential. She thought it was important enough to contact me. "Can you send me those pictures from Elaine's office? I want to study them some more, try to find a pattern."

"Okay," she said again. "And thank you for the ride."

"You're welcome."

She closed the door and I pulled away from the curb. I hadn't lied. I wanted to inspect the pictures from Elaine's notebook. The entries were written in some type of code and since the drawer was locked, it was important, at least to Elaine. I just needed to figure out why.

I drove to the StreetSmart office, parked and waited. Elaine's Porsche was in the lot. The woman was still here but if she worked regular hours, should leave in a little while.

My phone pinged with a message from Jessie; the pictures I'd asked for. I tried to figure out what the numbers and letters meant. If this information was so important to Elaine why would she have it at her office and not at home?

My phone rang from the shop. "Hi Sylvia."

"Hey there. I am about to close up but wanted to let you know you have an appointment with the security guy here tomorrow morning at ten."

"Thank you for doing that." I felt the need to reach out, to quell any misgivings my office manager may have had over what she'd revealed during our talk. "About what you told me and what I said…I don't judge. I try to live by the credo 'unless you live it, don't mis-give it.' I'm glad you're working for me."

"Hey, when you get to be my age, you really don't give a damn what anyone thinks," she quipped, then her tone softened, and I could detect a smile in her voice. "And I'm glad to be here too. I'll see you tomorrow."

A smile spread across my face for the first time that day.

Twenty minutes later the StreetSmart manager exited the building. She slipped into her silver car and drove off. I followed, hoping she would make a stop at a questionable location, something that might bolster Jessie's suspicions but the woman drove home. I parked across the street from her upscale apartment building and did a mental head smack that I should have brought something to eat because my stomach let out a growl loud enough that Moosie's head turned my way.

"Yes, I know. I wasn't thinking."

A scan up and down the street showed no eating establishments nearby and I didn't want to take the chance that I would miss my quarry should she leave. I had the woman's unit number from the information Will had given me but no idea if her unit faced the street or not. Going into the building and checking that out wasn't an option because the doorman's job was to announce guests.

I sat in the van, waited, petted Moose and gave him an envious look as he dozed off to sleep. It appeared my stakeout might be another bust like last night with Melinda until Elaine's Porsche appeared from the underground parking. I sat up straight, started the van and followed, leaving two car lengths between us. As her car maneuvered the streets, it seemed we were getting into familiar territory when she pulled to the curb in front of a house. I parked away from her and killed the lights but kept the motor running because Elaine hadn't left her vehicle. A few minutes later, a familiar figure walked down the driveway.

Melinda.

And she wasn't dressed for a job interview.

My curiosity was at full tilt as the sports car drove off. I hadn't seen what Elaine was wearing but Melinda had on a form-fitting, elegant dark blue dress. I followed them into downtown where the Porsche stopped at the front of an upscale establishment offering more than just fantastic steak, and Melinda hopped out of the passenger side. She strode to the entrance of the restaurant while Elaine drove away, searching for a place to park.

I took a right on Capitol, another on San Jacinto to Texas Street, then back to La Branch, slipping into a parking spot near the restaurant so I could keep the front door in sight. Apparently, the women were going out for dinner. First lunch yesterday and now dinner tonight. Were they an item? Dangerous ground, if that were the case, considering the professional impropriety of it with StreetSmart. Maybe they were related, like an aunt and niece. Mother and daughter? Elaine wasn't old, per se, but if she'd had a child young it was conceivable a daughter could be roughly Melinda's age.

I pulled out my phone and sent a quick message to Will.

Anything in background about Elaine and Melinda being related?

Since it appeared the women would be in the restaurant for a few hours, I went looking for something to eat I could share with Moose. A critical eye told me a meal in my price range wouldn't be on this block. And not in the next one either, as I made my way down the sidewalk. Four blocks later and almost faint from hunger I found a bistro that provided takeout and wouldn't make my credit card erupt in flames. I ordered a double burger, plain, for my companion and a taco salad for me. When I got back to the van Moose was practically drooling, no make that he was drooling. I used the paper napkins from the bistro, cleaned up his saliva and let him gobble down his dinner while I ate mine and continued to monitor the door of the restaurant.

Time dragged. Moose slept. I caught myself nodding off but still no appearance from Elaine or Melanie. I glanced at my watch and noted it was almost eleven. How long did it take for dinner? I hopped out of the van, jogged to the nearest parking lot to the eating establishment where I figured Elaine must have parked the Porsche because I hadn't seen it on the street.

The Porsche wasn't there.

I ran farther, checked every parking place along the entire roadway for Elaine's car, but didn't see it.

Dammit! They left while I hunted for something to eat!

Why? Did they not like the food? It could have been a million reasons, but it didn't matter because they were not here and I doubted they'd be back tonight.

CHAPTER TWENTY

Will's ex-cell mate, Mike Lavinksi was the epitome of a computer nerd. Whereas Will, with his deep blue eyes that would twinkle with devilish mischief, could stroll into the GQ office and land on the cover, nobody would notice Mike Lavinski.

He had a thin build, copper-shaded medium length red hair that framed a round face and square rimmed dark brown glasses over snapping blue eyes. With his button-down shirt, crisp ironed blue jeans and high-top running shoes, the guy about to install my security system exuded a bookish aura that was almost enduring. Until he opened his mouth and a deep baritone voice with thick Queens accent made me blink. Twice.

My face must have conveyed my surprise, because he grinned. "Yeah, I get that a lot. High school was a bitch."

I burst out laughing. "No doubt."

He opened box after box, removed wires, cables, sensors, keypads, the works. "I'm going to cut to the chase here. Will explained I have a record, right? You're okay with that?"

"You planning on robbing me?" A test, but my opinion of the person standing in front of me was already solid. I could see why Will liked this guy. He was honest and forthright.

"Not on your life. Will would kill me."

"Then we're good." His movements were efficient, practiced, not a single extraneous action, like watching ballet for hands. "Will mentioned you were caught breaking and entering."

"That's right." He stopped, brought his eyes to meet mine. "This is the point where most people ask what led me to a life of crime, what I usually stole, any regrets, etcetera."

I met his open gaze with my own. "If you want to tell me, that's up to you otherwise it's none of my business. I'm not worried because like you said, Will would kill you if you screwed me. I could also call on a few other friends of mine." That bit was added with an evil smile to see his reaction.

Mike nodded once. "Fair enough." No quivering, no trembling hands. Rock solid.

Yep, I liked this guy.

Since my presence was required in the office for the installation, I'd left Moose at home and gave Sylvia the morning off. My plan was as soon as Sylvia came in, I would follow Elaine again.

While Mike drilled, set screws, and ran wires I called Clayton to see what he wanted to talk to me about that he didn't have time for at the funeral. His secretary put me on hold and while waiting, I checked the calendar of upcoming jobs, which were lacking. Maybe Sylvia was right about the social media option.

"Sadie, how are you?"

Talking with Clayton put me at ease because we were still friends. Few people could say that about their exes.

"I'm fine, thanks. How about you?"

He paused and his next words held a note of pride and happiness. "I finally made partner."

"Oh wow, Clayton, that's fabulous! Congratulations!"

When we'd met, my ex was an overworked, underpaid public defender assigned to represent me. He'd won my case, which opened some doors for him and he became a prosecuting attorney. Clayton proved my innocence to charges of theft and murder of a local businessman a few months ago. He had worked so hard for this promotion, and I was thrilled the senior partner of his firm finally acknowledged how talented my ex-husband was.

"Was that the reason you wanted me to call, to share your news?"

"Yes, and no. There's a possibility to push some work your way and wanted to talk to you about it first."

"Okay."

"A friend of mine is starting a company that would provide staging for events. Festivals, concerts, exhibitions, that sort of thing and is looking for a logistics company."

My ears twitched. This could be huge. "How big are we talking? I only have the moving van and if they need something bigger, I'd have to lease a rig."

"Right now, what you have should suffice because they're just starting but I've seen the business model and it looks good with plans to expand out of state in the next year or two."

"Wow, okay. I'm interested."

"Good. I'll set up a meeting. You can talk to the owner and work out details."

I was stunned. This was perfect timing. "Clayton, I can't thank you enough for thinking of me and putting a word in."

"You're welcome." He paused. "I hear background noise, like banging and clattering. Are you at home?"

"No, at the office. I've got a security guy installing a system."

And as soon as those words slipped out of my mouth I wanted to take them back.

"Sadie." His tone conveyed everything in that one word. Caution, inquisitiveness, concern, apprehension. "What's happened?"

I couldn't evade the issue, so filled him in on the need to have the business monitored. When I was finished, there was silence for a second.

A beat passed before he said, "I'm glad you are taking precautions and am sure Blaine is relieved, too."

I would not go into details. "He's away for a while. This was a last minute-decision."

Another bout of silence. "Everything okay?"

Damn the man and his inquiring mind. He could read me like a book.

"Yup. Just off visiting the relatives before the baby is born." I crossed my fingers behind my back at the little white lie. The truth was for another time.

"Good for him. Listen, Sadie, I have to run. I'll set up the arrangements for a meeting and get back to you."

"Sounds good. Thanks again Clayton."

"You're welcome."

I ended the call and considered Clayton's preliminary proposal. Quite a boon for the business, a possibility to expand and get my name out there. I looked forward to speaking with his friend.

The rumble of Sylvia's motorcycle came closer and cut off outside. My office manager entered wearing full buff-colored leathers and removed her helmet.

Mike poked his head outside and broke into a grin. "Nice ride."

Sylvia's eyes grew large upon hearing the man's voice but she recovered quickly. "Got that right." She turned to me. "Anything I should know about?"

"Mike Lavinski meet Sylvia Brady, my office manager." They nodded and when Mike went back to his wires, my focus turned to Sylvia. "I'm heading out. I gave some thought to your idea of having a presence on social media. Although we have a website, and that has brought in some inquiries and jobs, it can't hurt to cast a wider net to get our name out there. I have no clue how to set up something like that. Can you take care of it?"

"No problem. I started on the basics of a page but haven't made it public yet."

My cell pinged with a text from Jessie.

Bromskey leaving for the afternoon. Can you follow?

I hit back, *Do you know where?*

No, but she won't be in for rest of day.

Not for lunch or a meeting unless it's a long one, as it was barely noon. I let Jessie know I wouldn't make it before the manager left. Hopefully, the woman would go home first or I'd be out of luck tracking her movements.

I spoke to Mike. "Would you mind instructing Sylvia on the operation of the system before you leave? I'd like it to be operational as soon as possible. Also, leave me an invoice so I can pay you."

He nodded, then continued working.

"Call me with the code in case I don't make it back in time," I said to Sylvia.

She took off her jacket. "Sure thing."

I hustled to Blaine's van and sped out the lot, aiming for Elaine's apartment and not the StreetSmart office.

Traffic did its best at pushing my buttons and I finally reached Elaine's place but didn't know if she was there or not. Waiting in case she left was a waste of time. I locked my purse in the glove compartment, hopped out of the van and strode down the block to her building. The uniformed doorman opened the glass door for me and I strode across marble flooring to the Concierge desk. My hope that whoever was working would have stepped away for a minute was dashed when an older, well-dressed man with a polite smile greeted me.

"Good afternoon. May I help you?"

"Yes. Would you ring Elaine Bromskey and tell her Melinda Tanner is here?" If this man knew Melinda, I'd be chased out of here faster than my great-great Uncle Cleetus dodging the deputies during a moonshine run.

"Certainly." He picked up the phone and rang upstairs.

The muscles in my shoulders relaxed until his eyebrows slightly and he replaced the receiver.

"May I see some ID, please?"

Crap. At least the woman was home.

"Of course." I made to reach for my purse and pretended embarrassment. "Silly me, it's in the car. Just a minute and I'll be right back."

I turned and strode away before the man got the idea to call the authorities. My even, confident pace carried me out the door, where I turned in the opposite direction of my vehicle. If the doorman was vigilant and he watched me leave, I didn't want him to know my vehicle and report what had transpired to Elaine and raise suspicion. I walked down a few blocks, then sped back, zipping from doorway to doorway. No laws broken but my heart still beat a heavy rhythm. I contemplated moving the van but didn't want to lose the vantage point. My eyes danced up and down the block checking for flashing lights but after twenty minutes and no boys in blue, I settled down.

Not wanting a repeat from last night, my focus didn't waver from the entrance to Elaine's building or the underground access.

My phone pinged.

A text from Will. *No evidence of foul play in other locations Elaine worked at. Other than both coming from Austin, no connection between Elaine and Melinda.*

Even biological or through marriage?

Nothing for a minute before he replied. *Neither. Elaine not married.*

Not surprising. It would have answered some questions.

I sent a message to Jessie. *Is Melinda at StreetSmart today?*

Yes, she's here now. Why?

Will explain later. Thanks.

I put in a quick call to Tanya, asked her how she was doing and after a bit of coaxing, she relented to seeing a movie tonight with Jessie and me but only if she could drive herself in case she felt like leaving early. Baby steps, I reminded myself and agreed. I texted Jessie the news and said she could ride with me.

Another long, drawn out, excruciating hour passed before my patience was rewarded and Elaine's Porsche appeared. She sped off and I followed, grateful for the first time that Houston's traffic would provide some cover. When she finally stopped and I parked to watch, I sat back stunned. Dressed in sleek black pants and a shimmery soft peach blouse, she entered the same restaurant as the night before. What, did she forget her doggie bag? Pretty late for lunch and way too early for dinner. Drinks maybe? A business meeting?

A smattering of people entered and exited the establishment before Elaine left on the arm of a well-dressed man. They stood at the entrance while the valet brought the car around but it wasn't Elaine's. The man helped her into the passenger seat of his dark blue Audi, tipped the valet, slipped behind the wheel and merged into traffic. I pulled in behind a few cars but the trip was short; down La Branch to Walker where the Audi pulled up to the Le Meridien hotel.

Well, well, well. Elaine was in for a delightful afternoon.

Deflated that today's escapade was nothing more than a tryst, I let the woman keep her secret and thought about going home.

A text came in from Jessie.

Melinda leaving. Thought you'd want to know.

A glance at my watch said although not end of the day, the young woman was likely on her way home.

Thanks. You need a ride home?

No, Erie coming to get me. Will see you at seven-thirty.

I acknowledged Jess, turned left and drove to Melinda's place, wondering what to accomplish. Was there a connection between her, Lewis and Elaine? Maybe I should focus on one between her and Lewis.

I beat Melinda to her place and watched as she entered her house but it was a quick stop, coming out ten minutes later and hopping back into her car. There was still time before the movie, so I followed Melinda. Before too long, I knew where she was going.

I made sure not to park too close, instead opted for around the corner, parked then ran to confirm my suspicion. From behind a tree, I poked my head out and kept the doorway in sight, a smug smile on my lips. Melinda stood at the front door of Lewis Woods' house, while Tanya's brother leaned one arm on the frame. His posture spoke of relaxed confidence, one hand on his hip, fingers splayed while he leaned in to speak with her. She showed no signs of fear but also didn't display any reciprocation to the unspoken invitation. She reached into her purse, withdrew a small plastic bag and handed it to him. My eyes squinted and I wished for binoculars to see the contents. It wasn't tiny, like those little bags you see on crime TV shows but that didn't mean the contents couldn't be drugs. Lewis flipped it in his fingers and stuffed the bag into his pocket. Was Melinda Lewis' supplier? If so, he'd be violating his parole and maybe that was what I'd overheard from his kitchen window between him and his gang friends, of how Lewis' sister would be upset if she ever found out. Melinda's hands launched on her hips as the two people continued talking, a clear sign she was not happy. Lewis shrugged. She leaned forward, fingers now balled in fists of frustration, and he finally lifted both hands in a calming gesture. The young woman huffed, nodded once and relaxed her stance, gave a half-hearted wave and walked back to her car parked at the curb.

The exchange took only a few minutes but it set my mind to whirling. The whole interaction was circumstantial and I'd have to wait a day or two, follow Melinda again but a theory formulated in my brain.

I went back to the van and drove home to grab a quick bite to eat, feed Moose and let him out the back before picking up Jessie and our girl's night at the movies.

* * *

With Tanya sitting between Jessie and me, we shared popcorn and laughed through a romantic comedy that was just what the doctor ordered to put us in a cheerful mood. I saw snippets of my fun-loving, witty best friend who used to get me out of trouble. The ashen pallor of her face when she arrived at the movie theater was gone and an honest to goodness grin lit up her face and stayed there when we exited two hours later.

"That was fun," Jessie said with more enthusiasm than I'd ever seen her convey.

"God, I needed that," Tanya said, heaving a vast sigh. "Thanks for dragging me out."

I linked both their arms with mine and marched toward our vehicles. "Ice cream, girls?"

"Absolutely!"

"I'm in!"

We were ten feet from where we parked when I noticed something was wrong. I dropped the contact with the girls, picked up my pace and almost ran the last few feet.

My mouth hung open at the four slashed tires of Blaine's van.

What. The. Hell.

Jessie gasped. "Oh, no!"

Tanya rushed around the van, as if she couldn't believe what she was seeing. She pivoted, ran to her car parked two spots away then came back shaking her head. "They didn't hit mine."

I sprinted up and down the line of parked vehicles. All of them were unscathed. I unlocked the van, checked inside. Nothing was taken or damaged.

"Pop the hood," Jessie ordered. She lifted and secured it. "Do you have a flashlight?"

I scrambled through the glove compartment and pulled one out. Thank you, Blaine. Jessie inspected the motor, moving to each side of the engine. Ignoring my protest, she scrambled to gaze under the vehicle.

After a few minutes, she turned off the light, handed it back, lowered the hood and brushed her hands on her jeans. "The engine doesn't seem to be tampered with from what I could see. Do you think this is connected to what happened to your van before?"

"Who would do something like this?" Tanya rasped out, shaking her head.

No clue, but I knew one thing. I was miffed when someone had monkeyed with the engine of the moving van. I was angry when they ransacked the shop. But this was different. Someone was watching me and this type of damage was very personal.

The scene of how angry Moose had been when Lewis almost attacked me reared in my brain; snarling,

lips curled back in fury, ready to strike. I could relate
because at the moment, inside me, I wanted to let
loose the Moose.

CHAPTER TWENTY-ONE

The next morning, my focus was about as clear as being twirled on a rope swing. I'd gotten three hours sleep because my thoughts ricocheted from topic to topic like a pinball game, never landing on one subject long enough to come to some concrete conclusion. Since Blaine's van was the only one in the lot that had its tires slashed, I was targeted last night while at the movie theater with Tanya and Jessie. By whom? Was this related to the shop break-ins? Would the culprit attack me physically next? If so, how could I stop them?

That led me to investigate ways and means to defend myself other than carrying a weapon. And to keep the hamster on the wheel during the wee hours of the morning, I'd studied the numbers and letters from Elaine's notebook so long they all blurred together but a theory had come together. Since none of the numbers in Elaine's ledger went higher than thirty-one, I figured they represented dates; first the month, then day of that month. The letters that came after didn't coincide with the names of the months so I assumed those represented either an item or a person. My money was on an individual. Unfortunately, I couldn't understand what the number after the letter meant. My theory was that Elaine was running some type of scheme or game. Today my plan was to corroborate that but I wouldn't be able to prove anything until the StreetSmart manager made a move.

Sylvia had called me in a panic after she arrived at the shop and assumed, given what had happened over the last little while, that the moving van was stolen. Once I explained why I had it, I purchased four new tires for Blaine's van, which put me back over seven hundred dollars and then had to have the van towed to the tire center. The technician said it could be picked up by mid-day.

While that was being done, I drove to a self-defense studio on Eastwood Street. Although the attack last night at the theater hadn't been to me physically, I was assaulted twice in my life. Should a third time arise, I wanted to be prepared. During the time the sandman eluded my house last night, research taught me one of the best methods to fend off attackers to people of smaller stature, short gals like me, was called Arnis also known as Eskrima. This martial art form originated in the Philippines. Besides unarmed combat, students learn to use sword, knife but more to my liking, stick fighting. The rattan sticks were twenty-six inches long, an inch thick and despite being much lighter than the ash bats used for baseball, wouldn't feel as unfamiliar as a knife or sword in my hands. Plus, they fit in my vehicle. Once the instructor at the studio understood why I opted to learn this form of self-defense and what my goals were, he gave me a schedule for the class and signed me up. I could feel bruises forming already.

A text came through from Jessie. *Bromskey and Tanner in office. Will try to hear what's going on.*

I sat parked in my vehicle. *Be careful. Remember what I said about having a reason to be there if you're caught.*

No answer.

Ten minutes later and still nothing from Jessie. My phone tapped against my thigh as I waited to hear from her. Another ten minutes and still no communication. Before acting on the decision to drive down to the StreetSmart office and barge in, my cell finally rang.

"Are you okay?"

"I'm fine." Jessie's tone was low, her breath coming short and quick, like she was walking. Fast. Then quiet.

My heart banged against my ribs. "Do you need help?"

A second of silence. "Hang on."

Boots echoed across the line, a swift clip but not running.

"Okay, I can talk now."

I released a pent-up breath. "What happened?"

"I had to get out of the building so no one could hear. Bromskey and Melinda are going somewhere tonight, something important because Bromskey said something like 'wear the dark blue one again' if that makes any sense."

The dress Melinda wore the other night? Another dinner?

"Did you find out where?"

"No, but Bromskey said she'd pick Melinda up at her place at quarter to eight."

Hmmm, late for eating by the time they got to a restaurant and ordered.

"What are you going to do?" Jessie asked.

"Follow Elaine. See where they lead me."

"Can I come?"

I had an idea of why the two women would meet but not where and my plan would be difficult enough to execute without having another person along.

"Sorry, Jess, not this time."

She burst out, "You don't trust me?"

"Of course I do, but trust has nothing to do with it."

"Why then? Are you going to do something illegal?"

Possibly.

"No, but the implications could be disastrous. Besides, Elaine and Melinda know what you look like."

Silence. I had her there.

"You'll tell me if you find out anything, right?" she asked.

"Yes."

She sighed. "Probably just as well. I am hoping to get together with Erie tonight and talk. She's sort of ghosted me."

My brain stuttered. Was that some type of haunting thing? "Ghosted?"

"You know, when you contact people and they don't get back to you."

That's the newest word for ignore? With a shake of my head and an assurance I would contact her unless the night was a bust, we disconnected. A quick call to Sylvia provided no updates regarding new clients, however the social media page was garnering some interest and she also agreed to come with me to pick up Blaine's van.

I went back home and took Moose for a walk, to kill some time but also get rid of the tense anxiety thrumming through my body. It felt like I was in a holding pattern, idly waiting for things to happen instead of making them happen; passing time until Elaine and Melinda acted. Hoping for word from Blaine about Jerrald and what his future would look like. Waiting for some type of evidence to fall into my lap and help clear Tanya of murder. And a small pathetic part of me waited to see if Wayne would ever contact me again.

"Stupid twit. Just move on." The guy passing me as I mumbled my self-condemnation walked hastily on, eyeing me like a creature from outer space.

The mechanic finally called to say Blaine's van was ready. I dropped off Moose at home and fed him, picked up Sylvia at work, drove to the garage where we switched vehicles and she took the cube van back to Hawkins Freight where her bike was.

I went to my condo, took a shower and opted on a specific outfit for tonight's surveillance of Elaine and her protégée. Since Melinda was told to wear her blue dress, the women's destination was bound to be something more upscale than a diner or a local bar and that meant I'd need appropriate attire as well.

There isn't an abundance of designer wear in my closet. I'm more of the jeans and shirt kind of gal but sometimes even a simple black dress won't cut it. My old HCC college jacket, similar to Jessie's friend Erie, lay on the floor where it must have fallen off its hanger when Jessie had gone through my things to select a dress for my date with Wayne. I hung it up and continued to flip through an assortment of dresses, stopping on the one from my date. I willed my brain not to travel down that road, reached to the very back and pulled out a plastic covered hanger.

Beneath the covering, a sleeveless, sleek, figure-hugging, emerald green with a high neckline and a slit up one side that came almost to my hip. I slipped the satiny dress over the silk and lace bra and panties of the same shade and completed the ensemble with silver-colored high heels and matching clutch purse.

Even my makeup required special attention to create the illusion of a perfect face. Once done, the visage reflected in the mirror, dressed to the nines, spoke of sexy confidence and that's what I needed to convey.

I grabbed a canvas bag filled with contingency items, just in case, and gave Moose a kiss on his head. "Hope I won't be too late, buddy, but don't wait up."

I arrived early at Melinda's house so as not to miss the StreetSmart manager's silver Porsche or the whole evening would be a washout. It wasn't long before the sports car pulled to the curb a hundred yards ahead of me and Melinda walked down to the car wearing the blue dress, as instructed.

The evening was pleasantly cool, the breeze from the lowered windows calming my nerves as I followed the two women while they drove onto West Loop South and continued to Uptown Houston before parking near the front doors of the Post Oak. I continued farther into the parking lot, got out of the van and walked to the entrance, giving the two women ample time to exit their vehicle. A low whistle escaped my lips at the thirty-eight stories of the visually striking building. I'd heard about this place but of course had never set foot in the only Texas Forbes five-star hotel and spa. The seven hundred square foot tower embodied the needs of business and leisure travelers with amenities like a twenty thousand square foot spa facility, a wine cellar offering one of the deepest, well-rounded collections in the country, a presidential suite big enough to host the entire high school class in my hometown in Alabama, and even sported a private helicopter pad on the roof. This was where the other half of the *other half* spent their time and money.

The doorman opened the glass entrance for Elaine and Melinda and I stepped through behind them, keeping my distance. Trying to blend in was challenging as I resisted gaping at the two-story lobby where a massive grand chandelier glittered with Swarovski crystals as it hung suspended over marble flooring that housed over half a dozen grouped seating arrangements.

The two StreetSmart women passed the reception desk without even a nod to the staff and continued onto the banks of elevators while my focus was on some of the floor-to-ceiling artwork that graced the walls. My eyes tracked the two as they waited and when an elevator car finally arrived with a soft ding, Elaine and Melinda entered. I meandered to the elevators, stared at the rising numbers of the car as it traveled until it stopped. I made note of the floor and pressed the same button in an elevator that arrived to deposit an elegantly dressed couple. On the panel inside the car, my destination was the Concierge level. A trickle of unease slipped across my skin. How closely monitored would this floor be? Did guests need a special pass to gain access? There was no slot or scanner beside the designated floor. When the car stopped and the doors opened, a large reception area lay before me with signage leading to the Concierge lounge and other rooms. And best of all, no security. If the two women entered any room, I might as well leave because I wasn't about to knock on every door. Various pictures of oak trees in sepia tones paneled the walls, leading me to the low rumble of voices punctuated with laughter that drifted down the hall. I steeled my quaking nerves, stopped to check myself in the mirror, hot stuff, and followed the sound to the Concierge Lounge.

A staff member, wearing the usual black pants, crisp white shirt and sporting a black bowtie—the requirement of most high caliber food service establishments—carried a tray of canapés among the people milling around the long, narrow room. I kept to the side of the doorway until I could assess what this soiree entailed. Elaine and Melinda were there, a handful of distinguished well-dressed men of various ages and as my eyes swept the room, they landed on four or five younger women, one of which I knew. I couldn't remember the name of the young woman but was positive she was a StreetSmart member, as I'd seen her various times when I'd gone to visit Tanya. My eyes widened at the mannerisms, attire and how the women interacted with the opposite sex. The subtle brushing of the men's arms, how closely they stood to them, their almost false smiles while they listened to whatever each man was saying. Elaine stepped away from the gentleman she was speaking with, caught Melinda's eye who then came to her, and the two women conversed, their heads bowed toward each other but they weren't smiling. When Elaine touched the middle of Melinda's back, the young woman tensed and recovered so quickly that if I hadn't been watching I would have missed it. Elaine nodded her head to three men clustered together with drinks in their hands, and then gave a quick nod of the head as her charge walked over to the trio and inserted herself into their conversation.

Voices neared from down the hallway so I continued walking, mimicking searching for a room number. A quick glance showed an elderly couple who entered their hotel room.

I returned to the elevators, rode down to the lobby, exited the hotel and returned to the van. What was happening in that large room upstairs was pretty obvious but I needed proof. To avoid getting involved in the party at the Concierge Lounge, there was an alternative way to monitor the situation. A pair of black pants, white top replaced my dress. These, plus black low-heeled pumps, came out of the canvas bag I'd thought ahead enough to bring along. No bowtie, unfortunately, but if a staff member at the hotel questioned me, I could get away with saying it was left at home.

The staff entrance was usually around the back of the hotel and are locked. I stood in the shadows and waited. Someone had to either come out or go in. After fifteen minutes, a young man left, eyes focused downward to his cell phone while he texted. I darted to the door and stopped it before it closed.

My plan was simple; pose as an employee and head upstairs to the Concierge Lounge. Watch and listen. Hotels of this size had a vast number of staff and it was unlikely that the current employees knew everyone that worked there. I walked down concrete hallways, following the clang and loud voices to the kitchen. Everyone rushed around me, not noticing another person dressed like one of them. I went straight to the dishwashing section. The steam and heat were suffocating but no one paid attention as I slipped out with a rubber-matted tray, some small clean plates and went to locate the service elevators. My stomach clenched at one point when a tall man dressed in a suit with nametag marched by me but he was obviously on a mission because there was no acknowledgement. It took me another few minutes to find a service elevator and I punched the floor to the Lounge.

At the Concierge Lounge, a flutter of panic whispered down my spine. Although Elaine and Melinda had never met me, would the young woman whom I recognized as belonging to StreetSmart remember me as well? I had to be very careful to stay away from her direct line of vision. Upon entering, the one server in the room cast me a curious glance and I told him it was my first day and was here strictly to clean up dishes. The lie appeased him and he went about his work.

When my tray was full, I chose not to head to the kitchen, then return with clean dishes. Frequent trips increased the chance of being questioned. I grabbed the tray of dirty dishes, exited, turned a corner, and left them on the floor beside a room. I went back to observing the lounge from a wall niche, listening carefully for any signs of people approaching. After what felt like an hour, although likely just ten minutes, a man and woman I was unfamiliar with departed and made their way to a room. Whispering to each other, they reached a door. He opened it and paused, allowing her to step inside. That meant nothing, as they may have arrived as a couple. A few minutes later, Melinda left with a man that appeared to be in his early forties. Her hips swayed seductively as she strolled beside him. When he reached to unlock the door, she leaned close, murmured something into his ear and trailed her hand down his arm before she entered the room.

That confirmed what I'd suspected and there was no reason to linger.

Last night, while I studied the pictures of Elaine's notebook Jessie had sent, I noticed some entries coincided with deposits in one of Elaine's bank accounts. And also dates of deposits a few days later into Melinda's account. I'd have to see if Jessie could get me another picture for any entries made for tonight just to be positive but I figured Elaine Bromskey was running an escort service using the young women from StreetSmart. If Will could get copies of communications between Elaine and her girls or if one of the young women would turn over on her, there might be enough evidence to contact the police.

In the van, I did a quick search on the internet using my phone and learned that prostitution was classified as a misdemeanor in the state of Texas. Depending on the amount of offenses, the guilty could spend up to a year in jail and fined up to four grand.

I texted Jessie and asked for a picture of any new entries in Elaine's notebook. Maybe the StreetSmart manager would receive payment for services rendered the same night and then add it to her ledger before too long. It bothered me to put Jessie in that position, to thrust her into danger but without the information as definitive proof, everything else was speculation. There was no response right away.

As I drove home, my mind buzzed with this new information. Elaine was profiting from using the young women from StreetSmart, whether they agreed to it or were forced. The multitude of bank accounts in different cities, and how the new StreetSmart manager bounced from job to job led me to believe the woman had been at this for some time. If the law or governing body that oversaw StreetSmart got wind of what was going on, Elaine would be behind bars faster than Florence Finkle ditching her coveralls every summer picnic back home in Alabama.

At Blaine's, I let Moose out and gave him an extra treat for leaving him for so long.

In bed, the questions still kept coming. Was Elaine tied to Crystal Sherridan's murder? I couldn't see it but that didn't mean it wasn't there. Had Tanya found out about Elaine's illicit ways? No, the woman came after Crystal's murder. Melinda was here before. Tanya said that a young woman had requested to come to the Houston location of StreetSmart prior to Crystal's death. Could the killer have been Melinda? If yes, did she want the transfer or was told by Elaine? Perhaps to clear her path into a new job and new prospects in a new city? And what was the link between Melinda and Lewis? Were they dating? What about the contents of the plastic bag? From how he'd inspected it, it appeared he didn't own it. Was she supplying him with drugs or something else? Maybe she was stealing from her johns and getting Lewis to fence the items. Regardless, was this little venture a sideline or under the direction of Elaine?

As good as it felt to tell Jessie she was right about Elaine, I was still no closer to figuring out Crystal's murderer and proving Tanya's innocence and that weighed on me as I lay in bed and stared at the ceiling, waiting for sleep.

287

CHAPTER TWENTY-TWO

A fine line rests between obsession and interest, one that blurs depending on circumstance and the obsessed.

Not sure which side of that line was attributed to me.

After almost two hours of restless tossing, turning, flopping and readjustment of the pillow under my head, it became apparent Mr. Sandman was giving me the finger. Again. With a sigh of frustration, I sat up, switched on my bedside table light and reached for my phone. A quick scroll through the contacts and I hit connect.

It rang and rang.

Interest or obsession?

Possibly obsession.

When the person finally answered, the voice over the line soothed me after the first word, and there was no possibility about it. Definitely obsession.

"KRDL, this is Jackson."

"Hi, Jackson. It's Sadie." I closed my eyes in resignation at my lack of restraint, at how pathetic my life had become that solace came from a stranger.

"Well, hey there."

Sinfully smooth, like being bathed in chocolate. It was that easy to be swept away by his voice.

"Can't sleep?"

"That obvious, huh?"

He chuckled. "It is the middle of the night and you could have called anyone else but chose me. That says something."

Did it? Was there someone else I could call who would make me feel special, appreciated, and listen to me?

When I didn't respond, he lowered his voice, as if reaching out a hand and touching my face. "Want to talk about it?"

Apparently, astuteness was a prerequisite for being an on-air personality. And I wanted to talk to him, tell him everything. A 'lay-my-heart-out, spill-my-guts, vent-my-frustration, full on confession' of how I was feeling, just so someone would listen.

Instead, I said, "Sure, but then I'd have to drive up there and kill ya because you'd know where the bodies were buried."

A heartbeat of silence ensued before a burst of laughter came across the line, so rich and full it tingled my skin and washed through to my soul.

"Sorry," I cut in through the last of his chuckles. "Warped sense of humor. You really don't want to know my drama."

Silence. Had he hung up?

"Maybe I do," he said softly, hesitantly.

A clock in my head went tick, tick, tick as speech eluded me. Did he just move the bar, narrow the disc jockey and groupie fan gap by a few inches?

"Sadie?"

"I'm here." My voice was ragged and soft. I swallowed. "I'm here."

"Good. For a moment, I wondered if you disconnected."

"No," I whispered, astonished at how my heart was thumping like a snared rabbit. "I just…I didn't expect that type of reply."

We didn't speak for a few moments until I said, "Why?"

"Why, what?" he replied.

"Why would you want to know what's going on with me? You don't even know me?"

"Because that's how two people get to know one another." The smile in his voice drifted over the line. "Are we going to get to know one another, Sadie?"

The thump of my heart skyrocketed into kettledrum category. "Why me?"

He didn't hesitate. "Because from our brief, sometimes off-beat yet enjoyable conversations, you come across as a smart, interesting, independent woman. Someone who I'd like to get to know better."

Okay. Like wow, the man knew how to compliment a woman. Not to mention leaving me tongue-tied enough that I shivered.

"Balls in your court, Sadie."

After a moment's hesitation, I pushed out in an exhale. "Okay." And again in a calmer tone, "Okay. What should we talk about?"

"What's keeping you up this night, not that I'm ungrateful," he added with a small laugh.

So, I told him. In between temporary breaks when he'd have to go back on-air to maintain his radio show, and keeping names out of the equation, I spoke about Tanya and her murder charge. I gave Jackson all the details, hoping he would have a different perspective, some insight I was missing. I relayed that my key suspect was the brother who did it as an act of revenge. Jackson plied me for opinions, details on Tanya's relationship with her brother, her family, her colleagues. When the conversation wound down, he gave a low hum in his throat and a picture formed in my mind of him stroking his chin in contemplation even though I didn't know what he looked like.

"I don't think it's the brother," he finally said.

"What? Why not?"

"Getting back at your sibling is one thing," he explained. "Actually framing that person for murder is something else."

"But—"

"Hear me out. The brother may claim he wants retribution, and no doubt he's angry, even livid with his sister, but from what you've told me regarding their relationship and upbringing, I don't think he'd want his sister in jail for the next twenty-plus years."

"He did time. Maybe he wants to give her a taste, see what he went through?"

Jackson made a sound that he wasn't convinced. "Did he ever deny the robbery?"

"No," I replied.

"Despite what he confessed to you; I think that was an act for his part in the robbery more than being turned in by his sibling."

I couldn't see it. "You think so?"

"Trust me," he commented sardonically. "With family, the male ego can be downright stupid but usually not cruel."

"If you ever tire of working the night shift as a DJ, you would make a successful shrink," I chuckled.

He didn't respond right away but eventually quipped, "Comes with the job."

"Somehow, I think there's more to it than that."

The DJ didn't deny my words and an awkward minute stretched between us.

"Thank you, Jackson. You've given me something to think about and I appreciate you listening to me and your concern for my friend."

Again there was a pause and I worried he felt uncomfortable.

"You're welcome." He cleared his throat and the tone in his voice changed. "Listen, Sadie. I…you know you can call me at the station anytime you want…but…would you mind if I called you? Like, when I'm not on shift?"

Thank goodness we were not sitting across from one another because one look at the stupid-ass grin on my face and the flush of warmth heating my cheeks, he would have thought he'd asked me to marry him.

I swallowed the squee of delight, which would have broken the poor man's eardrums, gave myself a mental slap to stop acting like a teenager and said with as much decorum as I could muster, "I'd like that."

"Great," he rushed out with a sigh. "Since the office receptionist didn't pass along your last message, I don't have your phone number."

I gave him the digits and he had to put another song on for his listeners.

"Guess you should try to get some shuteye," he said when he came back on the line.

The time on the bedside clock made me grimace. "Yeah. Umm, thanks again for your help and perspective. Gives me something to think about. "

"You're welcome, Sadie. I'll call you soon, if that's okay?"

I smiled. "You bet. Have a good rest of the night."

His voice lowered. "Sleep well." And he hung up.

With the light off and nestled under the covers, my emotions rebounded between desperation and elation. On the one hand, the prospect of a budding relationship with Jackson looked like it might be a possibility, but the flip side of my minor happy achievement was if I considered what Jackson said, that Lewis didn't frame Tanya for Crystal's murder, my list of suspects was dismally short.

Dang.

CHAPTER TWENTY-THREE

"What does the other guy look like?"

Sylvia commented on my appearance despite having to put on makeup.

"Not a mark on him." I touched the swelling on my cheek where it had come in contact with an errant rattan stick from my Arnis self defense class earlier. "You should have seen the skeptical glances I got while running a few errands."

I downed half the double batch of Live-Wire from the large plastic bottle in my hand.

"What's in the bottle?"

When I told Sylvia the ingredients, her eyes boggled. "And you're not in a diabetic coma?"

"Awesome metabolism."

"I would suggest you go back home and get some rest but you've got a move scheduled in few hours."

I did? Gees I needed to get my head back in the game of my business. The rest of the Live-Wire went chugging down my throat, which was followed by a slight shudder from so much sugar and caffeine.

Sylvia shook her head as she watched me tremble and shudder. "Hope your life insurance is paid up."

"Good to go," I croaked. "Do you have the details for today's job?"

From what my office manager told me, I'd need help with the move. I hit Jessie's number. The phone rang and a mechanical voice said the person was unavailable. I sent a quick text and asked her to contact me as soon as she could.

While waiting for a reply, I swept out the back of the cube van, checked the blankets and tie downs for the job, checked the gas level and peeked under the vehicle for drips or leaks. All clear.

Half an hour later, I still hadn't heard from Jessie. After a moment's hesitation, I called Tanya.

"I'm in a bind," I said when she picked up.

A gentle snort accompanied her reply. "When are you not?"

"Do you have time to give me a hand with a move this afternoon? I can't get a hold of Jessie."

"Sure," my best friend replied. "Erie is here. Did you want her help too?"

Guess Jessie was right about Erie spending a lot of time with Tanya. "No, the two of us should be able to handle it."

We set up a time and I left to get something to eat.

* * *

The move was uneventful; an estate that wanted furniture dropped off for consignment and a few pieces to an antique store. One item was a gorgeous mahogany desk but there wasn't space in my home for the unit.

Tanya sat beside me on the back bumper while we drank water before I drove her back home.

"Oh, hey. Did you ever call that woman who gave me her number to pass along? The one from the funeral."

"Yes."

I couldn't quite pinpoint Tanya's tone. Hesitation with a touch of irritation. Although it wasn't my business, my friend was vulnerable right now and the last thing she needed was someone taking advantage of her.

"Everything okay?"

Tanya paused with the weirdest expression on her face. "We had the oddest conversation." She waited a long time to continue, as if saying it out loud might make it true or offensive, before replying in a clipped tone, "She told me to be careful of Erie."

The water bottle stopped halfway to my mouth. "Okaaay. Be careful how?"

"She said Erie can have a temper."

"We all have a temper. It just comes out more in others. Wonder why she thought to voice her concern."

"Not sure. Other than the funeral, I've only seen Erie a few times and basically we've been helping each other deal with Crystal's death."

Then why had the young woman felt she needed to warn Tanya? Had Mandy been watching Erie or Tanya? Something Tanya had mentioned twigged in my brain.

"Didn't you say Crystal thought at one time she was being watched?"

"Yes, I did." Tanya's eyes narrowed. "You don't think Mandy...."

"Let's not jump to conclusions," I said to quell the fear and suspicion on my friend's face. "How does she know Erie?"

"They used to be roommates," Tanya provided.

"She didn't elaborate?"

Tanya shook her head.

"Did you mention this to Erie?"

"Yes," my friend said. "Carefully, because I didn't want something that trivial to escalate. I sort of fudged it a bit to Erie, said that Mandy ran into me, had seen me and Erie at the funeral and wanted to offer condolences but didn't want to intrude on the family's grief. Then kind of hinted that Mandy must have been a good friend."

"What was Erie's reaction?"

"She got agitated, said they had been roommates until there was a sort of falling out because Erie wanted to get her own place and Mandy couldn't afford to live on her own."

Nothing interesting there. "And that's it?"

Tanya nodded. "Yes. I didn't mention the real reason for the conversation with Mandy. Erie said she'd forgiven Mandy and that it wasn't a big deal anymore."

"Do you think it's a big deal?"

"Not really. I have seen no hints of suppressed anger from her."

I stood, stretched the kinks out of my back. "Guess that means it's not. Time to get you back home. Thanks for the help. I appreciate you stepping in when I couldn't get a hold of Jessie."

"Anytime," she said as she opened the door to the passenger side of the van.

I swung into the driver's seat and checked my phone, anxiousness crawling low in my belly. Still no word from Jessie. I could check on her, but wasn't sure of her address. Plus, I didn't want to come across as a mother hen. Jessie was a private person and although she worked for me and we'd gone to a movie with Tanya, I don't think she considered me a close friend. At least not yet. It had been less than twenty-four hours since we'd last communicated so I'd give it some more time.

* * *

Moose's leash was in my hand when Will texted.

Have stuff to share. Can we meet?

I didn't feel like going back downtown for a drink at Andros' so I asked if he'd be willing to meet at a park in Blaine's end of Houston. The dog could get his exercise. He agreed, so the Saint Bernard and I climbed into the vehicle and went to meet Will.

Will leaned against his silver BMW M4 convertible, legs crossed, watching Moose and me as we crossed the lot at the park on Allen Parkway.

He stooped and rubbed the dog's ears with a wistful smile. "I wanted a dog as a kid but my parents always said no. They thought it would be too messy."

Sometimes having tons of money didn't guarantee happiness, I mused.

I made sure Moose's leash was secure and had a water bottle for him as we set off into the park. "What did you find out?"

"First off, Stephanie Waxton. I used your idea and contacted her as a potential client. It was challenging to speak with her specifically because she's working for a company with several employees. I had to use some finesse and drop a few names, citing I'd heard she did great work, but eventually we had a meeting."

"And?"

"I couldn't come right out and say that I heard she used to work with Crystal but I maneuvered the conversation to her previous employment. She said there were projects she worked alone on and some with other employees. When I questioned what they were, she gave me details but nothing stood out. I went out on a limb and casually asked why she left that job and for a minute I thought she wouldn't answer. Then her voice took on a forced nonchalant air and said her current employer paid better but she wouldn't look me in the eye when she said it."

"Hmmm. Could still be nothing. Maybe she was telling the truth, or she could have left for personal reasons."

Will nodded. "Which was why I contacted her previous employer, said I was checking references and asked why Stephanie left. They didn't come right out and say anything disparaging because that would open them up for liable but they said they wouldn't hire her again. And I couldn't ask about Crystal without raising alarm bells."

I sighed. "Still flimsy."

Perhaps Crystal spoke with Tanya about Stephanie, their previous working relationship and why they left that company, apparently together. I voiced those thoughts to Will and he agreed it was worth a shot.

We rounded a corner and pulled off from the walking path onto scrubby grass. I opened the bottle of water and poured some into my palm for Moose.

I glanced up. "Have you seen Jessie recently?"

Perhaps the note of tension in my voice made Will's gaze sharpen on mine. "No. Haven't seen her at all today. Thought she might be with you."

Moose finished drinking and we made our way back to our vehicles. "I've had no contact with her since yesterday afternoon. No answer to texts and she's not picking up her phone."

He pulled out his cell. "I'll try pinging her phone." After a few seconds, he said. "No response. Her phone must be off."

"Is that normal?" I guess we all had days when we didn't want to talk to people.

His lips pursed. "Should I be worried?"

Good question. "I don't think so. When she gets in touch with me, I'll let you know."

If I still hadn't heard from Jessie by tomorrow I would call and speak to Elaine, despite my desire to avoid the StreetSmart manager as much as possible. And Tanya could check with Erie. Maybe Jessie and Erie left for the day while we did the move.

I was still concerned. It wasn't like Jessie not to reply in some form, especially when she knew I was waiting for pictures from Elaine's private notebook. My conscience couldn't help whispering that maybe I had put my newest employee in danger by asking for those pictures.

CHAPTER TWENTY-FOUR

First thing the next morning, I checked my phone but there was still no response from Jessie. A slow bubbling panic churned in my gut. Why wasn't she answering?

I had to wait a couple of hours before I called the StreetSmart office and when I spoke with Elaine, she said in a curt tone that Jessie wasn't due in today and she had not seen her. No concern, no 'if-I-should-see-her-I'll-contact-you' either. Humph, nice boss.

Next, I texted Tanya and asked if she or Erie had heard from Jessie. Her response a few minutes later was no.

Although I knew Will would tell me if he'd heard from Jessie, I just needed to be sure so I started punching in numbers.

The phone rang only once. "Have you heard from Jessie yet?"

Unease washed through me. "No, and I'm getting really worried. Tanya and Erie also had no contact with her."

"How about Bromskey?" Concern laced through his words.

"No. She said Jess wasn't due to come in today, anyway. Do you know any of her family?"

"She mentioned a brother named Tim who lives in Houston. Don't know about the other one but Tim shouldn't be too hard to find. Her mom died when she was young. She's never spoken about her father," Will provided.

"Do you feel comfortable enough to get in contact with her brother here?"

"For Jessie, yes. If I can't find out anything, we'll have to contact the police and file a missing person's report on Jessie," he said after a moment.

My stomach clenched. "I understand. Just do what you can, okay?"

"I'll keep pinging her phone and get back to you on what I find out with the searches."

"I presume it's still early for results about the searches we talked about yesterday?"

Before we parted, I gave him the location of the store near Crystal's and the traffic cameras between her and Tanya's place. And also the location of the convenience store by Tanya's apartment. If Lewis watched Tanya's place during the murder and was the smoker in the car, he might have entered the store for cigarettes. And if he was on the video feed, it would be another reason he was still on my suspect list. I'd told Will to search for anyone who might have a connection with Crystal and Tanya. A long shot but something could pop up as suspicious.

"Still working on it," he said.

"Okay. Last thing. Can you get me an address and phone number on Mandy Beckster?" I spelled the last name for him.

"Shouldn't be too hard with a last name like that. Trouble?"

"Maybe." I explained what happened at Crystal's funeral and the ensuing phone call between Mandy and Tanya.

Will was silent for a moment. His voiced lowered. "Do you want me to check out Erie?"

I wasn't sure. I had nothing against the young Goth woman but didn't want to discount the advice from Mandy because she'd been slighted.

"Sadie?"

"Sorry. I'm trying to justify invading the privacy of a friend of Jessie's based on an opinion of a disgruntled roommate." But for my newest employee's safety better to seek forgiveness later. "Yes. Please let me know whatever you can find out."

"I will. I'm sure Jessie is okay," he said, his tone one of comfort. "Talk to you later."

Will hung up and a part of me feared the young woman I cared about was not okay.

True to form, within minutes my tech genius friend sent me Mandy's phone number. I was about to call the woman when my phone rang.

"Hey, Sadie. How are you?" my ex-husband asked jovially when I answered.

"Hi, Clayton. I'm good. How are things?"

"Fine. Remember our last conversation when we talked about a friend of mine who is looking at opening a business to provide staging for events?"

"Yes." With all that had been going on, I'd completely forgotten.

"Things have been hectic and so we were wondering if you're free tonight. As this is just in the preliminary stage where you'll hear what the five-year plan is, how do you feel about coming over here and discussing it over drinks? It will be quieter than going out somewhere and there will be room to spread out," he suggested.

"That's a great idea. What time?"

"Eight okay?"

"Sounds good. See you then."

That quick call uplifted my spirits. What Clayton and his friend proposed could help my business.

I dialed Mandy. She picked up on the third ring.

"Hello," she said hesitantly. She wouldn't recognize the number and sounded reluctant to answer.

"Hello Mandy? My name is Sadie Hawkins. We met at Crystal Sherridan's funeral. You approached me to pass along your name and phone number to my friend, Tanya Woods."

Her tone eased. "Yes, I remember you. What can I do for you?"

"I was hoping we could discuss what you and Tanya talked about."

There was a moment's hesitation before she responded. "That's between Tanya and me."

"I understand and if it would ease your apprehension, Tanya told me about your conversation."

"Then why are you contacting me?" she said with a note of confusion.

"Not to dispute or verify what you spoke about, but I only have Tanya's version of the call." I paused, considered my words. "I'm not saying Tanya doesn't believe what you said but she may be…too close to the situation and not able to see things from a different perspective. Do you understand what I'm trying to say?"

Again, a pause before Mandy replied. "All right."

"You had said that you and Erie were roommates. Is that correct?"

"Yes."

"Tell me about that."

"Well, we met through a mutual friend who knew each of us was looking for someone to share expenses with. Erie had just moved out of her parent's house and couldn't afford a place of her own while she looked for work. We got along well, laid some ground rules and because I work full time, I offered to pay the first two months' rent as long as she found a job in that time and bought the groceries."

"She agreed to that?" Sounded like a nice deal to me.

"Yes. She started at the Beanery about a month later."

"And things were fine?"

"Mostly, yes."

"What do you mean? Something must have happened or else you wouldn't have felt the need to warn Tanya."

Mandy was silent for so long I wondered if we'd lost the connection. Finally, she spoke, hesitant at first. "It started shortly after she moved in."

I waited, not wanting to push.

"At first it was hard to pinpoint," the woman on the line said. "Erie would want to do things together. Don't get me wrong, we had fun. We went shopping and went to clubs and such, but I had other friends as well that I wanted to spend time with. After a while, Erie got a bit too....clingy."

"She wanted all your time and was resentful of your other friends?"

"Among other things."

That sounded ominous. "What other things?"

There was no response but I could still hear Mandy breathing.

"Did you mention this to Tanya?"

Again, silence.

Frustration made my next words come out in a rush. "Mandy, I only want what's best for Tanya.

She's my best friend and obviously there was something you felt strong enough about that you needed to warn her. Please help me help her."

The woman sighed. "Erie took an interest in me beyond friendship. Her attention didn't upset me or anything but I told her I wasn't gay. I thought that would be the end of it but she still continued to pressure me for more attention and when I wouldn't give it to her she would get upset—say and do cruel things. When I explained that I didn't have those types of feelings toward her, she either didn't want to believe me or thought I might change my mind. Regardless, it got to where I had to ask her to move out."

Interesting. Erie's spin on this subject, according to Tanya, was because Erie wanted to get her own place and Mandy couldn't afford to live by herself.

"Did you have to have her evicted?"

"No. One day I came home from work and all her stuff was gone. I haven't heard from her since," Mandy said.

We talked for a minute more but there was nothing pertinent from our conversation that would help me figure out who murdered Crystal. I thanked the young woman for talking with me and hung up with more questions than I got answers.

After confirming with Sylvia that the office was not busy, I went to visit my mother. The visit was brief, as she was tired and kept slipping into the past.

As I left the facility, Will texted he had info to share and to meet up at the Beanery. However, with the possibility of Erie being at the Beanery working, I suggested we change the location to Andros.

***

Will sat across from me at our usual table near the back of Andros', sheets of printouts stacked beside his coffee cup.

"First thing, I had to leave a message on Jessie's brother's phone asking him to call me," he said as I sat down.

"Okay."

"Next. Although you didn't ask for it, here's info on Mandy Beckster." He pushed one page toward me. "I did a bit of digging but didn't see any red flags. No trouble with the law that I could find, current and previous addresses, her phone number, which I already gave you, and an employment history."

"What?" he said to my quirked eyebrow. "I'm thorough."

I perused the page. Nothing stood out. "That you are, my friend."

"Same with Crystal," he said, pushing more pages my way. "What you told me checked out. I've also included shots from cameras on the night of her murder." He pointed to one image. "This is from the convenience store nearest Tanya's apartment. Recognize this person?"

Lewis, buying a pack of cigarettes. My eyes darted to Will's face, took in his grim demeanor and he pointed to the lower right-hand corner of the picture to the timestamp. An hour before Crystal's supposed time of death.

"It doesn't mean anything."

I gaped at him. "Pretty coincidental, don't you think? Given how many stores are in Houston and he goes into that one, on that day in the middle of the night?"

It seemed no matter what avenue I chased, Lewis appeared to be in the thick of things. Had he been meeting someone else in the area or was he stalking Tanya? Did he follow Tanya to Crystal's, wait outside until she left then saw an opportunity to exact revenge on his sister for her blowing the whistle on his part in a burglary and kill Tanya's lover? Could he be that soulless?

Icy dread spiraled through my veins.

"It's circumstantial," the young man across from me said. "Let's put that aside for now. I spotted Stephanie's white Volkswagen beetle on the traffic cams near Crystal's apartment. And yes, she went twice to the area within an hour on the night of the murder, which corroborates what the busker told you." He slid a few more pages across to me. "These are images from the store two blocks away from Crystal's place, the other one you asked me to tap into. The only saving grace is, at that time of night, there are few people out. Within an hour before and an hour after Crystal's death, there are five people who were captured on video. Oh, and before I forget, Lewis's car was nowhere near Crystal's place the night of the murder."

With that info, Lewis slid farther down my suspect list.

I scanned the photos. One of an elderly man with a cane, two were of men in their late twenties or early thirties wearing sweats and t-shirts. The other two people appeared to be women or maybe smaller males, one in a plain black hoodie, the other in gray with a logo stitched on the front but both individuals had the hoods up which obscured their faces.

"You can keep those. I have copies," Will said before he handed me the last page beside him. "This is some info on Erie."

Like he'd said, he was thorough. Erianna Layette went into the system when her mother committed suicide. Erie found the body. She was seven years old. With no mention of a father or other family, she bounced around from one foster home to another until the Sherridans adopted Erie. Under their love and tutelage, plus the help of counseling, the young girl dealt with the grief, guilt and pain of the loss of her mother. She had the odd brush with authority until after high school where Erie had found her stride, taking a few night courses, volunteering at StreetSmart and gaining employment at the Beanery.

"Nothing out of the ordinary."

Will pointed further down the page. "She does like to move around a lot."

A list of numerous addresses from the time she moved out of the Sherridans until her recent return a few months ago. I gave him a questioning glance.

"It took me a while, but each of those places was leased to different individuals. All female."

"Mandy said that Erie wanted to be more than friends, despite Mandy not being gay. Perhaps it was the same with the rest of these women?"

"Could be," he agreed.

"What's your take?"

He paused, weighed his words. "Nothing really. It appears Erie is looking for companionship, someone to take care of her, notably a female. Whether that's something Tanya has to be worried about it's not up to us to say. Tanya is a grown woman. She can take care of herself and her private life is just that-private."

"I know…but I don't want her to get hurt any more than she already has."

Will reached across the table and put his hand on my arm. "Nor do I, but unless Erie does something to physically harm Tanya there is nothing we can do about it. And," he added when he saw me open my mouth to reply, "We can't tell her our suspicions. People don't like it when you pry into their private lives."

"Okay. I have something else I want to talk to you about. It's Elaine."

I explained my theory of how the StreetSmart manager, based on the records we found, was running an escort service using some of the young people from the organization. Will's eyes widened as my explanation unfolded, and he suppressed a smile about me sneaking into the Concierge Lounge at the hotel.

He nodded his head. "Think you might have something there. Although it's a theory, it's pretty solid."

"What I really need is to get some more pictures from that ledger, which is why I've been waiting to hear from Jessie."

"Now that I know it's there, I could try getting that for you," Will suggested.

"You'd be okay with that?"

He grinned. "Piece of cake. But," he added, dropping the smile. "It can all be explained by a decent lawyer." He waited a beat before continuing. "What we need is testimony. Do you think Melinda would roll over on Elaine?"

"Your guess is as good as mine. Maybe. When I followed her the day she went shopping and met up with Elaine for lunch, Melinda didn't proudly show off her purchases, like she would if she valued a friend's opinion. It was more of an approval to the selection of attire. And the night in the hotel

Concierge Lounge, she definitely stiffened when Elaine put a hand on her back. She may throw the woman under the bus but can we take what we have to the police now?"

"It would be up to the DA to cut some type of deal," he pointed out. "If they couldn't prove for sure that Elaine was running a prostitution outfit, then Melinda might take off and we'd have nothing."

"We really need that ledger."

Will pushed back his chair and rose. "Leave that up to me. I'll either get pictures of the entire thing or maybe take it altogether."

I got up as well, put everything he had given me in my purse. "You might have a problem. The drawer is locked, Jessie told me."

He peered down his nose at me. "Really? You remember who my cell mate was."

Oh yeah. Mike Lavinski, the rehabilitated thief, turned security expert. I gave my companion a playful shove and we headed to the exit. Once outside, I touched his arm. "Please be careful, Will."

He winked. "Always am. Talk to you later."

Driving home, I gave some serious thought about approaching Melinda. Did we have enough for the young woman to report her supervisor? Or would she be frightened, perhaps thinking if she confessed she would be in more trouble and, because she'd been complicit, would go to jail? Maybe she was in the program because she'd been arrested previously for solicitation. Or, Melinda could inform Elaine to conceal the ledger, erasing all evidence and implicating Jessie who witnessed it.

I gave my head a severe shake as if to vanquish the hamster on the wheel. Patience. Wait to see if Will could get that ledger. I'd be on pins and needles until I heard from him, which wouldn't be until tomorrow at the earliest.

If there was no contact from Jessie by tomorrow, I would definitely file a missing person's report with the police. My stomach churned with worry over my young friend. Where the hell was she?

* * *

After feeding Moose, I got ready for my meeting with Clayton and his friend. A more professional look was called for so I switched to black pants and a blouse and swiped on some mascara. I told myself the change was because of a business meeting and not because I was going over to Clayton's but had Tanya been here, she would have arched her eyebrow in skepticism.

With a pad of paper and a pen, I headed out the door to listen to an idea on expanding my business.

When Clayton and I went our amiable separate ways, he kept our house after paying me out and I had expected him to stay there but he'd opted to sell it and purchase a condo closer to his office. The last time I was there he'd made me dinner after getting me released from jail and although the circumstances for that meeting hadn't been the best, the gesture meant a lot to me.

He buzzed me through the front of the building when I arrived and was waiting for me at his door. The green eyes staring down at me sparked with happiness and a grin spread across my face.

"Come on in." He swung the door open wider. "We were just setting up on the coffee table."

The person, who was sitting on the black leather couch perpendicular to the white marble gas fireplace rose, turned around and the smile that I still carried froze on my face.

It was the stunning blonde woman I'd seen with Clayton at the Italian restaurant when I was having dinner with Wayne.

Clayton's hand on my elbow propelled me forward or I'd still be rooted to the spot in the entranceway, gawking like an idiot and feeling like a fool.

Introductions were made and as I lowered myself into one of the accompanying black leather chairs. I made myself listen to what Candace Flemming had to say, kept myself engaged and considered what was right for my business. Over drinks of white wine, scotch for Clayton and cola for me, I took notes, made suggestions and perused her business proposal when all I really was to go home and get drunk on Wild Turkey.

After two hours of negotiating, we hammered out a deal and with a handshake to the lovely Candace, I left Clayton's place with some assurances. First off, I knew Clayton would make sure I didn't get shafted on this deal as he had both his client's and my best interests at heart. Second, this arrangement would be a tremendous help to my struggling local moving business.

And third, but most importantly, going by the subtle glances, how close the handsome lawyer sat with his beautiful client, the body language they both shared by leaning toward one another ever so slightly, it was more than apparent that my ex-husband had moved on.

Guess it was time to do the same.

CHAPTER TWENTY-FIVE

The morning after the business meeting with Clayton and his client-in-all-probability-love-interest Candace, I patted myself on the back for not finding the bottom of a fifth of Wild Turkey. Perhaps I was wising up, growing up or just plain giving up on how Clayton fit into my life. I'd accepted that he was my lawyer and my friend. And that's all.

I made a few phone calls, then decided with the evidence Will and I had gathered, that it was time to contact Officer Ramerez and let her in on the depth of Crystal's and Stephanie's association. And that Stephanie had visited Crystal twice the night of the murder.

I expected to leave a message and was surprised when she picked up the phone almost immediately.

"Officer Ramerez," she said professionally.

"Hello, Officer Ramerez, this is Sadie Hawkins calling."

The pause from her end of the line spoke volumes. I imagined the woman was pinching the bridge of her nose.

"Ms. Hawkins. What can I do for you?"

Well, at least she was polite about asking.

"I have some information that you might find interesting regarding Tanya Wood's case."

Another pause and an imperceptible sigh. "And that would be?"

Might as well start with a bang. "Did you know Stephanie Waxton actually visited Crystal *twice* the night of her murder? Both times within an hour after Crystal left Tanya's apartment."

That got her attention because she asked quickly, "How do you know this?"

"Eye witness account and her vehicle, a white Volkswagen Beetle was seen a block away from Crystal's apartment."

"Who's the witness?" she asked with emphasis.

Oh-oh. Put brain in gear before engaging mouth, Sadie. Although the city recently allowed busking, going by the street musician's comment about avoiding the local authorities as much as possible, he probably wouldn't appreciate me giving him up. "Umm, I promised them I wouldn't reveal their identity but the person described Stephanie."

Ramerez sighed. "If I can't speak with the witness that doesn't do me any good."

"The traffic cams in the area will corroborate what I've told you. And I have to wonder why Stephanie lied about visiting Crystal only once."

"And how do you know that piece of information?" she challenged.

"The police report from Tanya's lawyer." Well, sort of. I didn't ask Will how he got it.

Her muffled grunt on the phone before adding, "Anything else?"

"Yes actually. Stephanie and Crystal have a history. They worked together."

"We're aware of that fact," Ramerez said.

"Did you also know they were both let go from the company on the same day?" According to Will.

"No, I was not," the officer admitted. "There could be numerous reasons for that."

"Yes, but it sounds awfully coincidental and you know what they say about coincidences," I replied.

Another soft grunt of admission. "Is that it or do you have other information you want to share?"

"No, that's everything. Look, Officer Ramerez," I said in a placating tone. "I get that you're busy. You have the case well in hand and probably don't appreciate the interruptions. And by no means am I trying to tell you how to do your job. I just wanted to pass along some information you may not have had."

Her tone softened. "I understand your concern for your friend, Ms. Hawkins. I'll do what I can with what you've given me. Thank you for the info."

"You're welcome," I said and hung up.

She listened to what I said, but I hadn't made a friend. Or an enemy. I would take that.

***

At Hawkins Freight, Sylvia greeted me with a smile and handed me a glass of something green. "What is this?"

"Something to give you a little get-up-and-go instead of the heart attack inducing concoction you usually drink."

My eyes narrowed on her. "And the reason for your sudden interest in my health?"

Sylvia's eyes were bright. "Because the professor called."

The professor? Like Gilligan's professor? From an island in the middle of nowhere?

"Umm, who?"

"You know, Mr. Shamdi with all the books."

"Oh, that professor." And here I thought Gilligan and his crew finally got rescued. Come to think of it, didn't they?

"Yes, him. He wants to move the same shipment to a different location. Today."

Really? The man had mentioned the possibility of moving his load again but I didn't expect it to be so soon. Did he not understand the concept of scheduling? And why the sudden notice? An uneasy feeling squiggled in my stomach.

"That's…weird. He didn't say to where, did he?"

"No," she responded. "He said he'd meet you at the storage facility and would give you directions from there."

The queasy feeling grew. Maybe Erie had been right when we'd done the initial move; maybe something illegal was in those boxes. But money was money and I couldn't turn down potential business. Perhaps I should call someone official to let them know about my trepidation and then remembered there wasn't anyone official to call because Wayne was no longer here. And I'd be pushing my luck contacting Officer Ramerez twice in one day.

"Okay. Call him back and find out the time while I see who can give me a hand."

"On it." She reached for the phone.

I pulled out my cell, started texting Jessie and then remembered there had been no communication from her for days. I'd visit the police station and file a missing person's report on the girl before doing the moving job.

Yet said job still required more hands.

After punching in digits, Tanya picked up on the second ring. "Hi."

She sounded better. "Hey, how are you doing?"

"I'm okay." The words held a touch of optimism. "How about you?"

"Good, thanks but I really need your help."

"What kind of trouble have you gotten into now?"

The light teasing brought a smile to my face. I was sure there would still be days of intense grief and loneliness but it appeared my friend was finding her way back.

"The professor called."

"The professor? Like on Gilligan's Island?" she asked.

See, this was why she was my best friend. We thought alike.

"Oh, you mean the guy with the books," Tanya proclaimed.

"Yes, him. He needs to move the books today. Can you give me a hand?"

"Sure. It's not like I have anything else planned. What time?"

Sylvia was still on the phone. "I'll know shortly," I said to Tanya. "Still waiting to hear back from Jessie to see if she can help." If I didn't mention asking Jess to help, Tanya would question why and telling her that the young woman was missing would not help my friend right now.

"Okay," Tanya responded. "If you can't get Jess, I'll get a hold of Erie."

Sylvia covered the phone mouthpiece. "Twelve o'clock."

Two hours. I gnawed my bottom lip.

Sylvia must have caught my expression and spoke into the handset. "Short notice will cost you extra."

My eyebrows rose skyward. She mouthed the word 'what' then winked while listening to Professor Shamdi.

"You there, Sadie?"

"Sorry. My office manager is negotiating a fee for this last-minute booking."

"Office manager? When did you get one?" Tanya asked.

Right after you were arrested. But I kept that silent. "Recently. She's great. You'll have to meet her."

Sylvia replaced the receiver on the phone with a thumbs up. "You're good to go."

"The move is for noon."

"Okay," Tanya replied. "What about Erie?"

"If Jessie doesn't respond n the next hour, I'll text you to contact Erie if she could give us a hand."

Or, it would take Tanya and me longer, that's all.

"Sounds good. See you later," Tanya said.

I cut in before she could hang up. "Tanya. Did Crystal ever speak to you about Stephanie?"

"Stephanie? I don't think so. Who's Stephanie?" she asked with curiosity.

"Stephanie Waxton. She and Crystal used to work together and she was the woman who came into Crystal's apartment that night with the Superintendent."

"I can't recall if Crystal ever mentioned her. Why?" Now the curiosity was more pronounced.

If I told Tanya about Stephanie she would want to know how I got that information and I wouldn't jeopardize Will.

"I'm following up on some things I've learned. It's probably a dead end," I admitted.

"Sadie."

I sighed. "You asked for my help and that's what I'm trying to do. Just trust me, okay?"

"Okay," she relented. "Anything else?"

"No. See you at the storage unit and thanks again, Tanya."

"You're welcome," she said and hung up.

"I've got an errand to run," I said to Sylvia as I headed to the door. "And then I'll head to the storage unit to meet with Professor Shamdi."

"Okay," she replied. "And don't let him talk you out of the late-notice fee."

I drove to the nearest police detachment, fear and anxiousness forming a ball in the pit of my stomach. In the parking lot, I texted Will to see if he'd gotten a response from Jessie's brother, Tim. His reply was that he had but the man hadn't heard from Jessie either and thought a family member placing a missing person's report might lend more weight than an employer. Will had mentioned to Tim the last instance of anyone seeing or talking with Jessie without providing further details I texted him thanks with a thumbs up. Then I let Tanya know we needed Erie and asked her to pick the young woman up, gave the address and said I'd meet them there and went to get something to eat before heading to my moving job.

***

On the way to the storage unit, I made a special side trip to the cigar specialty shop on Times Boulevard for a package of Davidoff Pantellas, a premium slim cigar with a tobacco blend from three South American countries and Tanya's only vice. I'd be paying both Tanya and Erie as well but didn't know Erie well enough to get her something extra.

Everyone was already at the unit when I arrived. Professor Shamdi seemed apprehensive and tense, constantly checking the roadway between the units like he was doing something nefarious or illegal and looking at his watch.

"Thank you for slotting me in at the last minute," he said when I raised the back door of the moving van and lowered the ramp.

"Well, you mentioned you might need to relocate, although I didn't expect it to be within a few days."

He spun the combination on the lock and heaved open the storage door. All the boxes were as we had left them, stacked on pallets to keep the cargo off the concrete floor.

When he took off his suit jacket and rolled up his sleeve, I touched his arm. "You don't need to help. The three of us can get the job done."

"The faster the better," he said, grabbing a dolly.

My neck began to itch.

Chit-chat was kept to a minimum as my client was all business, stacking boxes with Erie while Tanya and

I unloaded and stacked in the van. Each time the professor came out of the unit to push the dolly up the ramp I caught him watching the roadway.

My neck went from itch to full-on twitch. Something was going on.

The man had set such a brutal pace that by the time we were down to the last remaining half dozen boxes all of us had removed our light jackets and were sweating. Tanya kept sending me worried glances and all I could do was shrug and give her a reassuring smile. Even Erie grumbled quietly at Shamdi's push to finish things.

When the last box was in the van, I secured the door, pushed the ramp back under and chugged the rest of the water that Tanya, in her wisdom, had provided. My client wiped his sweat streaked brow with his forearm and finally smiled…until he heard the roar of a car.

Make that cars.

His head whipped around and his eyes widened in fear. Five cars were careening toward us…and it looked like they were all filled with women.

"Get in the van and follow me!" He raced to his car.

Erie, Tanya and I must have looked like the Three Stooges, crashing into one another as we scrambled to do his bidding. I didn't know what was going on but from the command and pitch of his voice, I wasn't about to ask.

Tanya and Erie went to race to Tanya's car only it was boxed between Shamdi's and the moving van.

"We'll come back for it later!" I opened the passenger door of the van. "Get in!"

Once the door closed, I floored the gas pedal and followed the taillights of my client as we tried to outrun whoever was after him.

"What's going on?" Tanya cried.

"Damned if I know!"

Erie was doing her best to stay upright between the two front seats as the van swayed back and forth with each twist and turn of the wheel. I spotted Shamdi's car as it rocketed between the two chain-link gates that were lined with more women.

"Do you think he might have pissed them off?" Erie asked, her hands clutching the headrests of both seats for balance.

Tanya pointed out the windshield. "They're trying to close us in!"

I smashed down on the pedal and the van's engine roared. "Not if I can help it!"

A security guard was trying to stop women from closing the gates but became overwhelmed by the sheer volume of feminine bodies. As time seemed to slow to a crawl, everyone's eyes widened as I barreled the van to its destination of the roadway beyond. At the last second, sanity prevailed. The gates were hauled back and our vehicle skimmed through with mere inches to spare, leaving a sea of screaming, cheering women in our wake. Our vehicle crashed onto the road where it bucked and bounced and I yanked the wheel to the right where Shamdi had taken off. The stench of burning rubber accompanied tires screeching on pavement as the van tilted before straightening and rocketing down the street.

"There!" Tanya hollered, pointing to the professor's car and I pushed the engine harder, trying to catch up and hopefully losing any pursuers.

My heart raced against my ribs.

An odd, high pitched screeching sound started from the motor.

Damn! When Jessie had fixed the engine she'd said not to push it but whoever was chasing us didn't appear like they wanted to invite us to sit down and have coffee and sweet potato pie.

I'd closed the gap between our two vehicles and a look in the side mirrors didn't show anyone trying to get closer but my client still kept up a brutal pace.

"What's that noise?" Erie cried.

Shamdi finally eased up on his speed and turned into a vast parking lot of a strip mall. Box stores, toy stores, ladies' and children's wear stores all lined the three sides of the shopping center. On the far left, a large brick and glass structure had a banner hung along its face. Stands with nylon signs that bent and twist in the breeze stood flapping in the dull air. People formed a line from the doors all along the front of the store and continued down the sidewalk. It looked like a few hundred people were there.

A massive and horrific bang echoed and I braced for the airbags to deploy. Only there was no impact. The three of us lurched forward but the expected crunch of metal or shattering of glass never came. Perpetual motion carried the vehicle forward until it limped to a stop. Steam hissed from beneath the hood.

Well, hell.

My fiery red-headed temper hit the breaking point as I vaulted out of the van and marched to Shamdi's car. This guy had cost me my engine!

He stepped out of his car but kept the open door between us as I marched up into his face. "What the hell was that all about?!"

The calm, cheerful smile never left his face, although he said softly between clenched teeth, "Calm down Ms. Hawkins. We have arrived at the destination and all is well."

Anger flashed red hot. "Don't make me let loose the Moose," I warned.

He blinked at me. "I beg your pardon?"

Air went into my lungs in an effort to calm. "Never mind. No, all is not well!" I pointed to the van. "My engine blew trying to get away from people who wanted to murder you!"

He laughed a little too loud and waved to the crowd and pulled me aside. "No one was trying to murder me," he hissed.

"Well, they sure as hell wanted to murder me! They tried to lock us into the storage compound."

"Ms. Hawkins," the man said in a placating tone. "No one is trying to murder anyone." He turned to the store, nodding at the people. "Everyone is here to see me and what is in the back of your van."

"And what exactly *is* in the back of my van?" I ground out between clenched teeth.

"Books."

I rolled my eyes. "So you've said. But really, come on!"

"It is true. They are my books. My recent release." He pointed to the name on the banner at the front of a big name bookstore. "The release of my novel was slated for next week but when the title from another well-known author was due to come out the same day, I pushed the date to today and announced it on social media. And since the books were already here, well, I had to take advantage of the opportunity."

You could have knocked me over with the air from a butterfly's wing. The name emblazoned on the banner was for one of the biggest independent authors of super spicy romance. And since there was never an image associated with the writer's first global best-selling book, I hadn't realized my client was the author of that racy novel. I grinned. You never knew who was behind the pen.

"You!? You're…." and I repeated the name from the sign.

Despite our recent experiences, the man graciously blushed "Yes, that is me."

"And the…." I waved my hand at the line of cars from the storage facility tearing into the lot. "Them?"

Again, color rose in his cheeks. "Sometimes my fans can be…."

"Obsessive!"

"Eager," he supplied.

"How'd they find us at the storage compound?"

"Fans can be very resourceful and once something is put on the internet that information flies faster than the speed of light."

"What about my van? It can't be driven. I run a business."

"I am sorry for the subterfuge. Keeping my book a secret until the release day was of utmost importance." He waved to someone standing by the door that started making their way toward us. "I will take care of all expenses, towing, everything." He reached into his suit jacket pocket and withdrew a thick envelope. "The agreed-upon amount plus the last minute fee. My publicist will take care of everything. Now, I must go. My public awaits."

If the man hadn't been so sincere, I'd have stomped on his foot with my Dan Posts.

His publicist and I exchanged details and she called transportation to be taken to where we needed to go.

"You got me out of a bind again." I pulled some cash from the envelope and handed Tanya some money.

My friend waved the payment off, patting her pocket where the package of Davidoffs rested. "Well, that was exciting," Tanya grinned while we waited for our transportation.

A droll stare told her how my feelings were on the subject. "Thank you for your help, Erie," I said, passing her the cash. "I'm sorry it was so last minute."

She gave a light shrug in reply.

"Have you heard from Jessie lately?" I asked her.

The young Goth girl looked away and shook her head. "No, I haven't." She went to stand near Tanya's car. "Can I get another ride, Tanya? I need to get going."

"Of course," she replied and went to give me a hug, then paused. "What's wrong? You're frowning."

"Nothing," I hedged. "Something's niggling in the back of my brain but I can't quite figure it out."

My friend wrapped her arms around me. "Okay. Thanks for the adventure and the Davidoffs."

The tow truck driver hooked up the van. We drove to the shop and he backed the vehicle into the bay then left.

After I explained what happened, Sylvia shook her head. "That sucks."

Another thing to add to the crap pile.

I handed Sylvia the envelope and asked her to make the deposit when my phone dinged with a text and I prayed it would be Jessie.

It was from Will. *No ledger.*

My response was immediate. *You didn't get it?*

No, it's not there. It's gone.

Dammit! Without that, we had nothing. I wanted to scream.

Before I could text a response, my phone rang. The screen read Jessie.

Trembling fingers brought the cell to my ear. "Jessie? Is that you?"

Sylvia approached, her face pinched in concern at the panic in my voice.

Jessie's breathless tone came over the line. "Sadie?"

"Jessie! What's wrong? Where are you?"

"I don't know," she panted like she was running.

My breathing ramped up and my heart felt like it was about to explode. "Okay, hon. Tell me what you see. I'll come get you."

"No time. Meet me at Tanya's!"

"Tanya's? How will you get there?"

Silence except for her labored breathing. "I'm going to hot wire a car."

"What! You're on parole!"

"It doesn't matter!" More running. "Damn, someone's coming. I think Tanya's life may be in danger."

My gut clenched. "What have you found out?"

"No time to explain. Just meet me there!"

The line went dead.

CHAPTER TWENTY-SIX

Jessie's warning that Tanya's life was in danger catapulted me into action. I turned to race toward the van.

Sylvia latched onto my arm. "I don't know what's going on but we can take the bike, it's faster."

She had a point. Jessie's urgent voice meant there was no time to waste.

"Okay."

I ran to the van, grabbed my purse and was heading her way when she called from across the office. "I've got an extra helmet but not another set of leathers. You should wear a jacket just in case. Road rash bites."

From the van's passenger side, I grabbed the jackets lying on the seat, locked up and followed Sylvia to her bike. She tossed me the extra helmet.

I slipped on the helmet and jacket, put my purse and the other jacket between us as she started the Harley Davidson.

She released the clutch and gave a slight turn on the throttle. "Where to?"

I jerked a thumb to the left out of the parking lot and, over the roar of the engine, bellowed the directions to Tanya's place. "How do you feel about speeding?" I added.

"It's a Harley," she replied loudly. "What do you think?"

Sylvia swept the bike in and around cars and buses, weaving through multiple lanes of traffic like a pro. Buildings flashed by, horns blared and as we entered an intersection when the light changed from yellow to red, my driver opened the throttle. We zipped around a turning vehicle with a mighty explosion of power, the Harley fairly dancing under a master's hands. I closed my eyes and tightened the grip around Sylvia's waist, fear and adrenaline flooding my bloodstream.

She shifted into next gear. "Do you want me to stay off the sidewalks?"

God forbid. "Preferably."

I hung on as the engine roared and we flew down the streets; the wind buffeting us, and then it hit me. That niggling thought I'd had in the back of my brain now changed everything I knew about the case and all the pieces finally fell into place.

Between wearing a helmet and the engine's growl, conversation while sitting on the back of Sylvia's Harley was near impossible except for giving directions. But the ride gave me time to put my thoughts in order. Things could go in a myriad of ways once we reached Tanya's place and considering what the outcome could be, I needed to keep calm and lay out my suspicions.

We skidded to a stop in a light spray of gravel at our destination. Sylvia kept the engine running as I leaped down, yanked off the helmet and gave it back to her.

She flipped up the face shield. "You want me to stay?"

Although my office manager was someone I trusted, she was still a stranger to Tanya. "No. I should be okay and thanks for getting me here so quickly."

"No problem. Hope the owner of the trash can I ran over didn't catch my license plate." She grinned, lowered the shield and gunned the engine. "Call me if you need me."

I gave her a thumbs up and watched as the senior roared off. Hell on wheels.

Cell in hand, I punched Jessie's number.

The young woman answered after two rings. "Sadie? Where are you?"

"I'm here, at Tanya's." A quick scan of the area didn't show anyone coming my way. "How long till you get here?"

"A few minutes. Don't wait for me. What's Tanya's apartment number?"

I gave her the info and disconnected. The stress and seriousness in Jessie's voice propelled me to

Tanya's building and I pressed the button of her apartment.

"Hello?"

"Hey girl," I said in a false, cheerful tone. "Can I come up?"

"Sadie. Sure, of course," Tanya replied and activated the automatic lock on the front door.

I jogged to the elevators and waited impatiently for one to open. On the ride up, my hand tapped against my jeans in sync with my racing heartbeat.

From my sharp knock on her door, Tanya opened the portal with a quizzical expression. "This is unexpected." She stepped away to allow me entry.

"Are you alone?"

Surprise and a hint of concern flittered through her eyes. "Yes. Is something wrong?"

I didn't answer, instead went straight to her living room, paced between the window and her couch, too keyed up to sit.

"Sadie, what's wrong?"

I faced her and knew what she was about to learn would be hard on her, so very difficult to comprehend and get past.

"I think I know who killed Crystal."

Tanya's eyes widened and her face paled. "Who?"

"I…we need to wait for someone else to arrive."

She opened her mouth to argue when the buzzer to the front door of the building went off. Tanya strode to the phone unit by her door, listened then gasped before she pushed a button, releasing the lock.

She whirled to me. "Jessie! Is Jessie the killer?"

"No, hon. No. But she needs to be here because she has information. Please, just wait until she comes up and we'll explain everything."

My gaze wouldn't meet Tanya's as we waited for Jessie to appear. I had a hunch on who killed Tanya's lover but apparently so did Jessie. I wondered how she had figured it out.

The few minutes seemed like hours, the tension thick and taut and Tanya trembled. I wanted to hold her, to offer comfort but that would come later.

At a soft tapping on the door, Tanya allowed Jessie to enter. The relief of seeing the young woman unharmed almost knocked me to my knees and I had to restrain myself from giving her a hug.

"Will someone tell me what's going on?" Tanya asked, with a mixture of annoyance and fear.

"May I please have a glass of water? Jessie asked quietly. "I've had nothing to eat or drink in almost two days."

Tanya reared back. "Are you ill? Did you need to see a doctor?"

"I'm fine," the girl replied. "Just some water, please."

When Tanya went into the kitchen, my hand rested on Jessie's shoulder. "Are you okay?"

"Yeah."

My best friend returned with the water and Jessie drank greedily. "Thank you."

"Now, let's sit down and you can tell me why the two of you are here and what this is all about," Tanya said firmly.

I was about to speak when the unmistakable sound of a key in the lock made all three of us turn our heads.

My eyes flared as the person walked into the room. I hadn't expected Tanya to give them a key. "Hello, Erie."

She recovered from her surprise at seeing me and Jessie. Her eyes narrowed and her pace slowed. "Am I interrupting?"

"No. Sit down. We were just about to talk." I controlled my voice, as if speaking to a cornered animal.

While Erie sat in a chair opposite us, Tanya's gaze flew from me to Erie, uncomprehending. Jessie's brow furrowed with confusion.

I shrugged out of the jacket I was wearing. "I believe this belongs to you. You left it in the van after we moved Professor Shamdi's books."

Erie reached to take it but I held on. "HCC. Great college. I went there."

She looked at me with irritation. "Yes. I had the jacket on when we first met and you mentioned that."

My gaze never wavered. "I still have my jacket. I came across it the other day in my closet and noticed a slight variation between yours and mine and did some digging. Every few years, the college makes slight modifications to their insignia, such as changing the stitching style or color."

"Yeah, so?" Erie's tone wasn't quite defensive but held a bite.

"Sadie." Tanya interrupted.

I signaled for patience and focused back on Erie. "You see yours here." I tapped the smaller printing under the letters HCC. "SOC, for sociology, right?"

"Yes. That's what I'm enrolled in."

"According to the college when I contacted them this morning, their jackets don't have fields of study acronyms and the school doesn't do custom orders." I pointed again to the fabric clasped in my hand. "That would mean you had SOC added after you bought the jacket."

I gave Jessie the jacket to hang onto and noticed her hands tremble. I fished into my purse, pulled out photos, leafed through them, selected one and held it up for Erie to see.

"This is a picture taken from a convenience store camera two blocks away from Crystal's place. I had it blown up. Unfortunately, you can't see the face of the person because they are wearing the hood of their jacket but there is no mistaking the gray color and the logo on the upper front left. HCC, and the year. With SOC underneath."

Even Tanya's soft gasp wouldn't make me take my eyes off Erie.

"Okay. So I visited a convenience store. That proves nothing." She shoved the picture back at me.

"It does when the date and time stamp on the surveillance camera says it was within a half hour of the time Crystal was murdered."

Out of the corner of my eye, I saw Jessie reach for Tanya's hand and grip it. Erie also saw the movement and fiery anger flashed in her eyes before it vanished.

"I was staying overnight. I must have stepped out for something," she defended.

Jessie spoke up for the first time, her voice so strangled and hurt, she barely got the words out. "But you weren't. You were with me, Will, and a bunch of others from StreetSmart at the Indie movie festival. There was a group of us and we took up one entire row. In fact, you had to sit behind our crew in the aisle seat because you came in at the last minute. I was somewhere in the middle. The lights came back on when it was over after three in the morning and you were there. How could you be in two places at the same time?"

Erie's voice began trembled. "No, you're wrong. The camera is wrong. I was there through the whole thing."

"The bistro," Jessie half whispered, her face deep in thought.

"What?" Erie stared at her in confusion.

"The day Sadie called me to fix her van; we went to the bistro after. The one you said was closed for a private party that night so we both made plans to meet up with the StreetSmart crew at the Indie movie festival instead. How did you know it was closed on that specific night if you were at the theater with us the whole time?"

Erie said nothing.

"That's right," I added, spearing my gaze on Erie. "I remember that conversation. The place on Rice, isn't that right Jessie?" When she nodded, I continued. "And you also mentioned you hoped to see the musician. Probably the same guy I talked to, who was busking out in front of the bistro the night of the private party. He saw the police cars driving past with lights flashing and stopping a few blocks up the street. At Crystal's. And her place was on Rice."

Erie's eyes flared in panic.

I held up the picture still in my hand. "When I saw the convenience store photo and noticed the logo something triggered in the back of my brain but it wouldn't come into focus. It was bugging me for the longest time. Then I remembered you were wearing this jacket that first day when you brought Jessie to my shop. And again this morning with the move, and it got me thinking about other video surveillance cameras. Early today I drove by the theater where the Indie movie festival had taken place. There wasn't a camera at that location but there was one right next door. At an ATM where you stopped. Maybe to check your bank balance after your trip to the convenience store." I reached back to the stack of photos I had put down, selected one, handed it to Erie who took it with shaky hands. "It's a clear shot of your face, Erie. And you're wearing your HCC jacket, you can just make out the logo and SOC underneath. The date matches the night and shortly after Crystal's murder."

Thank god for Will's computer hacking magic. I had woken up the poor guy before the crack of dawn after I drove around and spotted the ATM beside the movie theater. It had been a really long shot but the picture was the last piece of evidence we needed to refute Erie's alibi that she was with the StreetSmart crew for the entire evening.

"My debit card was rejected at the store when I wanted to buy some snacks," Erie whispered, almost to herself.

The girl folded in on herself; like the weight of the world had crushed her shoulders and she couldn't bear it anymore. The picture fluttered to the floor at Erie's feet. "I didn't mean for it to happen. It was an accident. I'd seen Crystal and Tanya leave the theater. They'd been arguing and were sitting right behind me because there was no room in my row."

She turned her gaze to Tanya. "Even though you tried to keep quiet, I heard everything. Crystal shouldn't have forced you to let her move in. I got so angry because what she was saying was hurting you."

Tanya's eyes widened, her face paled and she gripped Jessie's hand tighter.

Erie caught the motion, looked away and rested her gaze back on me. "I followed them both, hoping I could convince Tanya that Crystal wasn't the right person for her. I heard the entire argument from the hall. Crystal said some mean, vile things, then she left. I confronted her but she just brushed by me, told me to mind my own goddamn business and stormed off."

She paused, clenched her fists tight in her lap. "I thought I'd let her cool off a few minutes and went to her place. Crystal had given me a key a long time ago, said if things got to the point at mom and dad's that I needed to just hang out and chat to come over anytime. But when I let myself into her apartment, she wasn't alone. There was another woman there. Another woman! Another lover! Like you meant nothing to her! Crystal was drunk, saying stupid things I didn't understand. They were arguing about some type of design plans that Crystal had stolen."

My eyes rounded. Another woman? Stephanie? I heard Tanya gasp and all the color leached from her face.

"This woman wanted the two of them to use those plans that Crystal had stolen from the place they both worked but Crystal said it was too soon, that they'd need to wait. The other woman got so mad. She freaked out, saying she needed the money they could make. That's when she saw me and left."

So that was what Stephanie was looking for the second time she went to Crystal's. Design plans.

Erie raised her eyes to stare at Tanya, tears slowly down her face. "I got so mad at Crystal. She stole from people and if you two moved in together, you'd get caught in whatever crap she was in and that would hurt you. Crystal wouldn't have stayed. She would have left you, hurt you like she's done with her other lovers. She had so many others. Did you know that?" When Tanya didn't respond, Erie continued. "I said I'd tell you what she'd done because I loved you in my way. And you know what she said…she said you wouldn't believe me and that I was a silly little girl who knew nothing about love. I got so angry I wanted to smack her so I..I grabbed the nearest thing…"

The creative design award.

Erie started sobbing, tears streaking down her ashen face. "I do know about love. I know that when you love someone, it doesn't matter how or in what way, you don't hurt them. You're don't kill yourself and leave them to find your body. You're not supposed to leave them all alone."

Her whole body shook, caved around itself, as if to cage in the pain. Tanya rose, gently pushed aside my restraining hand and went to sit beside the weeping girl. She enveloped the young woman in arms and rocked her, murmured hushed words and told her everything would be okay.

Tanya had commented to me when she was released on bail that she'd felt like she and Crystal were being followed. Apparently, that had been Erie.

I stepped into the kitchen and called the police, gave them brief details, asked if they could please come and have a female social worker on hand as well. And I didn't think sirens would be necessary.

I felt drained and so bone tired that all I wanted to do was sleep for a week. I felt Jessie's presence behind me, hovering in the background as if afraid to approach. Her face was so pale it was almost translucent.

"Not who you thought, was it?"

She shook her head, eyes brimming with tears.

"I'm sorry Jess. Wish this could have turned out differently."

"I thought it was Bromskey because of what happened," she murmured.

I was about to ask her to explain where she'd been the last few days then realized the police were on their way. "The car you stole. Where is it?"

The young woman blinked a few times, startled. "Down the block."

"What's the make and model?"

She gave me details as I called up Will.

"Will," I said softly so Tanya couldn't hear me. "Jessie is here at Tanya's with me but we need help. She commandeered a ride but if the owner hasn't already reported the car stolen, they will soon. Any way to move it and get rid of any prints?"

"Is she okay?"

"Yes, and I don't have the details of what's happened but the police are on their way to arrest Erie for Crystal's murder so we need to stay as witnesses to her confession. Can you take care of the problem for us?"

"Leave it with me."

I relayed the rough location from Jessie of where she'd taken the car from, where it was parked now plus the vehicle info and clicked off.

I rested my hands on my employee's shoulders, giving a light squeeze in support, grateful she was okay.

"And now, young lady, please tell me where the hell you've been."

CHAPTER TWENTY-SEVEN

Jessie's explanation of where she'd been the last few days had to wait because the police and social worker arrived at Tanya's apartment. Over the next couple of hours, with my best friend's lawyer present, authorities took our statements, phone calls were made and eventually Erie was taken away under the watchful eye of a social worker and two police officers.

Tanya's apartment was silent as the three of us sat, each grappling with the enormity of recent events. Dusk had fallen, smudging the last of Houston's sunset into grayish tones of red and orange and I watched the ebbing slivers of light recede across the floor, like life draining away.

"Can I get you girls anything?" Tanya finally whispered.

Jessie shook her head.

"It surprises me that you gave Erie a key to your place," I commented.

My girlfriend glanced at me with dull eyes. "I knew Crystal had given her one and since that option was no longer available, I told Erie she could come here if the need arose."

I stood. "We should get going, unless you want one of us to stay?"

"No, think I want to be alone for a while. This entire ordeal has been rough and the next week will be even more so as Crystal's family has to deal with another crisis. I need to be there for them, so I'll spend a quiet night at home and try to get some rest."

I embraced my friend and we held onto each other for a long time, expressing our emotions and love through touch. Tanya released me, then turned to Jessie and held her. The young woman heaved a ragged sigh and closed her eyes, leaning into my friend's arms, as if finally allowing herself the connection.

"Call if you need anything," I said in the open doorway with Jessie beside me.

Tanya stood with her hand on the knob. "Thank you, Sadie." Her eyes said so much more.

"You're welcome," I whispered back and walked down the hall.

It wasn't until we were on the sidewalk when I realized we had no vehicle. The car Jessie had stolen was, if not back in its original location, hopefully close enough. Sylvia had driven me here on her bike and my office manager had probably gone home for the day.

"Share an Uber for a ride home?"

"Not until we nail Bromskey first for kidnapping," Jessie spat.

My eyes widened. "Is that what happened to you?"

The young woman's eyes snapped fire. "Yes."

Without realizing it, we had both started walking and were now in front of a small diner.

"You must be starving, and I could use something to eat. Let's grab a bite and you can give me details."

Once we took a booth, ordered some food and Jessie drank a glass of juice, she told her tale. "The day when I overheard Bromskey and Tanner talking in her office, remember, and they were slated to meet that night?" At my nod, she continued. "Well, she either saw me or someone said something to her because while I was waiting for Erie to come give me a ride, she approached and said Erie called her to pass along a message that she couldn't make it."

"Maybe Elaine thought you had heard what she and Melinda were planning." I frowned. "Wouldn't Erie have phoned you herself?"

Jessie's eyes were downcast. "Ordinarily yes, but she'd been acting all strange and I thought she was avoiding me. Now I understand why," she added quietly.

Our food came and we started eating.

"Anyway, since I had no way home, Bromskey offered me a ride only she didn't take me home. She took me out to someplace on the outskirts of Houston. I tried to get out of the car and run away but she hit me on the head and then dragged me into an abandoned house and locked me in the basement. Thank god she didn't ditch my phone, just turned it off and left it upstairs."

"Was Melinda with her?"

"No. I don't know if she knew I was being held against my will or not. I never saw her. In fact, I never saw anyone."

I gaped at her. "Elaine never came back? She just left you there?"

Jessie nodded, grim-faced.

Ohhh, I wanted to get that bitch.

"How'd you get out?"

An eyebrow rose. "You know I can pick locks, right, like I did to get pictures of Bromskey's ledger? Only a door lock is harder, especially when you don't have the right tools and need to improvise with what was on hand."

"Speaking of the ledger," I said, taking a sip of coffee but would have preferred a Live-Wire. "When I hadn't heard from you after I tailed Elaine and Melinda, Will tried to get it but the book was gone."

My young friend reached under her shirt to the small of her back. "That's because I have it. I took it that morning before Tanner and Bromskey had their meeting. I'd hoped to make copies of all the pages and then return it but didn't have time. Why is it so important? Did you figure out what the numbers mean?"

"You naughty girl, good for you." I laughed. "Oh, that's right, you don't know. Well, the night when you were abducted and I followed Elaine and Melinda, they went to the Post Oak Hotel where the two of them plus a handful of other young women met up with rich, older men for…entertainment."

Jessie's eyes flared wide. "As in…"

I nodded. "Elaine was running a prostitution ring using some of you from StreetSmart, including Melinda. There was another girl there from your group, but I don't know her name, just recognized her from my other visits to the office."

"And the ledger?"

"Accounts paid by date and initials of either the women or the men, or both." I didn't let on that the financials Will had found corresponded with those numbers, nor that Houston, in all likelihood, wasn't the only location Elaine had been engaged at being a madam. "It's a good thing you grabbed it when you did."

"Do you think we have enough to go after her?" Jessie asked.

"Well, with the ledger and what I witnessed they might have enough to charge her with prostitution. She also took you and held you against your will so that's kidnapping and, according to the indomitable *Perry Mason*, forcible confinement as well."

"Perry who?"

"Never mind."

"I have a record and it will be my word against hers," Jessie pointed out.

"Unless the authorities can get Melinda to testify against Elaine. Come to think of it," I tapped my finger against my lips. "Melinda arrived prior to Elaine, and Tanya had mentioned that just before Crystal's murder, she had a request from a woman to come here. Melinda and Elaine both came from StreetSmart in Austin. Maybe Melinda was trying to get away. That's up to the DA to figure out."

Jessie finished her food and pushed her plate aside. "Now, can we go to the police and nail Bromskey's ass?"

I grinned evilly. "Absolutely."

***

It was almost midnight by the time I crawled into bed. Before heading to the police station I called Clayton for advice and after his usual silent pause followed by a sigh and "why am I not surprised" he met Jessie and I at the station and gave us guidance while we told them everything regarding Elaine Bromskey. The authorities took Jessie's statement about her abduction and mine about the Concierge Lounge. I never saw what happened in the hotel rooms but the police understood. We gave them the ledger and my theory of what the numbers and letters might represent but by the expression on the officer's face, they appeared to have come to the same conclusion. I wasn't about to state that the amounts from the ledger coincided with deposits into Elaine's bank accounts. Not even Clayton could keep Will or me out of jail for hacking into bank financials. Although they never said they would try to get Melinda to roll over on the StreetSmart manager, my guess was it would be the first thing they did tomorrow.

My eyes were gritty and my lids felt heavy enough to qualify as dumbbells, but the goldfish in my brain kept circling the bowl. Erie had confessed to killing Crystal so that mystery was cleared but who had sabotaged the moving van, ransacked Hawkins' Freight and slashed my tires? And why? Seems there were never enough hours in the day for a short, feisty gal to solve all the puzzles.

There was always tomorrow.

CHAPTER TWENTY-EIGHT

If you looked up 'sucker-for-punishment', you'd probably see my picture beside the phrase. I stood at the door of Lewis' house wondering if I would be the next poster child for that quip.

Before I could talk myself out of it, my hand knocked on the door and I prayed Lewis wouldn't greet me the same way he had the first time I'd visited him, with a sneer and his gun pointed in my face.

To his credit, Tanya's brother opened the door unarmed but the sneer was still there. Oh well, one out of two was better than nothing.

"What the hell do you want?" he barked.

Good question. World peace, but that would require everyone to be on the same page. Difficult. Being taller would be nice, however getting stretched on the rack sounded painful. I'd settle for Tanya's peace of mind, which is what had brought me here.

"To make a deal with you."

With a snort, he scanned me up and down and scoffed, "I don't make deals with chicks."

He said that to piss me off so I didn't take any stock in his words.

"Apparently Melinda Tanner is the exception to that rule."

He stilled and I knew the mark hit home.

His hand went to slam the door in my face, so I shoved my boot to block it from closing. "Just hear me out, Lewis. For what it's worth, I'm actually doing you a favor."

Lewis hesitated, then made his way down the hall and into the living room, taking a seat in the same chair as earlier. The dilapidated couch was still there so I remained standing.

"You have two minutes."

Two could play hardball. "I know that you're fencing stolen property for Melinda." Actually, I didn't know that for sure but I was hedging my bets.

"Bullshit."

"I have proof, pictures of the other day when she handed you a clear plastic bag right here on your doorstep." A lie, but he didn't know that.

"That could have been anything," he defended.

"Maybe. But with your record..." I shrugged, letting the sentence trail off on purpose. "Sometime today the police will take Melinda Tanner and her boss, Elaine Bromskey, into custody for solicitation, among other things. The authorities might offer Melinda a lesser sentence if she testifies against Bromskey and who knows, they may question her sudden influx of spending money in her accounts."

Okay, so I was stretching it, but I needed to sell this to him.

He paused, his eyes narrowing into slits. "What's the deal?"

"I won't give the cops the pictures or tell them anything I saw if you agree to sit down and talk with Tanya."

"What the hell, Sadie! What's between me and my sister has nothing to do with you."

"True, but what's happened to Tanya these past couple of weeks, what you and your family have put her through has placed a tremendous strain on her and because she is my best friend. *That* has everything to do with me."

He glared at me.

"It's a conversation, Lewis. Nothing more. Just talk to her. Take that first step. She'll meet you halfway."

He sat with arms crossed, saying nothing.

"I know you've been to her place. I saw you waiting outside in your car. You obviously want to reach out. Maybe you just need an invitation."

Stony silence.

My gaze swept the room. The empty pizza box was gone but the battered coffee table and the secondhand, third-hand, hell maybe even tenth-hand, furniture remained. My voice softened. "Is this what you want out of your life? Is this how you see yourself for the next five or ten years when you can be so much more? Tanya has contacts that can help you get out from under this and become the person she knows is still in there. If she hasn't lost faith in you, maybe you shouldn't either."

I mimicked checking my watch for the time. "Guess my two minutes are up. Deal's on the table, Lewis." I turned and headed for the door.

When I opened the door, he said from behind me. "Set it up." He was gone when I glanced back at him.

I closed the portal and walked down the sidewalk, bright sunshine adding to the bite of tears stinging my eyes. It was a step, a small step, but if it brought some peace to Tanya I would take that gesture and run with it.

***

On the way to the office, I called Officer Ramerez.

"Ramerez," the woman said when she picked up the phone.

"Hello Officer Ramerez, it's Sadie Hawkins."

No expected pause before she replied. "Ms. Hawkins. The Wood's case is closed and your friend cleared. Is there something I can do for you?" Professional but polite. I was making progress.

"Satisfy my curiosity, I hope. Did you ever question Stephanie Waxton on why she lied about the number of times she visited Crystal the night of the murder?"

Pause and a measured intake of breath. Oh well, my track record of trying the woman's patience was still intact.

"The case is closed so what relevance does this have?" she queried.

"I don't like loose ends," I quipped, hoping it would persuade her.

I thought I heard her mumble something like 'being an investigator' but wasn't sure.

"Please, Officer Ramerez. There has to have been a reason. And I promise I won't bother you ever again," I added with a solemn vow while I crossed my fingers.

"Are you going to let this go?"

Now it was my time to remain silent.

She sighed. "Okay but only because of your tip on Ms. Bromskey and her *alleged* prostitution ring, which was passed onto Vice," she relented. "I will not confirm or deny that Ms. Waxton returned to Ms. Sherridan's apartment directly after attempting to buy Rohypnol."

My eyebrows crept up. "The date-rape drug?"

"That is one of the street names for it, yes."

"Can I ask how you found that out?"

"Rohypnol has anti-anxiety and muscle-relaxant effects and is used to treat insomnia. The average person thinks they can get a prescription or that it might be sold as an over-the-counter medication. The drug is not manufactured or approved for sale in the

United States, which is why all pharmacies are required to notify the police if a person inquires about purchasing some," she explained. "That and the fact Ms. Waxton lied to us about the amount of times she visited the deceased, gave us the incentive to question her."

"And her reasoning why she said she'd been there only once?" I asked.

"She was extremely stressed at seeing her friend dead and had forgotten," Officer Ramerez answered.

"So, Stephanie was going to give Rohypnol to Crystal?"

"When we spoke with Ms. Waxton, she denied having made the request at a drugstore and since she had none on her person, we couldn't charge her. Her excuse for returning to Crystal Sherridan's apartment shortly after she left was for Ms. Sherridan's well-being. Ms. Sherridan had been drinking and Ms. Waxton was concerned her friend might fall and hurt herself."

I bet. More like she planned on slipping Crystal a roofie and then trash the place, hoping to find the plans her and Crystal stole. By the time she returned, Erie had killed Crystal, then left, and Stephanie had walked in on Tanya looming over the body. No wonder she acted jittery like the building superintendent said. Stephanie lost her opportunity to find her prize; the plans. Since she had lied to the police, she couldn't very well change her story about seeing Erie the first time she was there. Perhaps because the police might dig a bit more, find out about the plans, tell her former employer and she'd be charged with corporate espionage.

Erie couldn't mention Stephanie, as it would implicate her in the crime scene instead of being with the rest of StreetSmart members at the theater.

I didn't mention that because Erie confessed, freeing Tanya and that was all that mattered.

"Are we done, Ms. Hawkins?" the woman asked.

I put warmth into my voice. "Yes, Officer Ramerez, we're done. Thank you for the info and all the hard work on behalf of Tanya. You won't be hearing from me again."

The officer wasn't quite successful in muffling her snort of laughter. "Can I get that in writing?"

Nope.

"You take care now," I said and hung up.

***

"I have something for you," Sylvia said.

My office manager and I were standing in the garage of Hawkins' Freight, staring at the immobile van.

She handed me a postcard. "It came the other day."

The scene on the front was a generic map of Texas, a souvenir one could get anywhere in the state. I flipped it over. The message was short and cryptic.

Sadie. I'm sorry…about everything. W.

Wayne.

My eyes shuttered closed as a piece of my heart fell away, leaving an odd vacant ache. The miniscule bit of hope I had clung to evaporated like a thin wisp of smoke. At least he let me know he was sorry. I stuffed the card into my back pocket.

Sylvia cleared her throat and motioned to the van, the wooden bangles on her wrist making soft clunking sounds with each movement. "What now, boss?"

Earlier, when I'd come into work, Sylvia gleefully had dragged me over to the wall-sized calendar which she'd purchased and proudly showed the list of upcoming jobs. Apparently, she had named Moose as the official business mascot with pictures of him that were altered to portray his loveable personality. That, plus the story of his rescue on our main social media page, and our snappy tag line—groovin' to do your movin'-had garnered a lot of attention.

I wasn't about to lose those bookings. The vehicle had to be fixed and Professor Shamdi's publicist had already forwarded me the funds to cover all the expenses. My dilemma was whether to call Blaine and see how long it would be until his return or ask him for a recommendation on who could fix it. The other option was to hire Jessie full-time. I didn't want to make the major decision without contacting my brother.

"Call a leasing company and get the cost for a short-term rental of a van roughly the same size. Maybe ask around for pricing. We're going to need something temporarily."

She nodded and went into the office.

The phone rang a few times before Blaine picked up. His voice was strained. "You must have ESP. I was about to call you."

Trying to keep things light, I joked. "We *are* related. How are things going?"

Silence.

"Blaine? What's wrong? Is it Jerrald?"

He sighed. "The baby is okay but we got the test results. When the umbilical cord got wrapped around his neck, it had multiple loops and was tight enough to block oxygen to the brain. The doctors called it Nuchal Cord Birth injury."

"Okay," I said carefully.

"The doctor tried what's called a 'somersault delivery' which means pushing the baby's head to the side, toward the mother's thigh through labor. That didn't work so they had to do an emergency C-Section on Karen."

"Oh, god."

"The doctor was great; the team was right there and they worked really fast."

"Last time we talked you said they were going to run numerous tests to see the extent of brain damage, so what did they find out?"

"It could have been a lot worse," Blaine paused, sighed. "But it looks like Jerrald has Cerebral Palsy."

I sat down on the back fender of the van. "Wha..what's that?" It sounded so awful, so deadly that I couldn't breathe.

"From what I've learned, it's a group of neurological disorders and disabilities which can be from mild to severe with things like walking, speech, learning, hearing or eyesight. He may have emotional and behavioral challenges or epilepsy and spinal deformities. It's too early to tell how many or to what extent but...yeah."

"Oh, Blaine." I sobbed, unable to hold back the tears and the agony he must also be feeling.

"I know," he choked, his voice cracking. "We have no idea how long he'll have to be in the hospital or what care he'll need. I feel so helpless and I don't know what to do."

A few shuddering breaths later, I forced my voice to level out. "You'll stay there and be with your son, your little girl and your wife. That's what you need to do."

"But that could take months." Worry edged his voice. "The business..."

"A month, a year, it doesn't matter. You stay there until everyone is well and ready to come back. I presume Karen's parents are on board?"

"Of course. They're beside themselves with worry over Karen and the baby and Karen's mother has been a godsend with Shanty. They've offered us a place for as long as we need it."

"Then the only thing you need to worry about is loving and caring for your family." I steeled my nerves and put a hint of optimism in my voice. "Everything is fine. In fact, we've gotten enough work that I've hired a part-time person to help me with moves. She's been great so there's no need to worry. It's all good here."

"You're sure."

"Trust me, Blaine. It's all been quite boring," I lied. "Let me know how things go and send me pictures of my nephew. I can't wait to see what he looks like."

"He has my eyes but Karen's nose." My brother's tone held so much love that it speared my heart.

"Good thing it's not the other way around. Now go give my niece and nephew a kiss and hug Karen for me. Okay?"

"Okay. Love you, sis," he said quietly.

"Love you too."

I sat there for the longest time until Sylvia came, handed me a glass with amber liquid in it, a match to her own.

"I didn't mean to overhear but sounds like you need this."

The whisky burned away the tightness in my throat, gave me something else to focus on as I hung my head and thought about the ramifications of what

Blaine told me. My brother would not be returning soon, so that meant I either needed to have Jessie on full time, if she'd take the job, or hire at least another part-time mover and hunt for a new mechanic.

"Anything I can do?" she asked.

"Just tell me you're not planning to go anywhere."

"Are you kidding, no one could replace me," she smirked, tapped her glass to mine. "Come on, I've got some quotes for you to look at."

***

I'd called the one leasing company that didn't want a king's ransom and set up a time to pick up the temporary moving van the next day. There was only a couple of days' grace before the next job and I wanted to have the van cleaned plus get Jessie to give the engine a quick inspection.

If she took the offer.

The tone in her voice was lighter than usual when she answered the phone. "Hey Sadie."

"You sound upbeat."

"That's because they hauled Bromskey away in chains," she practically giggled.

"In chains, seriously?" Wow, the authorities were hard core.

"No. Just visualizing. What's up?"

I took a deep breath. A lot was riding on the young woman's answer. "I have another job proposition for you."

"Okay."

"I'd like to hire you full time, as the mechanic and to help with most if not all the moves."

"Oh. What about your brother?" she asked tentatively.

It wasn't like Jessie wouldn't learn about it eventually, so I told her about the complications from Jerrald's birth and that it might be a very long time before Blaine returned.

"I'm so sorry to hear about your nephew. Can't imagine how difficult that would be to face. Umm, yeah, sure I'll take the job," she said firmly.

"Great. First thing is to replace the engine in the moving van."

"What?! Didn't I tell you to take it easy? What happened?"

"I'll fill you in when you get here. When can you start?"

"Tomorrow, I guess."

Would Jessie even be allowed to work full time? "What about checking with the manager of StreetSmart?"

"There is no manager at the moment. Someone is coming in temporarily from another location in a few days. The office is closed right now," she said.

I wonder if they would give Tanya back her position. Would she even take it?

"Did you need to wait and run it by that person?"

Jessie hummed in the back of her throat like she was thinking. "I don't think so. There are a few people who work full time that are clients here. As long as we do our community hours, it shouldn't matter."

"Perfect. We'll see you tomorrow morning. Do you need a ride?"

"I can make my way there."

"No hot wiring cars."

She laughed and hung up without admitting or denying that would be her mode of transportation.

Before I even pocketed my phone, it rang again.

"Hello, my friend. How you holding out?"

"I'm okay. Sadie, I need to tell you something about Erie," Tanya said.

CHAPTER TWENTY-NINE

My hand tightened around my cell phone. "What do you need to tell me about Erie?"

Tanya paused, cleared her throat. "Her lawyer called me because I guess Erie asked her to. I don't know if what she said was under the guidance of a social worker or whether Erie herself felt the need to confess everything, but she admitted to slashing your tires on the night of the movie."

Okay, didn't see that one. "Did she mention why?"

"Out of anger, but according to what I was told, Erie felt left out because we didn't invite her to the movie. She envied our friendship, thought it would impede her relationship with me."

"Ahh…relationship?"

"Of which there isn't one. At least from me, but there was one on her side," Tanya explained.

Unsure of how to respond, I said nothing.

"It's sad, on so many levels."

"Any idea of what will happen to her?"

"Not at the moment," Tanya replied. "There is no doubt Erie has emotional and psychological problems." She was silent for a heartbeat, then sighed.

"You know, I'm not even angry. I just feel sorry for her. It's all so senseless."

"Agreed." There was something that still bugged me. "Did Erie admit to anything else, or just the tires?"

"No," Tanya replied, elongating the word. "The lawyer never mentioned it. Why?"

I explained about the sabotage of my moving van and the mess that was made at the office.

"How come you never said anything?"

"You had enough on your plate, Tanya. Besides, now that I think about it, the sabotage of the engine in the van was before I even met Erie."

"Given Erie's reasoning with slashing your tires because she felt left out, I can't see her vandalizing your place. It wouldn't make any sense."

"You're right." I'd have loved an answer, though.

"Just be careful. Did you get an alarm system?"

"Yes." And that should deter the culprit, whomever they were, from invading my business.

"Good. Anyway, I have to go. I'm on my way to the Sherridan's to see what I can do to help. That poor family."

"Tanya, before you hang up there's something....I....you..."

"Just say it, Sadie."

"Your brother is waiting for a call from you," I rushed out.

My friend gasped. "What? How..."

I interrupted, no wanting to explain. "Please Tanya, call him."

She didn't respond other than the soft sound of her breathing.

"He wants to talk. Trust me." I waited. "I'm here for you if you need me. Anytime."

"I know that, Sadie. Thank you." A pause. "Will you ever explain how you got Lewis to talk to me or about those pictures of Erie from the surveillance cameras?"

Air caught in my lungs. "You didn't mention those to the police, did you?"

The smallest chuckle hummed over the connection. "Of course not, but I'm still curious."

"You know what they say about curiosity. I'll talk to you later." And hung up.

***

I went to visit my mother since I hadn't called or stopped by in days. Because she was lost in thoughts of the past, we ended up discussing mundane things and I read to her until she drifted to sleep. She didn't bring up Blaine, so we didn't discuss the topic, and I concluded that my mother would probably never know she had a grandson.

Back home I found a silent and subdued four-legged boy who looked like he was suffering from abandonment issues. Poor thing, it had been so hectic for me. No wonder he was glum. I snapped on his leash, took him out to the van and we drove out to one of the dog parks where he could romp around off-leash and make new friends.

Later, while sitting in the backyard with a pooped pooch, listening to the soft sounds of the night my phone rang with a number I didn't recognize.

"Hello?"

"Sadie, this is Candace Flemming."

The woman who contracted me to haul staging equipment to different venues. I almost patted myself on the back because that was my first association to the name and not that it was Clayton's girlfriend.

"Hello, Candace. How are you?"

"I'm good, thanks. Listen, I know this is super last minute but I'm in a bind. There are two events that require staging but they're in two different cities. Would you be able to handle the transport of one?"

"How soon?"

"In two weeks." Her tone went up at the end, like she was asking a question.

Hopefully my van would be operational by then but if not I would have one on lease.

"Sure, which city?"

"Well, you can pick if you like. One event is in Odessa, the other in Pampa," she related.

Pampa. Why was that city inexplicably linked to my life? Mind you, I had a choice. Go to Odessa and tell the universe to kiss my hiney. The image of Clayton and Candace arose, of the two of them having dinner and their intimate yet animated conversation over her business proposal. Pampa. Where Jackson was working at KRDL. Perhaps this was fate's gentle way of offering me a hand to move on, as Clayton had done. Maybe it was time to grab that hand and see where it led me.

"I'll take Pampa," I said and crossed my fingers.

About the author

Pat is a playwright and award winning author who has had a love affair with the written word since childhood, many times immersing herself in the stories of Enid Blyton and Carolyn Keene. An active imagination gave inspiration to short stories and her first play as a teen.

Her full-length play *The Truth About Lies* was staged at a regional theatrical competition in 2006. She was selected in the "One of 50 Authors You Should Be Reading" contest in 2012. One of her novels achieved a finalist slot in the 2013 International Book Award Contest - fantasy category. *The Daughters of the Crescent Moon Trilogy* garnered 2nd place for best series in the 2016 Paranormal Romance Guild's Reviewer's Choice Award. She was also one of the winners of the 15th Annual Writer's Digest Short Story Competition for *A Holy Night*.

Although still in pursuit of a place truly called home, Pat shares her life with her husband and three cats, all of which claim rule over the house at one point or another. Besides dreaming up her next novel, Pat enjoys traveling, baking, camping, wine and or course reading - not necessarily in that order.

You can find her on Facebook, her website patriciaclee.com or send her an email at authorpatriciaclee@yahoo.com